The Wonder Drug

THE
WONDER
DRUG

SUSANNA BEARD

Joffe Books, London
www.joffebooks.com

First published in Great Britain in 2024

Cover art by Imogen Buchanan

ISBN: 978-1-83526-834-6

For Adrian

CHAPTER ONE

Michelle

She feels the plane's wheels drop, hears the crunch as they hit the ground. Her stomach lurches, but it's not from the landing. This is it — her big adventure. She takes a deep breath, gripping the arms of the narrow seat, and offers a silent greeting to Iceland.

Just the sound of it — *Iceland* — is thrilling, terrifying. Again she asks herself: *What am I doing, leaving my neat, familiar place in London for this strange, cold world?* At a time of life when most of her friends are settling into their second half-century, happy and secure in their relationships and jobs, here she is, alone, stepping into the unknown.

The man in the seat next to her glances at her whitened knuckles, gives her an encouraging smile. She looks away. Now is not the moment for conversation. As the plane drifts gently into its bay, she squares her shoulders, consciously relaxes her stomach muscles. She chose this. She will see it through.

Outside it's dark. There's not much to see as the passengers wait for the seat belt sign to give them permission to move — only illuminated patches of concrete, the dark shape of the terminal ahead of them. Again she feels a jolt of uncertainty. Why didn't she think to arrive in daylight? But maybe there is no flight that arrives in daylight. Another thing she'll have to get used to. The dark.

"Come on." She didn't mean to speak out loud, but her words echo in her ears and the man next to her glances at her again. She ignores him. She urges herself to be positive about this. This, right now, is the beginning of her adventure, an opening, like a secret passageway into a different life. She's going to embrace the experience, not fear it.

* * *

"What on earth's got into you, Michelle?"

Gail's squeal of horror reminded her of her own reaction to what she'd done. Or was planning to do.

In her heart, she knew what had "got into her", though she'd never have admitted it. For a very long time now, longer than anyone knew, something had been eating away at her. Slowly burrowing through her, finding its way to her centre. Once there, it had taken control, like some kind of parasite. Or maybe not. Maybe it wasn't a parasite at all, maybe it was her real self, insisting on being acknowledged at last.

She sighed. Gail would never understand. Her best friend, with her lovely house and perfect family, who'd never known rejection in her life — how could she understand? She wasn't even sure she wanted her to. It was one of the many endearing facets of Gail's character. She was an incorrigible optimist — and why wouldn't she be, with a life like hers?

Gail was very different from Michelle, but it made her love her even more. Sometimes Michelle wondered if she really did hate herself. She certainly had her moments.

"Nothing's got into me. Really, this is something I want to do."

"But — *Iceland*?"

She could picture the horror on Gail's face — her blue eyes wide, her eyebrows disappearing into the perfect blonde fringe — and for once she was glad they were talking on the phone and not in person.

Gail didn't bother to wait for a response. "Michelle . . . *Iceland*? You are, without exception, *the* coldest person I've ever met."

"Gee, thanks."

"You know what I mean. You shiver with cold when the rest of us are in shorts and T-shirts. You keep thermal underwear companies afloat. You adore the sun. Why the hell are you going there, of all places?"

"Look, I know it sounds mad, but this is my chance—"

"Your chance to freeze your toes off?"

"No. Seriously, I'm single now, Toby's at university and he can go to his dad's in the holidays. Or he can visit me — Iceland's not that far, after all. My job's boring. My life is utterly mundane—"

There was a pause. "I didn't know you felt like that." Gail's voice softened. "I'm sorry. Are you okay?"

"Yes, of course I'm okay. I just want — oh, I don't know — an adventure?" It was hard to explain. It wasn't really adventure she was after, but something was calling her, inside. "Something to take me out of myself, something completely new and different . . . before I'm too old."

Gail snorted. "Old? You of all people, you'll never be old. Don't tell me you're feeling your age. Has someone upset you? Because this isn't the Michelle I know."

"Oh, but it is. I need to get this out of my system, Gail. I want . . . *more*."

"I understand that, I do, but honestly . . . Iceland. I can't believe it."

"Well, you'd better believe it because it's all settled."

"What? Wait, when are you going?"

"Next week."

The squeal at the other end of the line was ear-splitting.

3

CHAPTER TWO

Michelle

As she walks past the gate, the uniformed security guard, Gunnar, pops his head out of his booth, his breath condensing in great white clouds in the icy air. She smiles at him, barely feeling her lips move, they're so numb with cold. Mornings have never been her strong point, and in Iceland they're doubly hard. Waking to the darkness, emerging from the warmth of the apartment into the freezing cold street — she's not sure she'll ever get used to it, even with all the layers and the expensive down-filled coat that reaches almost to her feet.

"Good morning," he says, lifting a takeaway coffee cup in greeting, the hand clutching it clothed in a fingerless glove.

She's in awe of the language skills of these people. Everyone here seems to have perfect, idiomatic English, while it's a struggle for most non-natives to learn even the basics of Icelandic. She's been here for only a few weeks, but some of her British and American colleagues have lived here for years and not picked up a single sentence. It's tempting to say they're lazy, but with Icelanders being so proficient in English, it's easy to live here without making the effort.

"How are you today, lovely lady?"

She nods, grimacing. "Pretty average, thanks. Wish I was rich and didn't have to work. And ten years younger."

"Nah," he grins. "You're perfect as you are. And money isn't everything, is it?" He waves her through. "Have a good one!"

The science park in Reykjavik is like a town within a town, with its own particular pattern of roads, car parks and delineations. An extension to the university campus, not far from the centre of the city and on the edge of a lake, the park sprawls across a large open area from which you can see the airport, the sea and the city all at once — on a clear day. The beautiful, iconic Hallgrimskirkja, Iceland's largest church, can be seen rising like a stalagmite to a high point among the buildings.

Small clumps of people walk along wide pavements, warmly dressed, files under their arms, laptop bags on their shoulders. Everyone here, in this part of the park, is involved in some kind of ground-breaking research. At times it feels as if the whole place is holding its breath, waiting for some astounding breakthrough when a lone chemist or biologist or inventor finally justifies their existence.

Michelle isn't one of those boffins. Her job is to ensure the right people know about her company's work at the right time. Or not, as the case may be. Often in this industry, the job is to keep the story out of the news, rather than in. This is corporate relations, or PR to some. It's not science, or ground-breaking — but it is important, and in this industry, it can be vital. That's what she tells herself, anyway.

The glass door swishes and she steps into the huge entrance to the laboratory. When she first came here, she was struck by the lack of ostentatious branding, being used to companies that had large, shiny signs and logos in prominent positions on their headquarters.

But this is Kimia. Things are different here. From the outside, it looks like an ordinary office building, but the majority of this structure is dedicated to highly sensitive scientific research. Whole floors are divided into large areas, with rows of workstations occupied by scientists in lab coats. Delicate, state-of-the-art equipment is housed in glass cubicles or screened off in small rooms where the temperature is closely regulated. Everything on these floors is bright, sterile and carefully monitored. Security levels are high; everyone has a pass, some areas use fingerprint recognition or other hi-tech entry systems, visitors are restricted.

There's an air of expectancy here, but also of secrecy.

* * *

It all started back in London on a very ordinary day. Too ordinary, as usual.

Her computer pinged at the arrival of each new email. She'd meant to change that for some time. It was irritating and unnecessary. But she wasn't sure how, and it was bottom of a very long list.

But this particular alert, on this particular day — when her spirits were low and the future looked, well, bland to say the least — seemed louder than most, drawing her glance to the screen. It was the internal update, sent round by the PR team. This missive, which came monthly, was supposed to inform, motivate, bring teams together. Mostly it was ignored. Here, people worked in bubbles. Their own work, their own team: that's all that interested them. And perhaps it was the only way to behave in a place where focus was so important.

Normally she wouldn't have given it a glance, but this morning she was restless and procrastinating. She scrolled through the usual self-congratulatory articles — a new project set up, approval gained for this or that stage of research, funding successes. Towards the end, though, a couple of short paragraphs caught her eye.

MATERNITY COVER NEEDED
We're looking for a Senior Manager, Corporate Affairs to cover for maternity leave in the corporate communications department at our state-of-the-art research laboratory in Iceland. The role will last for a minimum of six months.

The right candidate will have international experience in the pharmaceutical sector, including Government Affairs, Corporate Communications and Patient Advocacy.
For further details go to . . .

Her scalp tingled. It was exactly her experience. It could have been describing her. Except that she wasn't on maternity leave and, at her age, would never be again.

But — Iceland? She knew a little about it from novels she'd read, from dark TV dramas. Dramatic scenery — stark, threatening landscapes, snow-capped mountains, plumes of steam from strange underground places, tectonic plates colliding. Dark, volcanic rock, tiny villages with scarcely any inhabitants. Darkness for most of the day, for months on end. Two-thirds of Icelanders gathering in Reykjavik, the capital, with a population smaller than many English towns, and nowhere near the size of London.

But also art, design, creativity, excitement. Liberal, fun-loving, tolerant people. Book-lovers, writers, poets. Living close to nature, to that ever-present threat, the skies dark, the volcanic earth a thrilling reminder of what might come or what might have been. Folklore, ghosts, spirits. She started to picture herself: the step into the unknown, the thrill of the new, discovering a land so different from the humdrum safety of home.

She copied and pasted the advertisement, together with the link to further information. Later, at home and with no pressure, she would study the requirements, craft a brilliant CV and step into a new future.

There was a reason, at the time, that she needed a change. To escape from the conventional, to move something in her life to a new and different level. It wasn't just that she was divorced or that her son had started university, leaving her with fewer responsibilities and a persistent feeling of emptiness.

On that particular day she felt wounded, her confidence shaken. And not for the first time in her life as a divorced, forty-five-year-old British woman.

CHAPTER THREE

Michelle

Her boss calls her to her office for an "introductory" meeting. Ashley is the head of three departments across the company, making her one of the most senior managers. This will be the first time they've met, Michelle's recruitment having been, for the most part, online, via the HR department and her immediate line manager.

At Kimia, all new recruits are carefully monitored, their first weeks filled with a minute-by-minute induction schedule designed to ensure absolute understanding of the way the company works. Michelle has just completed her induction, and her head rings with rules and regulations. The security module alone took an entire week. Now she gets to meet her ultimate boss and start her job properly.

She finds herself nervous, wanting to make a good impression. She's confident she can do the work — she has all the right skills and experience. But Kimia is new and different, and there's an atmosphere here that she can't quite put her finger on. It makes her nerves jangle.

She makes her way to the fifth floor, checking her face and hair in a smoky mirror in the lift. In the lobby, she registers her name at a security desk before she enters the main floor, where an assistant meets her and escorts her to the door of Ashley's large office.

As she enters, the light dazzles after the gloom of the lift. Located on a corner of the building, the room's huge floor-to-ceiling windows overlook the vast science park. Michelle's eyes are drawn immediately to the scene beyond: a grey-blue sea, snow-licked mountains. She has to stop herself from gaping, forcing herself to drag her eyes away to greet the woman who stands and skirts around an enormous desk, one hand outstretched.

"Stunning, isn't it?" Her voice is deep and sonorous. Michelle nods, noticing how clammy her own hand is in Ashley's cool grip.

Ashley is glossy and groomed in the way that only American women can be. Everything about her is intimidating. Smart red trouser suit; make-up so perfect it doesn't look like make-up; long, red fingernails, no sign of any chips; not a hair out of place. The skin on her face is immaculate. To look like that takes a shedload of money, and Michelle imagines she earns it. Her next thought — in the instant that the first impression takes — is that she's remarkably young to be in her position. She'd put her at mid-twenties, early thirties at most. But this is Iceland, and things are different here.

She indicates a sofa to one side of the room, a coffee table in front. No coffee is offered, though. This is going to be a short meeting. They sit on velvet cushions, with enough space for two people to sit comfortably between them. Ashley drapes an elegant arm over the back of the sofa and sits sideways, her legs crossed, her feet encased in designer heels at least three inches high. Michelle feels gauche and untidy. Not to mention old. She shakes her hair forward over her face, a habit she got into when she'd first noticed the lines on her forehead, the beginnings of a droop around her jawline.

"So, a month in, how are you getting on?"

"Really well, thanks."

"How was the induction? Are you getting to know us a bit now?"

"All good. Yes, the company's doing some fascinating work." She cringes inwardly. Ashley won't be impressed by obsequiousness.

"Any issues? Or anything you'd like to comment on?"

"The job's fine, I'm settling in well. It's very similar to what I was doing back in London. Everyone's been very helpful, thanks." She hesitates, searching for something more intelligent to say. "I mean, there are obviously things I don't know yet—"

Ashley raises an eyebrow. "You can be honest, you know. It's important you feel you can raise any issues."

"I'm not clear on what each department does, or how the teams interlink. Is there much integration, or do all the groups operate separately? I haven't quite got to grips with it . . ." She knows the answer to this, of course, but she's relieved to have found something to say.

"Ah," Ashley says, nodding. Not a single strand of hair escapes from her perfect blonde bob. "Yes, I can see what you're getting at. It's probably different in London. Here, as you know, we work at the highest level. Our projects can be very long-term but each is full of potential. A lot of the research done here is speculative, futuristic — really pushing the limits of science. Sometimes a drug can take twenty, thirty years to get to market. Sometimes a project fails after decades of work. Much of it is highly confidential — at the highest possible level of sensitivity. Some of the leading entrepreneurs in the world are reaching out into new areas of research. Kimia is one of the only companies with the capabilities — the brilliance — to help them."

Michelle's done her research and listened intently during the induction. She knows most of this. Hearing it from Ashley only goes to underline what she's beginning to understand — Kimia's reputation for state-of-the-art research, and for secrecy. She's doubly intrigued by Ashley's words.

"Does that mean some parts of the business are no-go areas?"

"Something like that. Both in a physical sense and intellectually. The higher you go in the building, the more sensitive it becomes. Top-secret developments are heavily protected. This is a cut-throat, competitive arena. I can't tell you much more than that, I'm afraid. It's vital that our systems are secure and that we control information from start to finish. Our communications have to be planned and executed in the most rigorous way. That's where your department comes in."

"Are there some projects, then, that we won't know about?" Michelle wonders how much Ashley will be prepared to say. Not much, is her guess.

"Exactly. Your team's work is important, of course, and very much valued, but it's focused on the projects that are coming to fruition and can be talked about. But because you're here on a temporary basis, unless things change, you'll have no contact with the more sensitive work. At all." It sounds remarkably like a threat. Michelle, taken aback, studies Ashley's face. But she's smiling, her eyes clear and innocent.

"I see." She's not sure she does see, but she's read about the billionaires, the visionaries, the entrepreneurs. Their compulsion to discover, to be the first, to leave a legacy of riches — not just financial — linked with their name. It's intriguing, thrilling to know that in this very building, something enormous might be in development — something unimaginable, perhaps, to the ordinary person.

She's about to ask more but Ashley moves on. "And how about your accommodation?"

She nods. "It's fine, though it's only temporary. I understand there's a policy?"

"Indeed — did nobody give you the details?"

Michelle shakes her head.

"Ah. You should have been told." Ashley frowns, makes a note. "We always house non-permanent managers with senior executives of the company. That way you can access advice and guidance both here and away from the workplace for the duration of your term with Kimia. You need to talk to Kristin

Jonsdottir in HR — here, let me give you her email." She rises gracefully, consults the screen on her desk and taps a few times on the sleek keyboard. "I've sent you her details."

This is the first Michelle has heard of this, and she's taken aback. Sharing is something she did in her twenties, and she doesn't want to go back to that life. Though it would be different now — she can afford a much better standard of living than she did then, and the company is providing financial help — she is older, and she doesn't want to be clearing up someone else's mess.

Ashley seems to sense her discomfort. "Don't worry, all our senior executives live in spacious, top-quality accommodation — in the city centre, mostly. Kristin will find you something that works for you, I'm sure. Don't hesitate to talk to her, any time, if you have any issues." She rises from her seat.

It seems the meeting's done. Another firm handshake and Michelle is ushered politely to the door. She heads back down to the real world and her desk in the open-plan office on the first floor.

* * *

Every morning Michelle's first port of call is the kitchen — more kitchenette, to be truthful — for coffee. She's usually one of the first in — not because she's keen or trying to avoid rush hour. Rush hour here is a far-distant cousin of the madness of London, and she barely notices it. Her journey in is by bus — a pleasant half-hour journey daydreaming while gazing at the lights of the waking city. She arrives early because she likes the peace to settle at her desk and introduce herself quietly to the day.

Finding her way around the job hasn't been too bad so far. It's similar to her work in London, though the projects are higher-level. It's not so easy negotiating the rest of the work environment. It's not that Icelanders are unfriendly — quite the opposite, they're charming and polite and welcoming

— or they have been so far. The problem is, the workforce here, particularly the scientific community, is not local. The vast majority have come here from other countries — from the US and right across the world — resulting in a broad mix of nationalities, all speaking the particular form of business English that is strange and unfamiliar to native English speakers. Because of this, there are nuances, misunderstandings, assumptions made that she knows what's going on when she really doesn't. After a few weeks she has only a hazy understanding of how this part of the company actually functions.

Or maybe she's expecting too much.

"Good morning, Michelle." She's jolted from her reverie by a colleague passing her desk.

"Ah, good morning, ah . . ." He's part of her team, but she struggles to remember his name. It's complicated — a long Filipino name that she finds hard to keep in her mind. She curses herself. She must write it down next time she hears it and make sure she memorizes it, or he'll begin to think she's rude. Or maybe he puts it down to her age. The rest of the team seem impossibly young to her. She's "senior" in more ways than one.

She pushes that thought away. She's made a vow not to think about it — it's not relevant, either to the job or to her private life here. Back home, she was almost obsessed with it.

It didn't help when her husband ran off with a girl half his age, of course. That was a low blow, even though the logical part of her brain scoffed in hindsight, knowing how ridiculous he was.

The disintegration of her marriage was a bad time. Her self-esteem plummeted to an all-time low and it was then that she started to obsess about her looks. She spent a small fortune at the beauty salon, enduring needles and strange machines that shone ultra-violet light on her skin, inflicting pain on her body and her bank balance for the sake of a minor improvement. She dieted fanatically, spent hours at the gym, even considered major surgery to improve her figure and her face.

Her bathroom groaned with the weight of all the rejuvenating products she slavishly bought.

She longed to be younger. And she wasn't alone in that. Once she confessed to the plethora of treatments she'd tried at enormous expense, friends and acquaintances alike revealed their own flirtations with cosmetic "improvements" — some of which resulted in the opposite.

Her friends were worried about her. "You look great," they said. "Just because that idiot's gone off with someone young enough to be his daughter, it doesn't mean you look old."

She tried to believe them. She's still trying.

CHAPTER FOUR

Michelle

Michelle's new home is gorgeous. Situated not far from Hallgrimskirkja in a beautiful part of the capital, it's quiet and spacious, light-filled (when there's daylight) and beautifully furnished. It overlooks a row of stylish houses opposite, and from the living room on a clear day there's a stunning view beyond to the sea and the mountains. Her room is huge — big enough for a desk, a sofa and a coffee table in addition to the enormous bed. It has ample storage, and she has her own bathroom. The kitchen is fabulous, much better than her own at home, the open-plan living area tasteful and welcoming. The furnishings are expensive, tasteful and contemporary — just what Michelle would choose herself, if she had the money. It's warm, too; Michelle is comfortable in a thin top, however cold the weather is outside. It's one of the upsides of living in Iceland — geothermal energy provides cheap heating for everyone.

The owner — and Michelle's new flatmate — is a young woman called Helga Jonsdottir, a senior manager at the clinic attached to the laboratory. Originally trained as a nurse and a paramedic, she runs a large medical team that conducts the clinical trials that have to be completed before a new drug can be approved. Groups of paid volunteers are rigorously tested in advance for their suitability. Once in a trial, they're constantly monitored, their reactions to the drugs carefully recorded, day and night. This means Helga's timetable varies from week to week.

When Michelle first went to meet Helga, she was surprised to see she'd been matched with such a young woman, estimating Helga's age at late twenties. She worried about the age gap, imagining Helga bringing friends to the apartment, parties, loud music.

But her new flatmate isn't like that. She has a long-term boyfriend, Magnus, who lives in the north of the country, in Akureyri, the second-largest town in Iceland. Whenever she can, she flies up there to stay with him for a few days. Otherwise, she spends all her time working — long hours and many nights — and from what Michelle deduces from her belongings and her taste in decor, she earns a lot of money.

Helga has the fresh, sturdy look of many Icelandic women. She's blonde and blue-eyed, with crystal-clear skin, and she wears no make-up at all. The only adornment she wears is a rather beautiful silver snowflake dangling from one ear, a tiny diamond sparkling in its centre. She's not groomed in the way that Ashley is, but there's a steely look in her eyes that reminds Michelle of her American boss. She's charming and polite, and she gives Michelle plenty of space. Michelle hopes they can be friends.

* * *

Ashley's remarks about the rich, tech-savvy leaders and their ground-breaking, futuristic ideals have triggered something in Michelle. She dreams up incredible innovations and imagines where they might take the human race. Her mind roams freely into the realms of fantasy until she reminds herself that that's all it is. She's always had an active imagination.

16

She begins to notice things about the building that she didn't before. Things like elevators that only travel to the upper floors, high levels of security at the entry point. From the outside, the mirrored windows on those floors that stare like blank eyes gazing over the science park. The different types of security pass. People avoiding eye contact, hurrying through the common areas as if they're contaminated.

Over coffee breaks and lunchtimes in the staff restaurant, she brings the subject up with her colleagues.

"Does anyone know what goes on upstairs?" She's sitting with an American — Amanda — and Leif, from Sweden. Both are in her team and both have worked at the company for a couple of years.

Amanda shrugs. "Secret stuff. Nobody ever talks about it."

"Yeah, it's well-guarded," Leif says. "If you think the scientists we deal with are quiet types, try talking to one of them."

"When would I get the chance?"

"Never, not here. They keep themselves to themselves," Amanda says. "But Reykjavik is a very small place."

"Do we get to know what they're working on?"

Amanda glances sideways at Leif. "When I first got here, I tried asking, but you don't get anywhere. They're all under strict non-disclosure agreements, the highest level of security."

Michelle knows this from the induction — but she can't quite believe that nobody speculates.

"But haven't you got any idea?" Her curiosity isn't dampened. "Surely you've talked among yourselves."

Leif shifts awkwardly in his chair, looks around the room. "Not me. We shouldn't even be talking like this," he says, finishing his coffee. "I need to get back. See you soon." He pushes his chair back and walks away.

Surprised, she turns to Amanda. "You won't get anything out of him," she says. "And I don't know much either, but yes, I have speculated. If you look online at what the movers and shakers in Silicon Valley are doing — and I mean the super-wealthy founders of businesses like Apple and Google, you'll get an idea of what we might be involved in here. But I don't know anything for sure, and nobody here will confirm it."

"But wouldn't they be using US facilities — or labs wherever they're based?"

"No, not necessarily. If it's a specialist area, they have to use a specialist lab, doesn't matter where it is."

"So people in this building might be working on something that could . . . I don't know . . . cure malaria, solve world hunger, create a new species of some sort that would support humans . . ."

Amanda nods. "It's at that sort of level. Stuff that's beyond our comprehension. The amount of security alone makes you think that. If you look at the company accounts, there's nothing about that part of the business. But it's definitely there, and you can bet your life there's billions of dollars of investment going into it."

"Wow." Now she's even more intrigued. "How does that work then? Is it legal to hide parts of the business?"

"Don't even ask about it. People have been sacked — even arrested — for less."

"Really? How do you know this?"

A look of alarm crosses her eyes. "I shouldn't have said that. All I'm saying is, curb your curiosity, Michelle. It's not worth thinking about, even. The stakes are too high."

CHAPTER FIVE

Michelle

She can't help dwelling on the conversation with her colleagues. She's always been fascinated by the possibilities of huge amounts of money. Not in terms of what she could make of her own life — no, what interests her is the freedom to imagine the unimaginable. The extraordinary possibilities offered by massive wealth. The opportunity to test a clever but outrageous theory, to imagine the planet years ahead — and actually influence its future. To harness technology to make people's lives better, their world greater, their reach into the universe further than ever before . . .

She fires up a search engine and thinks for a moment. It's hard to decide what terms to use. But she has to start somewhere, so she enters the words *new technologies in Silicon Valley*. Even the first page leads to terms she struggles to interpret: *advanced diagnostics, life sciences philanthropy, catalytic impact, blockchain technology, artificial intelligence*. The numbers associated with them are eye-watering: billions of dollars dedicated to research in so many areas.

The biggest numbers of all are in medical and biological technology — where Kimia sits. Perhaps she can gain some insight into what might be going on in those quiet upper floors of the building. But it's a huge and complex arena, spanning every aspect of human life: disease, food, nutrition, genetics, molecular biology, agriculture . . . the list goes on and on. The kind of work being done at the laboratory could involve any one of these, and it could be as broad or as microscopic — nanoscopic? Is there such a word? — as can be imagined.

She allows her mind to drift. What's the most thrilling, most important breakthrough that Kimia could be working on?

What if they were researching a cure for one of the world's worst, most widespread diseases? Cancer, malaria, coronavirus, heart disease, diabetes, Alzheimer's? Or a food that's cheap to make, healthy and prolific, that will solve world hunger in a flash? How about if they could reverse global environmental damage? What if humans never had to suffer injury or illness, ever?

Or what if science discovered a way to slow or stop the effects of ageing?

She lets out a cynical laugh. Typical of her — she had to come back to the age issue. She removes her reading glasses and rubs at the lines on her forehead. Perhaps they could invent a wrinkle-eraser? Like a child's pencil-eraser, but for the face. One that really worked — no false promises — and was affordable. That would be worth a fortune. Women — men too — would queue up in their droves to buy a wrinkle-free future. But let's think big: what if they could solve ageing in a holistic way, so that human organs stayed healthy for ever? But if people's bodies didn't age, perhaps they'd never die, and she daren't even think of the implications of that.

She closes her laptop and flicks through the TV channels, barely focusing on the screen. There's not much there to grab her attention, as usual. It's at moments like these that she wishes she had a partner, a companion, someone in the next room. Even a friendly neighbour. She could pop her head around the door and say: "Fancy a quick drink round the corner?" or "Shall we watch a film?" or even just talk about the news, the day, their work, or hers.

Helga isn't here, or she'd search her out and see if she wants to chat or share a glass of wine. Helga's work schedule is such that they haven't had much time to get to know each other as yet; at this rate, they'll have to get a date in the diary if they want to have supper together.

She starts to feel sorry for herself, as she always does when she remembers she's single. To avoid the downward spiral, she jumps up from the sofa, determined not to become morose. She's in Iceland and this is her big adventure. Here, surely, she can behave differently. It's dark outside, but it's still early. She's going to have to get used to going out and about in the dark. It's October, with relatively long days, a bit like back at home, but by January there'll only be a few hours of light in the middle of the day.

She wants to use her time here productively — to explore, find a hobby, learn new skills even. To open her mind to new possibilities. Right now, maybe she can venture into the streets of Reykjavik, do a little window-shopping, perhaps even stop for a hot chocolate or something stronger. She feels perfectly safe here, after all. Then tomorrow, as it's Saturday, she'll spend some time deciding on a few things to do. Learn Icelandic, for example; there's a challenge. Book some trips to see the rest of the country; there are plenty of phenomenal places to visit, even in deepest, darkest winter. She wants to learn more about the culture, and she's been meaning to investigate the Reykjavik library, the many museums she has yet to explore.

She wraps up warmly, grabs her map of the city and turns the lights off.

* * *

She wanders for a while through the well-lit streets. A sharp breeze whistles around her head, bringing a whiff of sea air along with it. In Iceland, people live close to the seas; they're never far from water. In winter the middle of the country is inaccessible, out of bounds to most people, particularly once the snow comes.

As she makes her way towards the centre of the city, a soft glow emanates from some of the houses as she passes, and she glimpses people moving around inside, preparing their evening meals or sitting watching TV. Elsewhere sparkling lights give the town a Christmas feel. She's looking forward to the arrival of the snow, only days away: she loves the muffled sound of a town draped in white, the crunch underfoot, the sparkle of sunlight on snowflakes.

There are a few people around, some on their way home from work, others tourists taking pictures. People flock here in summer when the days are long and they can explore the mountainous region in the interior, and in winter for the Northern Lights, the frozen waterfalls and dramatic geysers. These are on her wish list for when she has the time.

Reykjavik is tiny compared with other capital cities. Even the centre is quiet, most of it easily walkable if you're happy to brave the weather. She likes to explore, but tonight it's dark and chilly, and when she sees a cosy, bright bar, it's hard to resist the temptation to stop.

Inside it's warm, the windows misty with condensation. The tiny room is filled with the glimmer of soft lighting, candles flickering on each table. Books line the walls on two sides, many of them leather-bound and dusty. A wooden bar fills the third side, while the window and door are on the fourth. Even with only a few people, the place feels lively.

She leaves her coat and hat on a small table by the book-shelves and steps up to the bar, where a young woman smiles at her. "I'll be with you in a moment," she says in English, pouring beer into long glasses. As always, Michelle wonders how she knows she's British. She must have that particular look about her. It's a look she'd like to change. She's always wished she looked more exotic, mysterious, making people wonder who she is and what she does.

Back at the table, she angles herself so she can see both outside and in. She enjoys observing people, and as the place fills up, the hum of conversation rises. Soft jazz plays in the background. A young couple takes the table next to her, apologizing with a smile for crowding her.

"Not at all," she says. She studies the bookshelf next to her table for something to do, eventually removing a small book of Icelandic poetry. It has a useful translation into English on every page, so she amuses herself for a while comparing the two languages.

Despite the hubbub, the couple is close enough that she can hear every word. They're young, perhaps in their early twenties, their skin fresh, their clothes casual: she notes the sneakers on their feet, despite the cold. The girl is blonde, her hair brushing her shoulders, and though she's speaking English, Michelle would guess she's Icelandic from her look and accent. The boy speaks with an American accent but there's a tinge of something else; what nationality he might be, she's unsure. He's dark, with an intelligent, serious face and wire-rimmed glasses. They're completely focused on each other, and the first exchange between them reveals they're on a date.

At once the memory forces itself into her consciousness.

CHAPTER SIX

Michelle

It was quiet in the bar when she arrived, only a few people sitting at tables alone, one reading a book, the others gazing at their phones. He wasn't among them. She knew his face from his profile and wondered if she should have waited. No, better to be settled in a quiet place, her back to the wall, than risk being seated out in the middle once it got busy.

She hung her coat on a nearby hook and approached the bar.

"White wine, please — anything dry."

The barman looked about twenty — tall, slender, hair flopping to his shoulders, soft smile. If she'd been twenty — no, thirty years younger, she might have fallen for him.

"Large or small?"

"Small, please." She didn't want to look like a lush before they'd even met, though she longed to down it in one. Nerves did that to her. She shook her hair forward over her face.

The barman placed a glass on a mat and poured the golden liquid. It swirled invitingly, catching the light. As she paid, he gave her a heart-stopping smile, lifting her spirits.

But the feeling of dread that had pulled at her ever since she agreed to this date returned as she sat at the table, trying not to glance up every time the door opened. She'd promised herself she wouldn't go through it again, telling herself she was fine on her own — no, better on her own. She had a good life, why would she give up that hard-earned independence? *To be with someone who made it wonderful,* her inner self replied. But she wasn't sure that person existed, and if he did, whether she would ever find him.

She squared her shoulders, took a deep breath and all of a sudden he was there, in front of her, an expectant look on his face.

"Michelle?"

"Yes . . . Jonathan?" Her chair gave a loud shriek as she pushed it back. A woody aroma of aftershave surrounded her as he gave her an awkward peck on the cheek, the sleeve of his jacket rough beneath her hand.

They sat, settling their clothes. She pulled at her dress to disguise the tummy she never seemed to lose, however many pounds she dropped.

"How are you?" he said, smiling. His teeth were clean and white, but the skin on his cheeks was more lined than she'd expected. Older than his picture, she calculated, for sure. But then, so was she. Her own carefully selected headshot had been taken eight, ten years ago. But it was a good likeness, she told herself when she uploaded it to the dating site, and she hadn't aged much since then.

"Oh, I'm fine, thanks. I was a bit early . . . got myself a drink." She indicated the glass, cursing herself inwardly for pointing it out.

"That's okay," he said, turning to inspect the bar.

"I think you have to go up."

"Okay." He stood, and in that instant she knew he wasn't for her. It wasn't just the extra weight around his waist, though he had to pull at his trousers to stop them falling below the protrusion of his belly, or the stiffness with which he walked, like an old man who never exercised. It was the fact he'd made no effort, opting instead for the usual fifty-something Englishman's unimaginative attire. Ill-fitting beige trousers, brown V-necked jumper, checked shirt, open at the neck. Old man's shoes — also brown, and none too clean. It looked as if he'd been wearing the same clothes all day, perhaps doing some DIY, and he'd added the jacket as an afterthought.

As he moved away, she could see the bald patch on the back of his head. Nothing wrong with that, of course — she liked a well-groomed pate — except that he had tried to cover it up with the remaining hair.

She worked hard to keep herself in shape — no, let's be honest, to keep herself young. She swam twice a week, subjected herself to Pilates and yoga, watched her weight like a hawk. She dressed carefully, applied make-up every day, made sure her hair was coloured and trimmed regularly. She wasn't bad for her age — not only in her own eyes, others had remarked on it — and she'd scrubbed up for this date.

But the rules were different for men. Single men her age didn't seem to be bothered about their appearance: she could tell by their dating profiles. Selfies taken in bad light, unsmiling, drooping faces, an ex's arm cut out of the picture. Nylon football shirts. Some of them looked terrifying. She wondered how those men got any interest — and if they did, who the women were.

Of course, she wasn't looking for a tall, dark, handsome man to carry her off. She wasn't being naive about this — she was forty-five and divorced. All she wanted was a kind, intelligent, interesting and amusing partner. She would have settled for a friend, a companion, if that was all that was available, to go with to the cinema or the theatre, for nights in over supper. But the least she could hope for was that the person she was meeting for the first time would try to make a good impression.

For a moment, she was overcome by a feeling of hopelessness. Was this, then, the best she could do? If so, she should stop trying to find someone to transform her good life to fabulous.

As Jonathan turned back from the bar, a drink in his hand, she did her best to rearrange her face. She should give him the benefit of the doubt — try to look interested and interesting, not downhearted and disillusioned. The least she could do was give him a chance.

* * *

She woke to a message: *It was lovely to meet you. Let's have dinner — soon! J xx*

She groaned and rolled over, turning the phone to hide the message. Men never seemed to get it. Jonathan had talked about himself with barely a pause for breath, then looked offended when she left. Barely a single question about her life, her needs, her hopes and desires, in all that time. Though she'd pretended to have no expectations, she was deeply disappointed.

How she'd missed her little dog when she got home last night, his joyful greeting when she opened the door. When he'd died only a few weeks before, thin and shaky on his feet — though still, as always, happy to be with her — she'd been bereft. For the first time since Robert and she parted, she'd felt not simply alone but lonely, and she was angry with Jonathan and his dirty brown shoes for triggering that feeling once again.

Though she'd been tempted to replace the old dog with a new one, she didn't want a dog to be the thing that held her back. Now she had the option to travel, to step off a plane into places that could astound her, teach her things she never knew she wanted to know. She had options, and was beginning to feel the need to find a new one.

But this latest experience started her thinking again. If she was to be on her own — of her own choice, properly on her own — a dog was a good companion. A daily walk had many advantages. Regular exercise, discovering new footpaths and country walks. A friendly community of dog-walkers. A chance to reset. Without a dog, though, a solitary walk lost its appeal. She'd tried it, and felt self-conscious, purposeless.

More than ever, she needed to change something now.

She picked up the phone and grimaced as she typed her response.

J — I don't think so. What did you learn about me? M

It took only a few minutes — in which she fell into a comfortable doze — for the reply to come.

No problem for me. I'm looking for someone younger anyway. J

She thought she was immune to that feeling. The jolt to her stomach, the blood rising to her scalp. *Younger . . . ?* He could have been hoping for children, which would explain his reason, but that made no difference. Even knowing he was utterly, hopelessly wrong for her, it hurt. The tears sprang to her eyes as she jabbed at the phone to delete the message. But she couldn't work out how to do it.

"Fuck!" She hurled the mobile onto the bed and turned away, as if the phone were somehow complicit in this cruelty.

"Screw you!"

Her chest heaved. Bastard. She hated herself for caring, but she did care. Not about him, not that he'd cast her off so easily, but that he'd mentioned her age. In her heart, though she tried to deny it, she believed — she *knew* — her age was an issue with men, with dating. Knowing it didn't help, though. Plus, how dare he? A balding, overweight, unfit old codger like him. At least ten years older than his photo.

She screamed into the cool air of her bedroom, making no effort to muffle the sound. The room seemed to throw the sound back, mocking her.

CHAPTER SEVEN

Michelle

Helga's working this weekend. It must be exhausting, but she never complains. Michelle can only think the rewards must outweigh the drawbacks.

But on Saturday evening, for once, she'll be home, and Michelle offers to cook for her. She wants to ask about Iceland and all the things she should see and do in the few months she has here.

Helga accepts with a grateful smile. "It'll be lovely to stay in and do nothing. I'm glad I'm not travelling this weekend — I love going to Akureyri, but when I do, I don't get much rest."

Michelle buys pasta, cheese, vegetables and wine. She'd never claim to be the best cook in the world, and she likes to keep it simple. There's a handful of dishes she can make a reasonable job of. Her son, Toby, tells her they're delicious. So she sticks to what she knows. She insists that Helga relaxes with a glass of wine while she prepares the meal, lays the table and lights candles around the room.

"Tell me about your job," Michelle says.

"I love my job, but I can't tell you much, you know."

"Yes, of course, sorry. But — broadly. The medical centre carries out clinical trials; that's all I know."

"Indeed."

"Are the tests different for different drugs? Sorry to be ignorant, but I don't know a lot about clinical trials. My department comes in at the very end of the process."

"Yes, the tests can vary quite a lot. But in general terms, we look at things like how long it takes for the body to absorb and get rid of a drug, how it interacts with food and other medication, how much can be taken without any undesirable side effects. That sort of thing."

"Don't you ever wonder what it is you're testing? You must speculate, at least a little bit. I'm sure I would, I'm so nosy . . ."

Helga laughs. "I used to wonder, but now I'm just doing the job. I think that's what happens to most of us who do this work. We know we're not supposed to talk about it, or discuss it with anyone outside the medical centre, so it becomes second nature not to mention it. I shouldn't really be talking about it now, even, with you."

"Sorry, I don't mean to put you in an awkward position."

Helga smiles, shakes her head, the snowflake earring catching the candlelight. "No problem at all. But it's best not to speculate, you know."

"Okay, I get it. Apologies again." She changes tack. "Can I ask about your boyfriend?"

"Yes, Magnus." Helga smiles. "You know where Akureyri is?"

"In the north?"

"Indeed. You should visit. It's the second city of Iceland and it's an interesting place — beautiful fjords, old turf houses, ancient settlements . . . If you decide to visit and I'm there, I can show you some wonderful sights."

"Brilliant! To be shown around by a native Icelander would be great. Let's arrange it soon."

"We can get a date in the diary tonight, if you like. I've just been given my schedule for the next few weeks, so now's a good time to put something in. Otherwise the time passes and the diary fills up."

"That would be great. Let's sort something out after supper."

Michelle's touched and heartened by Helga's offer, excited too. Perhaps they will really get to know each other on the trip and become good friends.

"I'm already looking forward to it. Will I meet Magnus?"

"Of course, if you'd like."

"Great. What does he do for a living?"

"His family has a restaurant. They opened in Akureyri twenty years ago. It's hard work, but business is good."

"I'll have to try it — what's it called?"

"Beck's. It's the family name. You can look it up."

"I will. At least it's a bit easier to pronounce than most Icelandic names — I was expecting it to be something complicated. So you'll be Helga Beck one day?"

"We want to get married, but I won't change my name. Women in Iceland keep their names when they get married."

"Really? How modern of them." Michelle took Geoff's name when they got married, though it felt a bit strange, as if she'd become someone else. But it was easier after Toby was born. Simpler to have one name for the school, the doctor, the dentist.

Helga smiles. "It's how it's been for a thousand years. There are almost no family names in Iceland. We're not a formal society. Everyone is called by their first name, except at certain events."

"It sounds very . . . equal."

"We're a very equal society."

Michelle hesitates. Her mind is still on Kimia. "What's it like to work for Kimia? I haven't been there long, but it seems particularly secretive to me."

31

Helga shakes her head, her pale hair shining against the light behind her. "I suppose it is, compared with other companies. But I can't discuss it with you, really."

Michelle has never come across such a tight-lipped workforce before. It's like Bletchley Park, but in Iceland. "They won't know what we're talking about between these four walls, surely?"

Helga shrugs. "We're both subject to NDAs, aren't we? I find it easier to say very little than to relax the rules, even at home. We do have to be careful. You never know what they could find out."

Michelle looks up, startled. "What do you mean — do they monitor their employees?"

"Bug them? Yes, they do. Not everyone, of course. But believe me, Michelle, they'll go to any lengths to keep their secrets."

"Gosh." She lets this surprising piece of information sink in. "Let's sit down, it's all ready."

Helga helps transfer the dishes to the table. "Lovely. Looks delicious. Suddenly I'm quite hungry."

There's a lull in the conversation while they help themselves to the food.

"Did you mean that — do you really think they'd go to any lengths? Even if it's illegal?"

Helga hesitates. "The pharma industry as a whole is pretty ruthless — you must know that from your work in London. There are many companies like Kimia, and they guard their secrets . . . vigorously, let's say."

Michelle thinks for a moment. "I know there's a lot at stake, of course. And I know the pharma industry has a reputation, but this . . . it's a whole new level for me."

"There's more money at stake than in any other industry in the world. And if the competition gets there first, it's all pretty much wasted. So yes, they're incredibly protective."

Michelle is beginning to wonder if this is a job she really wants. Perhaps she should have checked it out properly before taking the plunge. But, she reminds herself, it's only a short-term contract, and she'll be back in England before she knows it. She's doing this for the adventure, not the job.

She pours Helga another glass of wine.

tabbing the phone. But, she reminds herself, Oskar can't know where she is, and she'll return his friend before she leaves. She's doing this for the adventure, and for job prospects. He's another glass of wine.

CHAPTER EIGHT

Lars

Lars Andersson had been excited to join Kimia seven years earlier. He was young, keen to advance his career, hoping for great things. Joining a forward-thinking company like this was his dream, and he was proud to be part of it. Proud to sign the impressive-looking non-disclosure agreement, to promise not to impart in any way the highly sensitive work of the company, or to discuss it internally or externally with colleagues, family or friends. It was important work, and it needed to be treated as such. He thrived on it, working long hours, returning home every day to his tiny flat in Reykjavik, alone but fulfilled.

He couldn't have been happier when he was assigned to the project known, to a select few only, as PAN12. He joined a small, specialist team of experts who worked separately from the rest of the scientists in the highest-security area in the building. This team was tasked with carrying out the final stages of the decades-long development of a new drug — a drug rumoured to have massive potential, with millions, if not billions, of dollars invested in it. It represented the fulfilment of a long-term dream of a young technology billionaire from Silicon Valley, a man determined to change the world. So it was treated with reverence. It was the most important project the company had undertaken, ever.

Lars has worked on this project every day for more than three years. He's dedicated his life to it.

But today is different.

He's not overly concerned when he discovers the discrepancy — it's most likely a simple mistake. Something's gone wrong with the software, that has to be the explanation. He's in the process of analysing the results of a set of clinical trials, but the data doesn't add up. This happens from time to time, and it's usually down to a simple issue with the software or the way the information has been input. He tries various routes to solve the problem, but every time he runs the data, he gets the same result.

His anxiety growing, he checks, double-checks and checks again. He runs it through various different software packages. But the results are always the same. Could it be him — has he missed something? He's tired, but he knows it's not that. The computer doesn't lie or make this kind of mistake. He's spent days on the same set of data and he's exhausted all the options.

Sweat breaks out on the palms of his hands. Something's badly wrong. Whichever way he looks at it, the results are disastrous. If they're correct, the company has wasted huge amounts of money on decades of research. The fact that the tests have got to this stage is evidence that the drug is expected to make the grade. Not only to make the grade, but to be extraordinary. To break ground in ways that can only have been imagined before.

These results will not only kill the project, they'll kill the company. It'll be a global scandal for the industry.

This is way beyond his pay grade. The blood drains from his face. He can't deal with this on his own — no way, he has to tell someone. He quails at the thought, his stomach churning. The director of his department, Robert, is not an easy man. Though outwardly he's polite — charming, even — he can be unpredictable and prickly. But this isn't something Lars can sit on, not even for a short time. He has to go and tell him, right now.

He picks up the telephone.

But Robert's in a meeting, and not to be disturbed. Nobody seems to know how long he'll be, and it's already late in the day. Lars emails an urgent request to meet first thing in the morning. He goes home carrying the burden of his knowledge with him.

A response from Robert comes late in the evening, a simple *Yes, come to my office at 8 a.m.*

Lars is awake almost all night.

* * *

He arrives early the next day, very early, his nerves shot, the burden of his terrible news sitting heavy on his shoulders. He can only hope he'll feel better once he's told his boss — there'll be a simple explanation, or a way through this, a light-bulb moment, and all will be well.

Or maybe not.

There's something he needs to do first. He takes the elevator to the ground floor and heads for the cash machine. Only a few people are in the lobby, hurrying in and out, taking no notice of him. But the security camera in the corner blinks its red eye at him as he punches in the code. He draws as much cash as he's allowed in one transaction.

Pocketing the notes, he heads for the medical centre, a three-storey building linked to the main headquarters via a covered pathway. Inside, it exudes calm and cleanliness with soft lighting and muted colours. It operates twenty-four hours a day, every day. Testing takes no account of night or day.

The young woman on reception looks up with a smile as Lars approaches. His lab coat and his security pass are evidence of his position, and he smiles back, hoping he looks confident and relaxed.

"How can I help you?" Her teeth are Hollywood white, her eyes the brightest blue. He wonders if she has coloured lenses — if so, they do a good job.

"Ah, I'm picking up the samples from the Athena trial, and from Hebe. Let me see . . ." He opens his file as if to check something. He hopes she can't see the slight shake in his hand, hear the deafening beat of his heart. "AT/742990 and . . . HB/456023." Each clinical trial has a code name and is strictly controlled. Nobody here knows the identity of the drug that's being tested.

The woman turns to her screen. "Just a moment . . . let me get someone to help you. Do take a seat, they won't be long." She types, her long nails clicking.

Lars turns away, aware of another winking security camera. He pretends to be reading the notices displayed on a wall to one side of the reception desk, doing his best to fade into the background. A cold sweat breaks out on the palms of his hands. He doesn't want to be seen here.

"Hello?"

He flinches at the sound of her voice. A young woman in the blue uniform of the medical staff looks questioningly at him. "Sorry to startle you. Did you want to collect some remaining samples?" she says.

He nods, keeping his face turned from the ceiling camera.

"This way," she says, leading him through the double doors behind them, scanning a pass on the way through, and again at a door to the right. He's led into a large, bright room. Shelves fill the entire space, holding lines of identical boxes, each neatly labelled. At the front, barring entry to the shelving, is a large desk. She negotiates a security gate and pauses behind the desk. "Do you have the approval slips?"

"Ah no, but I have the security level . . ." He recites the code, holding his breath. It's possible they already know he's found something. But she nods, making a note on an invisible sheet behind the desk.

"Wait here, I'll just grab them for you." She disappears into the warren of shelves. Though she's only gone a couple of minutes, it feels like an hour, and he has to stop himself from calling after her to hurry. But she returns in a moment with two small packets.

"Not much left of either — just these." She passes him a list for his signature and hands over the packets. He slips them into his file and clips it closed.

CHAPTER NINE

Michelle

As the winter deepens, Reykjavik turns whiter, its streets muted by sprinklings of snow and ice. On the mountains, snow caps spread downwards. The days are getting shorter, but Icelanders take it all in their stride. Buses run smoothly, whatever the weather. Planes come and go at the airports — local and international — without fuss, and life goes on as usual.

Michelle had expected to hate the short days, but she finds the light as it fades quite fascinating. Darkness creeps in throughout the afternoon, and before the light disappears entirely there's a period of strange, still twilight. It's almost like a daily eclipse. The light is flat, the sun invisible as slowly, slowly, night falls. It doesn't lift again until mid-morning. It feels odd to have the city awake and open before dawn, while the moon and stars are still visible.

She finds herself liking this place more and more, despite the freezing temperatures. There is so much to discover here. Icelandic art, design and culture are everywhere. The food's good — lots of fish, of course, and a surprising range of international cuisines. The people go out of their way to be friendly.

True to her promise to herself, she books day trips at weekends to the popular tourist attractions. She visits Iceland's frozen waterfalls, boiling geysers, volcanoes and hot springs that make natural jacuzzies, where people bathe despite the icy temperatures. Outside the towns and cities the landscape is wild and thrilling, danger never far away. Rather than being intimidated by this, she finds it energizing, and longs to explore further into the mountains.

She's been out with Helga a few times too: a museum visit, supper and drinks, and she's beginning to feel like they're proper friends now. On a shopping trip, Helga shows her the best place to buy gifts, and they try on ridiculous hats together, laughing at their reflections in the shop's mirror. She learns more about the "real" Iceland from Helga than she does from the organized trips or exploring on her own. There's a date in the diary now for their trip to Akureyri, a few weeks hence. They're flying from Reykjavik and Michelle's looking forward to getting away from the capital for a couple of days.

She sends pictures of her travels to Toby and to Gail. Toby's response is gratifying. "Wow, Mum — that's stunning. Can't wait to come over!"

"We said Easter, didn't we?" They've agreed that Toby is to spend Christmas with his father and stepmother. Michelle doesn't like it, but she's looking forward to Christmas in Iceland — it'll be another new experience for her. "The rest of the time I'll be working, and so will you. That reminds me — how's the coursework going?"

"It's fine, Mum, don't worry. I'm working pretty hard, actually."

Michelle smiles. She trusts him, but she also knows how distracting university life can be.

"I'm on track for at least a predicted two-one at the end of the year."

"That's great. How are you getting on with your flatmates?"

"Fine, Mum. Sorry, gotta go. Easter, right?"

"Send me the holiday dates, okay?"

"Will do. Love you, Mum."

Gail has a rather different response to Michelle's enthusiastic stream of photos. *It looks cold*, she texts.

—It is, the clue is in the name (smiley face). But there are hot pools everywhere. The Blue Lagoon, near Reykjavik, is wonderful. You swim in warm water and put mineral-rich mud on your face. There's a bar in the middle!

—Huh. How do you get in the water without freezing your fingers off?

—Very quickly!

—Not my idea of fun (emoji with icy face). How's the job?

—It's . . . interesting.

* * *

It is interesting, her work, despite the high levels of regulation, though there's not much creativity about it. Reading the editorials about Kimia, you get an impression of a brilliant, innovative company helping to solve some of humanity's most intractable medical problems, to save lives by developing ground-breaking drugs. Allowing people to live longer, better. That should make it a source of pride for those who work there.

But there seems to be a dark side to it all. The secrets, the security, the draconian rules.

She tries to understand, to give the company the benefit of the doubt. She reasons if they're pushing the limits of science, it's not surprising that sinister implications come to light. Artificial intelligence, robots, genetic engineering — each one is a moral minefield. She knows she's not alone in thinking that. It doesn't take much effort to find reports, studies and opinions about the more unsavoury side of scientific and technological development. But she can't help wondering, privately, what possibilities the human mind can barely imagine that companies like Kimia might bring about. For instance, what would be the pinnacle product right now for Kimia? A cure for cancer? Too simple, maybe. Mind-reading? Quite a frightening prospect. A drug that makes you invisible? The further she takes her imagination, the more terrifying it all gets.

She feels on edge whenever she enters the building. Before, its white spaces and minimalist styling seemed classy to her — understated glamour. But now, even the structure takes on a menacing air, and the spaces seem threatening. She wonders if there are hidden cameras in the stylish pattern on the walls, in the elevators. Even the toilets.

She starts to look more carefully wherever she goes.

CHAPTER TEN

Lars

He holds the slim file under his arm as he weaves through the workstations on the way to Robert's office. He has printed out the top-line results as a report: they take up very little paper, but what they signify is devastating. The file feels like a dead weight in his hand as he knocks on the door.

"Come."

Robert stands as Lars looks around the door. He's British, middle-aged, slightly overweight, a scientist turned manager, and a long-standing employee of the company. Though he's dressed casually, there's an air of authority in the way he presents himself: his shirts always neatly pressed, his greying hair carefully groomed. Leather shoes, probably handmade.

"Come in, come in. How are you? I trust all is well?" He indicates a chair in front of his desk. The desk, Lars notices, is paper-free. A large screen and a sleek keyboard dominate the space, complemented by an iPad on a stand and a mobile placed carefully in line with the other gadgets. A controlled environment.

He clears his throat. All is most certainly not well, but how should he put it?

"Ah, yes, everything's fine," he says automatically, then realizes what he's just said. "At least . . . I mean, except . . ." He shifts in his chair. It's hard and uncomfortable, designed, he reckons, to make its occupant squirm. Perhaps an indication that Robert doesn't like long meetings.

Robert fixes steely eyes on his. "What is it? Is there a problem?"

"Well, yes, there is, I'm afraid. With PAN12. I've looked at it every which way, run all the tests, checked and double-checked, but the results are always the same." He hands over a single sheet from his file. "This summarizes the problem."

Robert places wire-rimmed reading glasses on his nose. He pauses, his eyes skimming the figures. His expression remains unreadable. Then he places the report carefully on his desk, leans back in his chair and removes a handkerchief from his pocket. He shakes it out, places the reading glasses in the centre and slowly polishes the lenses in a circular motion. Lars waits, his heart pounding.

At last Robert puts the glasses back on his nose and revisits the document. After a few moments he says, his eyes still on the report, "In your own words, please. And I don't have all day."

Lars, taken aback, stammers: "The tests show — seem to show — well, they do show, conclusively, a serious problem with PAN12. I've spent days checking the software, the procedure, the initial results against the final results, but it's not the software. There's something badly wrong here."

Robert's voice is cold, penetrating. "What exactly do you mean — wrong?"

Lars takes a deep breath. "What the results show is that, in years two and three, PAN12 begins to break down, in a small but significant number of test subjects. You can see the numbers in the report. In those cases, the effect is the opposite of what we were expecting. Rare illnesses occur, sometimes severe. Ageing speeds up dramatically, leading to . . . to—" he hesitates, then lowers his voice to a whisper — "premature death."

There's a long pause. Robert's face remains impassive, his eyes focused on the sheet of paper in front of him. Then, slowly, he removes his reading glasses once more and rubs the space between his eyes. Lars holds his breath. The silence stretches into the room.

But the peace is shattered when Robert stands abruptly, his chair rolling back, crashing into the cabinet behind it. Lars almost leaps from his seat. Robert walks with slow steps to the window and stares out. The sun has broken through dark clouds for a moment, and the sea beyond the buildings sparkles silver in the distance.

Robert turns, a thin smile on his otherwise unreadable face. "Thank you for coming to me with this. It is certainly an interesting report. So, you did all the usual checks on the data?"

Lars nods, dumbfounded. Robert's reaction is not at all what he expected. It's almost as if he knew about the discrepancy already. But if he did, why are the clinical trials still under way, and why haven't they halted the project?

"Did anyone else help you check the results at all?"

Lars shakes his head. "No, there's no one else in my team who's—"

Robert holds up a hand, cutting him short. "And you've told nobody else about this? Good man." Robert nods. "Let's keep it that way, shall we? I'll take it from here." He walks back to his desk, picks up his mobile and taps once. He speaks quickly, his voice neutral. "Yes, two minutes. Mr Andersson is leaving shortly." He taps again and turns, his face unreadable.

"I'll be keeping this." He flicks the flimsy report. "What else do you have in that file?"

Shocked, Lars stammers "I . . . nothing. You have the only report."

"It's wrong. A glitch in the system. Delete the report, and anything else that mentions it. Delete it everywhere — today. Don't talk about it, don't mention it to colleagues. Is that clear?"

45

Lars opens his mouth to object, but Robert shakes his head.

"Forget about it. We'll deal with it. It's out of your hands now." He takes a step towards Lars, one arm outstretched, ushering him towards the door.

Lars grabs his file and stumbles to his feet. "But—"

"Your involvement with this drug is over," Robert says firmly, holding the door open. "As far as you're concerned, you've never had anything to do with it. Are we clear?"

"That's . . . that's clear, thank—"

But he's cut short by the closing door.

* * *

Lars returns to his workstation, his stomach twisting into knots. Bile floods his mouth. He swallows, grimacing, holding a tissue to his lips. Luckily his colleagues are engrossed in their work.

He's on borrowed time here, he knows it. They won't reassign him. They won't be pleased with him for discovering a problem with their star drug. On the contrary, he'll be out. It won't be long before they home in on him, in a pincer movement he can't escape.

As he sits, stunned, at his workstation, oddities begin to fall into place — behaviour he didn't understand, practices that seemed strange. It all makes sense, once you take in the implications. If you can take them in.

"Lars, good morning."

He starts at the sound, his body tensing, his head whipping round. His colleague Martin greets him as he passes, his lab coat pristine in the silvery morning light. Martin looks at him strangely. "You're jumpy today," he says. He doesn't break his stride and is soon at the door, swiping his security pass without pausing.

Lars places his hands flat on his desk and leans in, waiting for his heart to slow. What is he supposed to do now? He can't go back to Robert — that's clear. But PAN12 is the only project he has; without it he has nothing to do. A sense of dread settles on his chest, squeezing his ribs until he can barely breathe. His hands shake, his heart starts to palpitate. For a moment he thinks he's having a heart attack.

With nowhere else to go, he heads for the toilets. But there's a cubicle in use, and all he can do is run the water until it's icy cold and splash it over his face, his head.

"Okay, Lars?" A young man emerges from the cubicle and stands at the row of basins, washing his hands with vigour.

"Yeah, all good." Lars avoids the man's eyes as he wipes his dripping head with some paper towels. "Just a bit of a headache. I'm fine now."

"You look pale — you need to get out more, get some exercise." The man claps Lars on the back as he leaves. The door swishes shut behind him.

A wave of nausea rises from Lars's belly. He's been unable to eat properly in days. He drinks water from two hands, slurping noisily, wiping away the stream of drops from his chin. He faces himself in the mirror. Steady.

What the hell just happened? Robert is difficult, hard to read at the best of times, but he gave no indication of what he was thinking. Did Lars do something wrong? If so, what? And why not discuss it, work through it together? He would have expected an explanation, even an excuse, for being taken off the project. He has no idea what to make of it.

Lars has been shut down, there's no doubt about that. He's been taken off PAN12 — in fact, he's been forbidden to go anywhere near it. He did everything right. He couldn't have been more diligent, completing all the reports as required, checking and double-checking, interrogating the results until he was absolutely sure he'd done everything correctly. It's not his fault they're not what the company was hoping for. He's one of their best, most loyal scientists — surely he's well placed to resolve the issue, even if it means delaying the launch. He has an impeccable record and has worked on PAN12 for his entire time at Kimia.

It can only be — he hardly dares think it — a cover-up.

His legs feel weak as he stumbles back to his workstation. He sinks into his chair. Perhaps Robert doesn't trust him. But there's been no indication of this, none. His track record is whiter than white. Perhaps Robert already knew there was a problem, so what seemed a shocking outcome to Lars served only to underline what had already become clear. Robert didn't seem happy to be reminded, if that was the case.

None of it makes sense, though. PAN12 is a special case, but there's no question of Lars breaking his non-disclosure agreement. He's always behaved in an exemplary manner as regards security.

The simple answer must be that Lars's results are right, and the news is as devastating to Robert as it is to Lars. But you wouldn't have known it from his demeanour. He was cold and uncommunicative, and he clearly wasn't going to discuss it. Lars imagines that when the door closed behind him, a very different Robert emerged. The man will have to face the board of directors with the worst possible news.

Or perhaps he won't.

Perhaps he's going to hide Lars's report, deny the results. Maybe that's why he behaved so strangely when he saw the report? But surely not. The implications are enormous. If Kimia goes ahead and releases the drug, people could die. Not a handful, but in huge numbers.

To ignore Lars's report would be criminal. More to the point, to go ahead with marketing the drug would be inhuman.

If PAN12 is unsafe, Kimia is finished. The money at stake is eye-watering. All of a sudden, Lars knows what will happen. The company has a reputation for ruthlessness. If they decide to ignore these results and go ahead, they'll make a fortune in a very short space of time — before the flaws become obvious. By the time the world realizes what's happening, Kimia's investors and directors will be gone. It'll be a global scandal, but the perpetrators will be impossible to find.

Lars is in the most difficult position imaginable. There's no way he'll survive this.

But what is he expected to do now? Keep his mouth closed and wait for something to happen, without question? There's no point — he's finished. They can't have him knowing what he knows if they're planning to put a lid on it. At best, they'll pay him off, and he'll be unable to work in the sector again. At worst — he daren't think about that.

It will be the end of life as he knows it. A small, angry flame begins to flicker and grow.

There's no time to lose. Security will check on him imminently, and he needs to show he's deleted the report. He turns to his screen. In a matter of moments the job is done. He looks around. No sign of anything unusual. With the file under his arm, he walks casually towards the elevators and takes the first one going down, its doors already open.

CHAPTER ELEVEN

Lars

Dread takes hold as he exits the elevator at the ground floor. His throat tightens. He's surely on borrowed time now. His left hand closes over the file.

At the security gate, a receptionist calls to him. "Mr Andersson?" He flinches, stops walking. She walks around the desk and approaches him. He clutches the file to his side. Sweat breaks out under his arms, on his back. They can't know about the samples yet, surely.

"You have a meeting on the ninth floor," the woman says, pointing behind him to the bank of lifts.

"Ah, I was just—"

"They're already waiting," she says, with an apologetic gesture. "Ninth floor. You'll be met there."

He turns to see two security guards walking towards him. Any wrong move now and they'll be on him.

This is it, then. He's being cancelled.

He nods, unable to speak, heads back to the elevator. The security guards shadow him a few feet behind. At the lift, one man stations himself close, his back to the wall, hands folded in front. He looks ahead steadily, avoiding Lars's stare. The other stands next to him, his eyes on the floor numbers as the lift approaches.

The doors slide open. Lars steps in. The second security guard makes a move to follow, but in that moment a woman appears from nowhere, lunges for the doors and pushes past. Startled, the man stumbles, and before he can recover, the doors glide shut and the lift is moving.

Lars closes his eyes. A small moment of freedom before they close in.

"Oops," the woman says. "That was close. Was he with you?"

Lars shakes his head, unable to speak.

Dark, shiny hair to her shoulders. A black down-filled coat, reaching almost to her ankles. A colourful scarf, artfully arranged over a black shirt. Brown eyes gaze at him with a hint of concern. A security pass reveals her name: *Michelle Turner*. He thinks fast — perhaps she can help him, perhaps—

But before he can speak, the lift shudders to a stop. The lights in the ceiling begin to flicker, then dim. They're stuck between floors.

The woman looks up in alarm. "No, no. Not now, please . . . I hate lifts." She turns to Lars. "Should we press the alarm?" She makes a move towards the bank of buttons, but Lars places a hand on her arm, holding it gently. She hesitates, startled.

This might be his only chance. "Not yet. It's okay, it's stopped because of me. You'll be fine, it's me they want. The security guard — he was meant to follow. I've got something. Please, take this, get it out of the building."

He grapples with the file for a moment, almost dropping it in his haste. "Listen, Michelle. My name is Lars. Lars Andersson, but that doesn't matter. This — this, in this packet — is incredibly important. It's evidence. Take it. Hide it." He folds the packet into her hand, closing her fingers around it.

"But what is it?" Her eyes widen. "Evidence of what?"

"There's no time." He pulls a single sheet from the file and folds it into a small square, his fingers fumbling. "This will explain. Don't show it to anyone here, you mustn't. Take it to the police — no, wait — take it to the media."

"The police? No, I can't. I don't—" She tries to hand the packet back to him but he won't take it.

"Not the police — the media. I discovered something and I'm being cancelled because of it. After this meeting, I'll be out on my ear, and I'll be silenced. I won't be able to say anything about it."

"But—"

The lift lurches, the lights brighten. A whirring sound indicates they're on the way again. The lift inches slowly upwards.

"Hide it, quickly!" For an instant she hesitates, her eyes searching his. Then she seems to make a decision. With sudden acuity, she slips the packet and the paper into the waistband of her trousers, covering the small bulge with her shirt. By the time the lift clicks into place, she's standing alone at the door, Lars in the far corner, as if they've never spoken.

"Oh, thank goodness for that," the woman says as the doors slide open, revealing two burly security guards. "I thought I was going to be stuck in there all day."

The closest one directs a cold smile at her, holding the door open with a large boot. He ushers her out, his eyes on Lars. "No need to worry. Just a temporary problem," he says.

In a moment, she's gone, and the two guards are in the lift, facing the doors.

"Ninth floor, I believe," the first one says, without turning. He presses the button and the lift departs, smoothly, upwards.

CHAPTER TWELVE

Michelle

She walks slowly back to her desk, unsure what just happened. The man looked frightened — no, terrified — and her instinct to help kicked in. What had he said? "I'm being cancelled." He must mean he's being sacked — or censored. He was clearly being escorted by those security guards — up to the ninth floor, where the directors have their offices, where the big meetings take place. Where he'll hear his fate, whatever that might be.

She takes a quick look around. Nobody's interested in her, everyone getting on with their work. She slips the packet and the fold of paper from her waistband. She holds them gently in one hand, resisting the urge to look at them now. If they're that important — "evidence," he'd said — then she should keep them safe until she's out of the building. There could be cameras on her right now. She checks the time: it's eleven fifteen, a long way to go until she can leave. She must find a hiding place, fast. If they want to track her down, they will. They'll know the man had a few minutes alone with her in the lift, before he was accompanied to the upper floor by the security guards. Once they discover he's taken something, she'll be in trouble before she knows it. There could have been hidden cameras in the lift, even.

There's no point putting it in her desk, or anywhere near her workstation. Not on her person either, or even in the ladies' room, which would be the first place she'd look if it was her doing the searching. No, she needs to be cleverer than that. The kitchen? Also too obvious. She gazes around, her mind racing. There's no time, someone could come at any moment. She slips the paper into the back of a file bulging with reports, gathers it up and balances her mug on top. In the other hand she still holds the packet. A short distance from her workstation is a desk usually occupied by a colleague who has been off sick for a few days. She won't be returning until next week. Without hesitating or looking around, Michelle places the file on the desk and, as if as an afterthought, drops the packet into an in-tray, hiding it from sight beneath some papers.

That's the best she can do until later. It's unlikely anyone will notice either item for the next few hours. She can keep an eye on them from her workstation and collect them safely on her way out later.

She heads for the kitchen and a strong cup of coffee. She has no idea if she's doing the right thing or not. It's possible that the man had done something criminal, that he had no right to take whatever's in the packet — but instinct tells her there's more to it than that. She doesn't trust Kimia's motives, and given a choice between David and Goliath, she'll take David any day.

Michelle's curiosity is piqued. She's already suspicious of Kimia's ethics, and the words *silenced* and *cancelled* are still ringing in her ears.

Luckily the rest of the day is quiet. There's a big event going on elsewhere in the building — a number of her workmates are involved. A hush settles over the area, and she's able to keep watch on the empty desk and the secrets it holds. She achieves very little, too shaken by what's happened to work.

At last the end of the afternoon arrives and she can leave. She's surprised she hasn't been sought out, strangely disappointed that her hiding place didn't need to prove itself. Perhaps they didn't know he had the evidence with him when he entered the lift — or perhaps he was able to sidetrack them somehow.

She wonders what will happen to him. He's probably been marched out of the building already, leaving any personal possessions behind. They'll examine his workstation, erase his hard drive, delete all evidence that he was there. That's how this company works. They've probably already got his mobile phone and any other work-related gadgets. The poor man will go home with nothing. No job, no phone, no references. Maybe they'll bribe him to stay silent, and he'll have something to keep him going. Or perhaps all they'll need to do is threaten him.

* * *

On the bus she keeps her bag on her lap, the packet and the folded paper safely stashed within. Reykjavik is a small place, small enough that anybody could be sitting next to her on the bus — someone from Kimia who she doesn't know, a journalist, a scientist.

Helga's out when she gets home. She throws off her coat, extracts the packet and opens it with shaking fingers. Inside is a tiny bottle containing a small number of blue pills, the contents pressed in with a ball of cotton wool to stop them rattling. There's no label on the outside, and nothing stamped on the pills to indicate what they are. She turns to the sheet of paper. *This will explain*, he'd said. But all it reveals is four sets of figures. There's no title to the page, but the rows are labelled with codes. She knows enough to know that the codes mean certain types of test. But what do they refer to? The data and the pills must be linked, or the man wouldn't have said what he did.

55

He wanted her to go to the police but corrected himself. "Take it to the media." Should she? She needs to know more about what she's got. If she simply hands the items over, they'll look at her blankly. Most likely they'll suggest she hands them back to Kimia. But they seem too important. The man looked scared, his hands were shaking, he told her not to show this "evidence" to anyone in the company.

"Evidence" is a weighty word. It implies wrongdoing, and Michelle is convinced the frightened man has found exactly that.

She's still puzzling when the door opens. Helga brings with her a swoosh of cold air, her hat and shoulders sprinkled with wet snow. Michelle looks up, relieved to see her friend. Helga could be the perfect person to help her. She's been with Kimia a long time, and though she's not a scientist, she understands much more than Michelle does about how it all works.

Helga stamps her feet on the mat, pulling off her snow boots to reveal pink woolly socks. "Wow," she says, as she joins Michelle in the living area. "It's getting really cold out there. Windy too. We'll have a lot of snow tonight. There's a storm coming in." She struggles out of her coat, scarf and hat and leaves them in a heap on the arm of the sofa. "I'm shattered. Cup of tea?"

"Yes. Yes, please. I'm glad you're home, Helga." She hesitates, the words of the desperate man echoing in her ears. *Don't show it to anyone here, you mustn't.* But she needs to share this with someone — she's way out of her depth. "I need your advice."

Helga returns in a few moments with two large mugs, steam curling into the air above them. But her smile fades when she sees what Michelle has put on the coffee table. Slowly she places the mugs on the tabletop.

"So, what can I help you with?"

Michelle reaches for her drink, but it's still too hot. She puts it down again. "This is really weird, Helga, and I don't know what to do about it." Taking a deep breath, she describes the scene in the elevator — the security guards, the frightened scientist and what he said to her. The unexpected responsibility he handed over to her.

"So, here they are, the pills and the sheet of data, and I'm none the wiser."

Helga frowns. "That's very strange. Let me see, I might recognize them."

Michelle pushes them across the table. Opening the tiny bottle, Helga drops a single pill into her hand and walks back to the kitchen area where the light is brighter. The pause that follows is so long, Michelle begins to wonder what's wrong. "Any idea what it is?"

At last Helga walks back to the sofa. There's a strange look on her face as she replaces the pill in the bottle, screws the lid tightly and picks up the sheet of data. Her skin is pale in the glare of the artificial light. The single earring flashes as she studies the page.

"What should I do, Helga?"

Helga shakes her head, reaching for her drink with trembling fingers. Her eyes are wide with shock as she cradles her mug in both hands. "Oh, Michelle," she says.

A feeling of dread creeps over her. "What is it?"

"This isn't good. You shouldn't have brought this back, you know. You should have handed it in straight away. It's against the rules to remove anything from the building. There are tight controls — they'll soon find out it's gone. If they haven't already."

"What is it? What's the drug — do you know it? Why do you think he took it? There must be a reason—"

"I'm sure he did have a reason. But this is theft, you know. It should never have left the building."

"But why do you think he was so perturbed? He told me to get it out of the building, not to mention it to anyone internally. It makes no sense to me." She gathers up the bottle and the paper, meaning to take them to her room.

Helga holds out her hand, her eyes anxious. "Don't worry, I'll sort it out. I'll hand it in for you tomorrow."

"That . . . that's kind of you." If Helga takes over, it'll be a weight off her mind. She can forget it ever happened.

But at the last minute, she hesitates. The look on Lars's face, the fear in his voice. She can't simply ignore his pleas. He was desperate, there's no doubt about that. "Actually, let me think about it. I'll decide what to do in the morning."

"Wait, Michelle." Helga's eyes are pleading now. "You could lose your job over this. I could lose mine, just because I know about it. It's dynamite. Please Michelle, we'll both get into terrible trouble if you don't take it back."

Michelle sinks down onto the sofa. She runs her hands through her hair. The last thing she wants is for Helga to lose her job because of her. Right now, she has no idea what to do. "God, Helga," she says. "What have I stumbled into?"

CHAPTER THIRTEEN

Lars

This is the first time he's been this high up in the building. Scientists are rarely invited here. This is where the billionaire clients come, a luxury elevator speeding them directly into the clouds. This is where world-changing decisions are made, where the big money resides.

Alongside spacious offices for the most senior executives are presentation rooms and boardrooms. The rest consists of open waiting areas, tastefully furnished, oriented towards the windows and the stunning views. It's as if the air is thinner up here, all noise muffled. You wouldn't want to raise your voice or have heels that clicked on the tiled floors.

The security guards guide Lars towards a seating area beside a door. A discreet sign indicates this is the office of Christophe Blanchet, CEO of Kimia and his ultimate boss. Lars is even more intimidated. If he's been summoned to Blanchet's office, then it's even worse than he imagined. Nobody gets to see the big boss — ever.

The uniformed men stand to one side of the door. Lars sits gingerly on a low yellow sofa that looks as if it's never been used. There's next to no back to it, no cushions at all — it's too hard to be comfortable. Nerves prevent him from settling anyway, but he finds himself wondering if it's a conscious strategy by the board. This is not a place for relaxation.

His eyes stray to the window, a huge floor-to-ceiling pane of glass. The whole of Reykjavik is stretched out in front of him, disappearing into the thin mist that shrouds the mountains beyond. Ominous black clouds threaten from the east. It'll snow on the highest peaks later, as the temperature drops with the arrival of darkness.

Later, when he's lost his job. What will he do? He daren't think about it now. The worst is yet to come.

He wonders if he should risk looking at his phone. Probably not. They'll probably take it away before he leaves the room. Or maybe before he even enters it — but he doesn't want to remind them.

When at last the door opens, Lars flinches, a flush rising through his entire body. He is ushered in by a woman, who exits as soon as he's in the room, closing the door quietly behind her. In his heightened state of nerves, Lars wouldn't be surprised to hear the sound of a key being turned, locking him in.

He stumbles as he enters, unused to the carpeted floor. It takes a moment or two to register the other occupants. Five of them altogether, and he recognizes two, a man and a woman, from their director profiles on Kimia's website. They're even more youthful than their headshots suggest — the skin on their faces smooth and fresh, their eyes bright.

Also at the table is Kimia's head of security, easily identifiable by the name tag on his lapel. Of course. The implications are not lost on Lars.

At the head of the enormous table sits a well-groomed man he's never seen before. It can only be Blanchet, a man known for his secretive nature. There are no pictures of him in the glossy brochures or on the slick website, no video of a smiling captain of industry shaking hands at a corporate function. The fact that Lars is present in a room with this man is in itself a dark signal of what's to come. He can barely move his legs as he approaches the table.

Blanchet indicates for Lars to sit opposite the line of directors. They take their seats in perfect synchronisation, like a group of automatons — and in absolute silence, except for the faint rustling of clothes on furniture. Not one of them makes eye contact. If he wasn't already terrified, this would have him shaking with fear. Nobody says a word of greeting.

He's acutely aware of the file in his left hand. He doesn't want to draw attention to it, so he places it under his seat. When he straightens up, all eyes are on him.

"I'll take that," the head of security says, holding out his hand. It's the hand of a twenty-year-old, the objective part of Lars's brain acknowledges, soft as a child's. Lars reaches down for the file, passes it over the table. His phone will be next, he's sure of it.

Blanchet leans forward. He looks slightly older than the others, perhaps in his early thirties, his brown hair carefully groomed, his fingernails immaculate. From his face you'd imagine his life's path has been smooth and privileged, with barely a misfortune to cause a wrinkle on his brow. A large watch sparkles on his wrist. His eyes are a bright, piercing blue, the whites around the irises almost impossibly clear. He fixes them on Lars.

"So, Mr Andersson — can I call you Lars?" Only a trace of an accent. From his name, he could be French, but he could pass as born-and-bred American.

Lars nods. Politeness seems unnecessary right now.

"Lars, I understand you've been involved in assessing the data from a set of clinical tests, the results of which seem . . . anomalous. Is that right?"

Lars hesitates. It seems pointless to argue his case, when it's so obvious what's about to happen. He takes a deep breath. A part of him can't let them get away with this. "Alarming, I would say."

The row of executives opposite Lars seems to shimmer as they shift uncomfortably in their seats. As one, they look at Blanchet, as if a ball has been tossed in his direction.

Blanchet's eyes narrow. "That's because they're incorrect. As you know, we're looking into it. Unfortunately, there are implications for you. You've run all the tests on this drug, which is, as you also know, classified at the most sensitive level. Now that you've been taken off the project, I'm afraid there is no position in Kimia for you."

The words fall like stones into a pond. All eyes turn on Lars. They're clones of each other, robots obeying the same instructions. Though he knew it was coming, it feels as if someone has tipped a bucket of icy water over his head.

He clears his throat. "I really don't feel—"

Blanchet cuts him off. "This has nothing to do with your feelings, I'm afraid."

"The situation was not of my making," he says, keeping his voice steady with an effort. "I ran the data multiple times. I checked again and again. There's no way I could have made a mistake. You know my record — I don't make mistakes. The results were conclusive."

Blanchet smiles, his eyes cold. "You see, that's where you're wrong. My colleagues here had them run again. There was no issue at all."

"But—"

"I'm afraid that's the end of it, Mr Andersson." He stands and strolls over to the enormous window on one side of the room. Today, it looks out over dark seas and heavy clouds, though on a good day the view must be breathtaking. Even while he's waiting for his sentence, Lars's mind strays, and he wishes he'd had the chance to contemplate that view.

"I'll take you through the necessary procedures," the head of security says, holding out one hand. "Your mobile phone, please." With difficulty, Lars drags his gaze from the window and the man who wields such power yet is never seen. Is the fact that Lars has seen his face his death sentence? He fumbles in his pocket for his mobile, hands it over without a word.

"Then you'll be escorted from the building."

Lars barely hears the drone of the security director's voice. But he understands the implication perfectly. "I'm sure we don't have to remind you of your non-disclosure agreement, Mr Andersson. Breaking that agreement would have serious consequences. Very serious indeed."

CHAPTER FOURTEEN

Michelle

"Listen, Michelle," Helga says, urgency in her voice and eyes, "think about it. You don't know this man. He could be a criminal, or a spy, trying to steal Kimia's secrets. It happens, you know, in this industry. That's why Kimia's security is so stringent. He could be getting you involved in something terrible. You just don't know."

Michelle's eyes widen. "My God, Helga!" It hadn't occurred to her that the scientist might be a thief, or worse.

"You can't get involved, believe me. Honestly, you could end up in prison!"

"But — but he was so credible, and his fear was genuine, I'm sure of it." Now she doesn't know what to believe.

"These people are clever. He could have been frightened because he'd been found out."

This is worse than she'd imagined. "I don't want anything to do with this. It's — it's too big. Way beyond me."

But something inside her resists returning the sample to Kimia. Her gut feeling tells her something's wrong. What if the scientist is genuine, and he's trying to do the right thing? "Perhaps I should take it to the police."

"No!" Helga gasps. "Why would you do that? Just let me take it back to Kimia for you."

"Surely, if he's a thief or a spy, Kimia would involve the police anyway?"

"More likely Interpol, or Europol. The local police couldn't handle something like this — they don't have the capability."

Helga's probably right. This whole thing is so far beyond Michelle's experience. But the scientist trusted her with the sample, and every bone in her body tells her he was honest.

Helga interrupts her chain of thought. "Did you get his name?"

Michelle shakes her head. "I'm not sure. Did he tell me? I think he did. But — no, it escapes me."

"Try to remember. Did he look like a scientist to you?"

"Yes, definitely. He had a blue lanyard."

Michelle's head begins to spin, and it's not the wine. "Wait — Lars! His name was Lars, I remember now."

"Lars what? What was his last name?"

"I can't remember. But Helga, let's give him the benefit of the doubt, just for a minute—" Helga starts to object, but Michelle holds up a hand. "*If* he was right and he was about to be cancelled, there must be a reason for it. Had he learned something about the drug that he shouldn't have? Had he found something wrong with the drug, or the tests?"

"We don't know. How can we know why he was seeing the directors? It could be any one of a hundred reasons. We're not scientists, Michelle, or detectives. We're not going to get to the bottom of this. We just don't know. You need to hand it back."

"But he was terrified, I could see it in his eyes. He was desperate for me to take the sample — *desperate*." She bites her lip.

"I can't help you, Michelle, except to say, please, *please* take it back to Kimia," Helga says, her eyes beseeching.

"I don't want you to lose your job. That would be awful. Don't worry, I'll sort it out. I'm sorry I involved you. Listen,

I don't know about you, but I'm exhausted. That wine's really gone to my head." She takes the tiny pill bottle and the report and puts them in her pocket. "I'll sleep on it. Maybe things will be clearer in the morning."

* * *

It's the worst night's sleep she's ever had. She tries to read her book — a book she was enjoying before this. But now she can't focus on the words, let alone force her mind back into the narrative. She gets a hot chocolate and watches TV for a while, the sound down for Helga's sake, hoping that the warm drink will make her sleepy. It only seems to make her more twitchy. Her head spins with questions, but there are no answers. She covers herself in a blanket and lies on the sofa watching one of her favourite films. But she's wide awake — nothing seems to take her mind off her situation.

After an hour or so, something makes her look up — the smallest of movements in the corner of her eye. A figure in a long robe stands at the door to Michelle's bedroom, one hand poised to push the door open.

"Helga? Are you okay?"

The figure starts. "Ah! I didn't see you there." Helga glides away from Michelle's door, her bare feet soundless on the floor. "You okay? Can't sleep?"

"Not so far, but I'll drop off soon. Were you sleepwalking?" She indicates her bedroom door.

"No, not sleepwalking. Only I . . . I was worried about you, wondering if you were still awake. I saw your door was ajar." Helga pulls a glass from a cupboard, pours herself some water. "See you tomorrow," she says, and pads back to her room.

Michelle gazes after her, her mind working. Was Helga about to creep into Michelle's room — was she after the sample? Why else would she be so furtive, knowing Michelle was there? Perhaps she shouldn't have trusted her. But she shakes the thought away. Helga's her friend, she was worried about her, that's all. Michelle's exhausted, anxious, and quite possibly becoming paranoid. Suspecting everybody isn't going to help.

A little later, while the film drones on, Michelle remembers Lars's last name. Andersson. That's it. Not that it'll do her much good. She searches online and discovers how many Lars Anderssons exist in Iceland — a lot. She adds *scientist* and eventually finds a photo of a much younger Lars with a short caption about his career. It's not helpful, and sleep is still not coming.

Finally, having exhausted all the other options, she takes a big swig of a cold remedy that helps induce slumber. After half an hour it does the trick.

She's awake again before the alarm goes off, her head heavy, her eyes clogged. As she makes her way to the bathroom, she feels nausea rise from the pit of her stomach. The wine and the cold remedy were a bad combination on an empty stomach. She retches over the basin, her stomach cramping, but to no avail. There's nothing to throw up. A tic over her left eye blurs her vision. She sits on the closed toilet for a few moments, gathering her strength. This isn't going to help; she needs a clear head today. She must decide what to do.

She takes a long shower, forcing herself to stand under cold water for two minutes at the end. It does the trick, because her head clears and her energy level improves. She decides to go into work and behave normally, try to forget what happened yesterday. One thing she's learned in life is that knee-jerk reactions are inadvisable. If you let a problem simmer in the background for a while, take your mind off it completely if possible, your decisions are likely to be more objective.

A black coffee is all she can face in the way of breakfast, her stomach still aching. She needs to decide what to do with the little bottle and the data sheet. She'd rather not take it with her, but it feels wrong to assume it will be safe in the apartment.

On her way to the bus stop she takes a swerve through a small sculpture park. When she first came here, before the weather grew too cold, she would linger a while on her way home. Her favourite piece is a small bronze of a woman embracing a child, and while sitting on a bench nearby one day, she spotted a mouse investigating a small hole in the trunk of a tree. She watched for a few minutes as it explored. Eventually, it left the hole and she looked in to see if it had nested there, but it had clearly rejected the idea and moved on, because the hole was shallow and empty. But her searching fingers found a very slight bend in the cavity. Perfect for a small packet in a waterproof bag. She clears a handful of wind-blown snow, places the packet out of sight and replaces the snow.

The cold wind batters her as she walks on to the bus stop. Overnight, a good few inches of snow have fallen and her boots crunch fresh footprints into the white powder. By the time she reaches the bus shelter, the tips of her fingers are frozen despite her gloves, and she's glad of the windbreak it offers. Stamping her feet, she's reassured by the sign telling her the next bus will be along in three minutes. Even muffled up as she is, she doesn't want to be out too long in this.

While she waits, two people join her, huddled against the cold. From their height and build, she'd guess they're men — there's no way of telling otherwise. In this weather everyone looks the same, heads and faces covered against the cold, long padded coats, snow boots, their faces invisible under scarves and hats.

She's relieved when the bus arrives, its bright lights warm in the dark of the early morning. It's half empty. She sits as far away from the other passengers as she can, beside a window, her bag on the empty seat next to her implying her need to be alone.

As she gazes out at the snow-covered streets, she can't help wishing Lars hadn't handed his problem to her. He must have known the implications. But then she remembers the look of desperation in his eyes. Who knows what he'd found out? Without being able to interpret the data, she has no way of knowing what was so terrible about the drug — or the report — that he'd handed them over to an unknown person.

She gazes out at the passing city, pleading with it to give her an answer. But it's frozen and silent, keeping its secrets close.

CHAPTER FIFTEEN

I like this kind of assignment. Easy target, good money. Very good money — quite possibly the highest paid job of its kind ever, though of course there's no way I can prove that.

No drama. Retrieve the item, eliminate the target, cover the tracks. Job done. Don't even have to get my hands dirty — free rein to use other operatives if I choose.

Gathering intelligence, surveillance — they're crucial to what I do, but they don't give me a buzz. I like being in the field, at the front line. Learning to be a sniper with the Marines, that was a buzz and a half. I found something I was really good at, and for the first time in my life I worked hard. But killing from a distance didn't quite do it for me.

What works for me is seeing the fear in their eyes.

My first one was the best. I laid the groundwork, studied the terrain, put all the pieces in place and pop! The work of seconds. I cleared out, holed up and analysed my success. I always study my successes and my failures, equally — even now, after all these years, all those jobs completed. What worked? What didn't? How can the process be improved?

I think of myself as a consummate professional. That's how I got this job.

CHAPTER SIXTEEN

Michelle

"May I?" a man says in English, indicating her bag.

"I . . . of course." Startled, she retrieves her bag, hands fumbling. He's dressed like everyone else, a scarf over his face, a woolly hat almost covering his eyes. He puts a small bag beneath the seat in front and looks directly ahead.

There are plenty of empty seats on the bus. Why would he choose to sit here, force her to move her bag? She starts to tremble, inching her body away from his.

"It's all right, there's no need to be frightened."

The slight accent gives him away. She risks a glance at his face, but she can't see enough of it to know.

"It's me, Lars. Yesterday I—"

"Yes, I know. How did you find me?" She's still suspicious. What does he want now?

"I watched you leave the building yesterday and get on the bus. I guessed you'd be on this one this morning. But — please listen, I don't have long. I'm leaving the country today, right now."

"I'm listening."

71

"The sample — you have it with you?"

"No. I didn't think that was a good idea."

"Is it safe? Did you leave it at your apartment?" His voice is low, urgent.

"It's safe. No, not there. Not anywhere it can be found easily. But — can you tell me what it is? Why is it so important?"

A couple takes the seat in front of theirs, snow dappling their shoulders.

"Let's move." They move right to the back, out of earshot.

Lars drops his voice to a whisper. "Its code name is PAN12. They're planning to release it, but they can't. If they do, people will die in their thousands, maybe millions."

Michelle gasps, her hand flying to her mouth. "What? What are you talking about?"

"It's a bomb. Not literally. But it could be more important than the atomic bomb in the history of the human race. And Kimia is the only company to have developed it."

She can hardly believe her ears. "What does it do?"

"This drug has one of the richest men in the world behind it. It's been in development for many years, probably decades. I've been working on it for all my time at Kimia. It's this man's lifelong dream, and it's almost ready to be released. What it's supposed to do is almost unbelievable." Lars pauses, takes a deep breath. "It combats ageing in humans. Not only that, it reverses it."

At first, Michelle is struck dumb. *Reverses ageing in humans?* Surely that's not possible — all the slowing down of the human body, the drying skin, the hair loss, the onset of arthritis, the wearing out of joints, the failing of organs. She's heard of drugs designed to delay the effects of ageing, though none has been proven to work.

But never to *reverse* ageing.

"You mean, actually reverse ageing? Not just delay it?" She has a vision of herself taking the drug. Her wrinkles magically disappearing, the annoying grey hairs going dark again, her body, with its tell-tale signs of childbirth, rejuvenated. It would be a miracle drug indeed if it were capable of doing that.

Lars bites his lip. Nods. "Yes, reverse."

Michelle gulps. "Jesus Christ Almighty. Sorry. Wow, that is . . . incredible."

A million questions run through her head. If the tiny blue pill really can reverse ageing, what are they looking at? Humans living for centuries? Centenarians playing professional football? People never growing old? Death only by accident or by fatal disease? A Benjamin Button existence? How far would people be able to go — back to their childhood?

"My God — you gave me a sample of that drug?"

"I had no option."

There's no time to be angry. They're getting closer to the science park, and in a moment she'll have to get off.

"Wait — but you said people will die?"

"In a significant proportion of people, serious diseases occur, even death. And they're still planning to release it in the next few weeks. Which is why you need to get the sample — and the report — to someone who can stop that happening."

The bus draws to a stop. Michelle looks out of the window, trying to see where they are through the ice and condensation. It's not far now.

A group of teenagers gets on and heads towards the back of the bus. Lars sits forward, leaning on the back of the seat in front. They glance at him and decide to sit elsewhere.

"I can't say more now — I need to get to the airport." He removes a glove, fumbles in a pocket and passes a business card to Michelle. "Here, find this man. He's a journalist. Tell him what I've told you. I have to go." He rises, pressing the button for the bus to stop.

"No, wait, why me? Why can't you call him yourself?"

"The chances of me surviving this are slim. They'll be after me — they might not even let me leave the country. They'll make sure I don't blow the whistle."

It's beginning to dawn on Michelle. "But if you're in danger, then surely that means—"

73

"I'm sorry. But you mustn't go back there. To Kimia."
For a moment, his eyes meet hers. In them she sees fear and urgency.

Shocked, she's about to protest. "But I—"

"Don't go back." He turns away, heading for the door. In an instant, as she wonders whether to follow, the bus has drawn to a stop and the doors open. Cold air rushes in. Two or three people follow Lars off the bus, blocking her exit and her view. In a flash, he's gone and the bus has moved off.

She cranes her neck, trying to catch a glimpse of him, but he's disappeared into the gloom. That's when she realizes she's missed her stop. The science park passes on her right, and, illuminated in the distance, the airport.

She slumps back into her seat. He's gone. Worse, she can't go into work, not now he's warned her against it.

Things have just got so much worse.

CHAPTER SEVENTEEN

Michelle

She's frozen to her seat in the back of the bus, unable to move with the weight of what she now knows. Suddenly what was a safe place to live and work feels very dangerous indeed.

This drug — PAN12 — is far, far more significant than she could ever have imagined. Now that she knows, it's not about losing her job, or Helga losing hers. Or even going to prison for helping a criminal. What she knows now is, quite simply, mind-blowing. Whatever the implications of a drug like this, they're gigantic. Unimaginable. Life as people know it today: gone. The future as it's understood today: shattered. People would pay a fortune to get this drug — the poor wouldn't have a chance. There would be a massive human divide: the underprivileged would age and die, while the rich would survive and grow younger, taking over governments, countries, continents. It's the stuff of science fiction.

She believes Lars. There's no question about it. He's a hunted man, and he's risking his life to do the right thing — she's sure of it. And she can't possibly go back to Kimia now.

Luckily for her, the bus is on a circular route, so if she stays put she'll end up back where she started. It will give her some time to decide what to do. The little bus feels like a sanctuary amid all the madness of the last couple of days. People come and go, the doors opening and closing, blasts of cold replacing the warm air every few minutes. She wishes she could stay here for ever, going round and round the streets of Reykjavik.

But as she begins to recognize the area close to her apartment, she realizes she has to move, and very fast indeed. Soon people will notice she's not at work. If they're already looking for her, the logical next place will be Helga's apartment. She needs to get her passport at the very least. Maybe an overnight bag, though she has no idea where to go next. She alights at the familiar stop and hurries through the snow back to the apartment.

Everything is quiet in the lobby, and on the stairs to the first floor, but she makes as little noise as possible, just in case. There's no sign of Helga as she enters the apartment, though her bedroom door is ajar, indicating that she's left for work. Michelle has a sudden sense of extreme urgency. Are they watching her apartment? There could be someone outside right now, or she could have been picked up by CCTV in the street — in which case, she has no time at all. She can only hope the bad weather will be on her side, shrouding everything in snow and ice.

Shaking, she reaches for a backpack stored under the bed. She doesn't want to be hampered by a heavy bag — for the moment, all she needs is the essentials. A couple of warm jumpers, jeans, thermals, underwear, her phone charger, toilet bag. She pauses for a moment, weighing an expensive pot of "age-defying" cream in her hand. Frivolous, given the circumstances? Perhaps, but it's only small. It gets thrown in with everything else, no time to waste. Passport, of course. At the last minute she rummages in a drawer, pulling out some British banknotes she's kept for visits home. It might be better to survive on cash for the moment.

She's ready in moments. She thinks about leaving a note for Helga — but she mustn't. She's already put her in danger, albeit unwittingly. Knowing what she knows now, she would never have risked it. She'll just have to hope they won't be interested in Helga once Michelle is out of the picture.

But as she closes the front door behind her, she realizes she has no idea where to go, what to do. There is no plan, only the overwhelming instinct to flee.

Outside, the weather's worse than ever and she bends her head against a bitter wind. She walks towards the centre of town, with a vague idea to stop somewhere quiet for a coffee, to think. Within minutes the cold gets to her, ice forms on her eyelashes, her fingertips turn numb. At the first café she comes across, she dives in, opening the door with a sigh of relief. Warmth hits her as the door closes, and she takes a few moments to stamp the snow from her boots and take in the surroundings. Few people are out this morning, it seems, and only one table is taken, an elderly couple hunched over steaming mugs, talking quietly to each other. There's an armchair at a low table tucked away in the corner. With a sense of relief she removes her backpack and her coat.

A girl approaches from behind the serving bar. "What can I get you?" she says in perfect English, though it's clear to Michelle from her demeanour and her clothing that she's local.

"Large black coffee, please. And a pastry of some sort?"

The girl smiles. "Coming up."

Michelle slumps into the chair. Already she's exhausted, both physically and mentally. If the strain is this bad now, how will it be in a couple of days' time? A couple of days could be a terrible understatement. How has this happened to her? She's not someone who breaks the rules or takes risks. Admittedly, she came to Iceland for adventure, to jolt herself out of her humdrum life in London, but she wasn't looking for this. This could be — no, this is — life-changing. And potentially very, very dangerous.

But this kind of thinking isn't helping. Things could move very quickly — they almost certainly will — and she's not ready in any way for what might await her. Whatever she might feel about fate being unkind to her, this has happened, and she has to deal with it. Andersson is gone and there's nothing she can do about it. She hopes he's safe, wherever he's going.

What should she do now? The "evidence" he passed over is secure for the moment. But he told her not to go to work — did he tell them she has the sample? Are they really after her, or is she just being paranoid? If only she'd had more time with him on the bus.

The simple solution, if she wants to stay here and keep her job, would be to hand the pills and the report back to Kimia, feigning ignorance. Forget everything Lars has told her and try to carry on. Would they believe her, though? If there was any doubt in their minds, she'd still be in terrible trouble.

Also, if what Lars says is true, then she could be handing back evidence of serious wrongdoing to the very organization that committed it. Not only that, but the consequences could be disastrous. If the company is planning to release a drug despite its terrible flaws, if Kimia is as ruthless as its reputation suggests, then she's been given a massive responsibility. She doesn't want it — but she could be the only person to prevent a massive human catastrophe. Is she being melodramatic? She doesn't even know the answer to that.

She closes her eyes, resting her head on the wing of the chair. This is so huge, she can't even think straight. When her coffee arrives a moment later, she almost leaps from her seat.

"I'm so sorry," the girl says, taking a large mug and a plate from her tray. "I didn't mean to startle you."

"That's okay," Michelle says, making an effort to smile. "I had a bad night."

"I hope the coffee helps. Enjoy your pastry."

The pastry is enormous. Michelle feels her stomach protest. She'll wrap it in a napkin and take it with her if she can't eat it. Though she knows she must eat, or she won't feel strong enough to deal with this. She tears off a corner and chews it slowly. It's fresh and warm and suddenly she's hungry. She devours most of it and starts to feel better.

That's when she remembers the card that Lars passed over. A journalist. She fumbles in her pockets, eventually finding it bent in two in her jeans pocket. The name on the card looks familiar. *Richard Bamford, freelance journalist.* Where has she come across that name before? If he writes for the pharmaceutical sector, then it would be on one of her many media lists. She pulls out her mobile and types his name into a search engine.

A picture comes up. He's a forty-something man with clear, intelligent eyes, no distinguishing features that she can see. She scrolls down the results. A short profile is all she can find. It claims he's an investigative journalist who has written for many national newspapers across the western world, including the UK and the US. There's not much detail on the profile. That makes sense — an investigative journalist wouldn't want to expose himself online, it could compromise his work. If Lars is right, Bamford could be very interested in what Michelle has to tell him.

Should she call him? She contemplates her mobile for a moment, then stands and approaches the girl at the serving station. "Can you tell me — is there a mobile phone shop nearby, please?"

There's one very close, fortunately. Michelle tells the girl she's coming back, and could she keep her place for her? Leaving the remainder of the pastry on the table, her gloves and hat on the chair, she pulls her hood up and leaves the café.

It's less than fifteen minutes before she's back, brushing fresh snow from her shoulders at the door.

"That was quick," the girl says with a smile. "More coffee?"

"Yes, that would be great." She opens the box and removes the new handset.

* * *

She dials the number, wondering again what she's getting into. But she has no choice now. She's not "getting into" anything

79

— she's in already, right up to her neck. It's getting out of it that she needs to worry about.

After a few nerve-wracking moments, when she begins to wonder if he doesn't answer unsolicited calls, a man's voice says: "Yes?"

"Richard Bamford?"

"That's me."

"My name's Michelle Turner," she says, her voice cracking. She glances around the room as she does so, checking there's nobody in earshot. It's all very calm in the café, and soft music muffles any conversation. She's safe. "You don't know me, but I work for a company called Kimia."

"I know it." His voice is gruff, but not unfriendly.

"Look, I know this sounds melodramatic, but please bear with me. There's something going on, with Kimia, that isn't right."

A pause. "How do you mean?"

"I believe it's about to do something really, really bad. I'm not exaggerating. I'm out of my depth and I need your help. You are an investigative journalist?" Her words sound naive, even to her, but she has to pique his interest. As she speaks, she begins to understand precisely how much she needs to share this with someone.

"I am. But how did you get this number?"

"I was given your card by a Kimia scientist who seems to have uncovered something. I'm not sure what exactly, but it involves a top-secret drug, backed by the biggest money you can imagine . . ."

There's a pause, as if he's taking notes. "What did you say your name was again?"

She gives him her name and explains that she's in Reykjavik. "This scientist — he gave me something. Then he told me not to go back to work. I'm very frightened, I don't know what to do. Do you think you can help me?"

"Can you give me more about the drug? Is it safe to talk?"

"I think so, I'm just in a café down the road from my apartment. I can't go back there, but I have my passport and a few things with me. I'm talking to you on a new phone."

"Hold on, I'm going to call you back. Give me two minutes, don't go away." The connection drops.

The two minutes feel like two hours. Two minutes in which she contemplates her ruined life, imagines being on the run in cold, remote Iceland, being caught and tortured for the information she barely understands. But at last the mobile lights up, displaying a different number.

"Richard?" she says tentatively.

"Yes, it's me. This is a burner phone. You're the only person who has this number. Now, can you tell me the gist of your story? Start with the drug."

This is a risk. She knows next to nothing about this man. But it's a risk she has to take. Right now, she has very few options. In as few words as possible, she explains what's happened to her, the conversation with Lars on the bus. He asks a few questions as she talks, but otherwise lets her offload it all.

When she's finished, there's a pause. Then a long whistle. Then he says, "You have to leave the country. Today."

CHAPTER EIGHTEEN

Lars

By handing the sample to the woman — Michelle Turner, that was her name — he's almost certainly put her life in danger. But he had no choice. If his results are correct — and he's one hundred per cent sure they are — then many other people will be in danger too. This drug is too dangerous, too desirable, too *everything* to ignore. Forget addictive drugs like Oxycontin, heroin, cocaine — these are nothing compared with PAN12. What it could lead to in global terms includes death, destruction, disease — even war. His own life is worth nothing compared with the catastrophe this drug could cause.

As he hurries through the airport, looking over his shoulder at every turn, he knows he's in real danger, every moment from now on. They might lull him into a false sense of security by letting him leave the country, but he's under no illusions. This will cost him his life, innocent or not. Compared with their ambitions, Lars Andersson is nothing, a speck of dust to be brushed away.

Already he feels exposed, watched. When he looks around, he sees people disappear from view, watching from

82

the upper level, following him on the escalator. Any one of them could be a Kimia spy. There are cameras too, everywhere he looks — normal airport security, no doubt, but Kimia's tentacles reach far and wide. Anybody could be in their control. With money like that, you can bribe, influence, threaten. Even if he gets as far as Sweden, the chances of him reaching old age are zero.

He's sweating long before he reaches the check-in desk. He wipes at his damp forehead with a sleeve — that alone makes him look suspicious. He has a small bag and his passport — no phone. He could buy another here, but there's no time. He's heading for the first plane out to Stockholm, and it's already boarding.

His only hope is that the woman takes his advice to call Richard Bamford. Bamford has a reputation for hard-hitting investigative journalism; he's won awards for exposing malpractice by companies and individuals. He's not intimidated by powerful people or organizations. If anyone can uncover the truth about PAN12, he can.

Michelle has a small window of opportunity before they track her down — which they will, when they notice the missing sample. Only she has a chance to get the story out.

Kimia must be stopped. They can't go ahead and release this drug, not after the results he found, and it's the only way to stop them. Otherwise it won't be Lars alone who suffers. It'll be that innocent woman — and possibly millions of other unsuspecting people.

* * *

To his enormous relief, he boards the plane without incident and takes his seat by the window. Nobody pays much attention to him. He watches as the line of passengers progresses slowly down the centre aisle, pausing as people stop to put their luggage in the overhead lockers. A woman and her young daughter — about nine or ten, he'd guess — take their places beside him. They don't seem to be a threat to him, and he relaxes a little, silently urging the doors to close, the engines to start, the plane to get in the air. To his surprise, these things happen, and he's undisturbed. Perhaps he's going to be allowed to get as far as Sweden, after all.

He allows his head to fall back against the seat, but keeps his eyes open, alert for danger. He needs to decide what to do once he's back in his homeland. It's not going to be easy to disappear, but disappear he must. For once in his life he's glad he hasn't married, had children, and that his parents have passed away. At least he's not putting them in danger. But with that thought comes the realization that his life as he knows it is over. Work, his career — those are the things he's lived for over the last nine, ten years. He has few friends, next to no interests — only work. Losing his job at Kimia in this way will ruin his chances of working in the same sphere, anywhere in the world, for the rest of his life. Kimia will make sure his reputation is wrecked.

For Lars, this is almost as bad as losing his life. In a way, it is losing his life. If he's to survive, he'll have to find another purpose, abandon any hope of pursuing a scientific career. The best he can hope for is to disappear. He will have to change his identity, his appearance, his habits, his work. He has no idea how to do that — it's the stuff of fiction for him, and fiction isn't something he's ever had much interest in. He deals in facts, evidence, empirical results.

He doesn't even know where to start with this situation. Where to go when he leaves the airport, even. Tears start to fill his eyes as he gazes out at the concrete surroundings of the airport runway. He can't remember the last time he cried, and the loss of control is a terrible shock. For a moment he wonders if it would be better to take his own life. At least that way he could deny Kimia the satisfaction of erasing him.

But that would be exactly what Kimia wants. Moreover, he wants to be alive when the truth is revealed. Kimia must be stopped, and it's his job to stay alive until it is.

CHAPTER NINETEEN

Michelle

Though the worst has begun to dawn on her, Michelle is shocked by Bamford's stark statement.

"Today? But . . ." Leave the country? Leave Reykjavik? She understands that's probably necessary, and that's bad enough. Abandoning her home, losing her job, all in the space of a few hours — she can't process it all.

"Yes, today. And don't go to the airport. That's where they'll expect you to go. Don't even try the domestic airport. You need to get back by boat."

"By boat?" Her voice rises to a squeak. A boat, from Iceland. That doesn't sound easy, or pleasant. Or fast.

"Yes, I'm pretty sure you can get out by boat. They used to go to Scotland, but I don't think you can do that anymore. I'll do some quick checking for you . . . hold on a sec . . . yes, you can get to Denmark, apparently. Do you have money? By which I mean cash."

"Some. But the weather here is terrible. We're in the middle of a snowstorm. Gale-force winds. Temperatures are dropping. I don't know how I—"

"You must. Even if it takes a few days to get out. If you take an unusual route, it'll be safer. I'll work something out, call you back in a few minutes. Are you sure you're safe right now, where you are?"

"I think so. The weather's so bad outside, there aren't many people around. Nobody knows I'm here."

"Sit tight. I'll get back to you."

Michelle sits tight, consciously trying to relax her shoulders, which ache with tension. Luckily the café is quiet, because every time the door opens, she flinches. She watches carefully for people looking in or pausing outside, but there's nothing to make her suspicious. After what seems like an age, the phone buzzes.

"Okay," he says. "It looks like the best route is to take a boat from the east of the country to Denmark, then drive back to the UK from there. Do you have a car?"

"No. I suppose I could hire one, but . . ." She hesitates, her eyes drawn to the window. Through a haze of condensation she can see the snow falling in huge flakes, flurries swirling across the empty street. Already a car parked outside is covered. Inches must have fallen since she left the flat this morning. "But the weather . . . I don't know about driving in this."

"I see what you mean. I'm looking at the weather for Iceland right now. Reykjavik has the worst of it, but driving anywhere could be tricky until the storm's over."

"What am I going to do?" She's horrified to hear the tremble in her voice. But if she can't get out of Iceland, she's going to have to hide, and she's not sure how she can do that either. Her heart rate begins to rise, panic threatening. She wants to weep at the sheer enormity of it all. But it won't help anything.

"Okay. Try to keep calm. I tell you what we're going to do. We'll do it another way. I'm going to get on a plane to Iceland — today if possible, if not then tomorrow morning. Then we're going to meet and decide what's next. The longer-range forecast doesn't look too bad, so perhaps we can leave on the boat together. It'll be safer — they won't be looking for a couple."

She can hardly believe it. "Are you sure? That would be . . . brilliant, if you can."

"Easier for me to get in than for you to get out. I'm a seasoned traveller — and I like Iceland, under normal circumstances. But in the meantime, you need to lie low. If you can change your appearance that will help."

"Right now, you can't tell who's who anyway, beneath all the clothes we're wearing. I think I'll be okay. But I'll see what I can do."

"Find somewhere for tonight, just in case I can't get in because of the weather. Preferably somewhere where you don't need to show your passport. Pay with cash if possible — and I'll bring more when I come. Don't go to a bank or draw cash or use a credit card anywhere. Do you understand? Don't be tempted — that's the first thing they'll check. I'll go now, and call you back shortly. I need to book a flight."

"Thank you. I can't tell you—"

"No problem. You need help, and I need a story. Works both ways."

* * *

The girl in the café couldn't be more helpful. Saying she's unable to take a flight today because of the weather, Michelle asks if she knows somewhere to stay locally.

"You can stay here," the girl says. "We have three rooms we let out, with breakfast. They're empty at the moment — it's not busy this time of year. I can let you have one, if you like."

A heaven-sent piece of luck. She needs whatever luck she can grab, right now.

"That's brilliant. Thank you so much, you've really helped me out."

"Would you like to see? I can't leave the café at the moment, but here, take this key, room three. It's the nicest, and it's all set up. Shared bathroom, but there's nobody else staying, as I say. Up the stairs and to the left."

The room is clean, bright and warm. It overlooks the street, but that won't matter. There won't be a lot of passing traffic here, especially with the snow. Back downstairs, she says to the girl: "It's perfect, thank you again. I'll just finish my coffee then go up, if that's okay. I have some calls to make."

"Of course," the girl says. "Breakfast is until ten in the morning. I hope you get your flight sorted out. Can I take your name and a card please?"

"Uh, Catherine," she says, her mind grasping the first name that comes to the surface. "Catherine Johnson. And I have cash, if that works for you."

Straight away, she wishes she'd chosen a different name. Her middle names have rarely come in useful but she wasn't quick enough to think properly. Luckily, it's unlikely anyone could trace her here, but she's going to have to be a lot cleverer than that. The girl nods and types her name onto a screen.

"Enjoy your stay," she says. "Just come down if you need anything."

Smiling her thanks, Michelle almost hopes Richard won't be able to get to Iceland today. She feels safe here, at least for the moment.

CHAPTER TWENTY

Michelle

It's no surprise that Richard is unable to fly straight away. The weather has set in for at least the next twenty-four hours. He's booked on a flight for the next day, arriving at the airport mid-afternoon, snowstorms permitting.

"I'll come straight to the café," he says. "Remember, don't call anyone, stay put. Don't use a laptop or your old phone. I'm going to do a bit of clandestine digging on Kimia while I'm here. I remember there were questions hanging over them a few years ago — it'll be useful to see what that was all about."

"Okay," she says, trying to control her voice.

Her imagination, fuelled by years of reading psychological thrillers and watching TV dramas, runs riot. She could have been caught on CCTV in the street, even entering the café. If they get access to that footage — and she's sure this will be worth plenty of money in bribes, if bribes become necessary — they could track her down easily. The police might already be in their pockets.

"Try not to worry," Richard says. "The weather's on your side. Let's just hope it lets up tomorrow. We'll get you out of there, I promise."

Try not to worry? All of a sudden she feels a terrible pang of homesickness. She longs for the mundanity of British life, the scruffy street she inhabits in London, the corner shop, the growl of a London taxi. She misses Toby. How long will it be before she can see his sweet, boyish face again? She misses her friends, especially Gail, and longs to hear her voice, to laugh with her, to share this ghastly problem with her. But she can't, and it feels like an enormous loss. When will her life return to normal again? Will it ever? Will she always have to run and hide, looking over her shoulder, unsure of what might be waiting around the corner?

Why, why did she have to be the one person in the elevator, the only person Lars Andersson could appeal to? Why did she accept the sample, the report, so unthinkingly? Right now, she can't imagine what her future will be like. She lies on the bed, clutching at the pillow, tears seeping into the soft cotton.

But feeling sorry for herself doesn't come naturally. *This isn't you*, she thinks. She sits up, dries her eyes and squares her shoulders. She's not going to let this happen. If it's true that Kimia is planning to forge ahead with a lethal drug, then she's going to do her utmost to expose it. If, as she suspects, Andersson has found something badly wrong with the clinical trials, and she has the proof, then she's going to find a way. Life doesn't always work out how you expected, but you have the choice. You don't have to mourn what could have been, and you can make the most of what will be.

If this, right now, is her life, then she's going to have to deal with it.

* * *

So she waits, cocooned in her little room, watching the snow swirl in great white gusts in the street outside. Already Reykjavik looks like a scene from a Christmas card, the roofs of the buildings opposite heavy with snow. She's relieved to see the street lamps and road signs obscured. Any CCTV footage will be foggy and indistinct.

90

People trudge by, bent against the wind, their eyes half closed. A man walks his dog along the pavement. The dog is excited, sniffing the snow, dancing in the drifts that form against the walls of shops and houses. Every now and then a vehicle passes slowly, its windscreen wipers sweeping away sprinklings of melting flakes.

A dark, heavy sky looms over the city, even after daylight appears around mid-morning. This is proper Icelandic winter weather. Daylight hours are few, night-time stretches out for two-thirds of the day. Now the mountains will be inaccessible. It'll be dangerous to drive anywhere except on the main roads, those that encircle the island, reaching only the larger communities. She hopes they'll be able to hire a car. Perhaps Sigrun, the helpful girl from the café, will help them find one. A four-wheel drive, preferably, that can cope with the conditions. She's not an unconfident driver, but this — wind, snow and ice all together, in a strange country — is daunting.

On a visitor's leaflet she took from downstairs, she studies a map of Iceland. The ferry from Denmark appears to stop only at a place called Seydisfjordur on the far eastern coast, about as far from Reykjavik as you can get. It barely makes any difference whether you travel north from Reykjavik or south — the distance looks the same. Whichever way you choose, it looks like a very long journey to the other side of the island. Then, once that's over, it will take hours to cross to Denmark, no doubt in the same challenging weather. And how long does it take to drive from northern Denmark to a ferry crossing to the UK? Days, probably. She can't bear to think about it. She only hopes that Richard turns out to be a good companion. If he doesn't then the next few days will be dreadful. Even more dreadful.

She sleeps surprisingly well, considering. Perhaps it's the feeling of safety, holed up in her room, or perhaps it's the muffling effect of the snow. Then next day, she locks her room and walks slowly downstairs, pausing to check the occupants of the café before she takes a table to wait for him.

It's quiet again, the snow deterring customers. Icy fingers frame the large window at the front of the café, and though the pavement has been cleared at the entrance, the snow piles up at the side of the road as cars edge through.

Sigrun, however, seems as cheerful as ever. "Good morning," she says. "I hope you slept well?" Michelle skipped breakfast, thinking it safer to drink the instant coffee in her room than risk it. Come to think of it, she'd skipped supper too — she'd been too keyed up to eat anything last night. Hunger strikes her as she remembers, as if her brain has set an alarm for her stomach.

"I did, thank you. Can I get something to eat, please? And coffee."

"Of course. Breakfast is done, but we have pastries and toast if you'd like."

"Both, please. I could eat a horse."

CHAPTER TWENTY-ONE

I was destined for an unusual life.

I grew up in a family that kept on moving. By the time I was eleven, I'd lived in eleven different countries. My father, a distant, cold man who took very little part in bringing me up, was in the army. We travelled where we were ordered to. Germany, Greece, Cyprus, the US — all was a blur when I was small. I soon realized that home wasn't a safe haven and making friends was pointless.

So growing up was a lonely business. There were no siblings to play with, and my mother suffered with all the moving. My father's lack of empathy — abuse, I call it — took its toll on her, and she died when I was thirteen years old. What happened after that, I buried deep in my mind.

At sixteen, I joined the Marines.

I was an angry teenager, a loner with a huge chip on my shoulder and hate in my heart. When I read the job description I knew, one hundred per cent, that was what I wanted to do. "Plan and lead beach assaults; be in charge of weapons deployment and tactics; carry out special missions; fly aircraft and helicopters" — this was music to my ears. I could be working in a war zone, on a ship or at a military base. What could be better? I had no family I cared about, and they certainly didn't care for me. I had no home. I was perfect material for the Marines.

By the time I left the service, I was a killing machine.

I could have stayed. I could have chosen to become institutionalized, following the rules like a robot. I could have risen up the ranks, been a military man for life. But it wasn't for me. I learned my craft, milked it as far as I could, but then I'd had enough. The orders, the yelling, the dedication to king and country . . . I grew cynical. I was surrounded by idiots with no more than a couple of brains to rub together, and most of them were my superiors.

So I bailed out. For a while, I drifted, unsure who I was or where I belonged. I had no friends, no family to speak of, no purpose in life.

Five years later, the message arrived. By then, I'd made my way across Europe, working where I could, never staying long in one place. I learned karate and jujitsu, German, French and Spanish, even some Arabic. I learned to play pétanque and blackjack, and how to cheat at cards. I lived one day at a time. I picked up some skills — pickpocketing, thieving, shoplifting — and I was good at them.

How they found me I don't know, but I'm glad they did.

CHAPTER TWENTY-TWO

Michelle

Richard brings with him a gust of icy, snow-laden air. It could only be him: a man in a donkey jacket, woolly hat pulled down over his ears, snow-spattered jeans and walking boots, a large backpack on one shoulder. Somehow he looks British: something about the pattern on his hat, the ordinariness of his clothes marks him out. Quite apart from the fact that he's the only person to have come into the café in the last hour.

"Michelle?" he says, dropping the backpack on the floor. He draws a hand from its glove and holds it out to her.

She stands for a moment and takes his hand. It's cold and dry, enfolding hers in a firm grip. "Richard. Thank you so much for coming. I'm glad you didn't get held up at the airport."

"The weather doesn't seem to have improved much. It's pretty hideous out there. But they're used to it here." He throws his hat onto a chair and it's soon joined by his jacket and gloves.

Sigrun asks from the counter: "Something to drink?"

"Coffee, please, strong and black." Richard rubs his hands together. "How are you doing, Michelle?"

For a moment she can't answer. A lump in her throat threatens to turn into a sob. She takes a deep breath. "I'm okay." She nods. "It's not the best situation, but now you're here, I'm hoping it'll improve."

Sigrun arrives with a steaming mug of coffee. "Anything else?" she asks.

"Not at the moment, thanks. I'll warm up a little first."

Sigrun returns to the counter and Richard pulls his chair closer to Michelle's, so he's right next to her. Normally she'd retreat from this, but everything's different now. With music in the background, nobody can hear what they're saying.

"Kimia has a reputation," he says. He's clearly not one for small talk. "Ruthlessness, stretching the rules, working its people hard. At the same time, it's done some ground-breaking work, and its scientists are world-class. It makes a lot of money. A lot." He extracts a laptop from his bag and opens it up. "There was a bit of a scandal some years ago. An ex-employee accused them of malpractice. It almost went all the way, but they paid him off. It must have been a good payout because I couldn't track him down. He's gone under the radar."

"You don't think . . ." There goes her imagination again.

He shakes his head. "They bumped him off? No, I don't, actually. But I do know they have huge resources. Their lawyers are cut-throat, they take no chances. He probably got a pay-off big enough not to need to work again."

"Do you think they've done the same to Lars Andersson?"

"Maybe. Though from what you say, he seems to have principles. He wants them exposed for what they are, and if he's disappeared, it'll be because he wants to see it through. Perhaps via you."

Shivers run down her spine at that. She tries not to think about what it might mean.

"So you think Lars is genuine? The drug's dangerously flawed?"

"We don't know that. I'm here because I think there's a strong chance that you've stumbled across something really important, but we have no proof. Yet."

"I realize that, and I'm grateful that you trusted me enough to come here. Gosh, I hope it's not all for nothing." She runs her hands through her hair. "That would be very embarrassing."

He smiles. "Look, don't worry about me. I've been on wild goose chases before, travelled a lot further than this, only for the story not to work out. I was at a bit of a loose end, your story sounded genuine, and I wanted — I want — to help. Iceland is easy to get to from the UK. Despite the weather. It all came together."

"So how are we going to prove that what Lars says is true? We're neither of us scientists, we don't have the skills—"

"We're going to have to find someone who does. Not here, back at home. Or wherever we can — the US, the Far East, if it comes to it — and we need to be quick. Kimia will be after that sample, and the test results, right now. We have to assume it's in their interests to stop us exposing them. That's if the report reveals what we think it does."

"Do I have time for another cup of coffee?" She tries, and fails, to smile.

"Yes. But then we must get going. We need transport, supplies, we need to book a crossing. The weather's on our side in some ways, but it'll make travelling slower."

She waves to Sigrun. "Another coffee, please. And Sigrun, we need to book a car. Is there somewhere nearby—?"

"I can book something for you, I know a good car hire business. What sort of car?"

Michelle looks at Richard.

"A good four-wheel drive, please," he says. "It's probably best I speak to them myself, if you could give me a number?"

"Of course."

In a few moments, she's back with a leaflet and Michelle's coffee. "Make sure you mention my name," she says.

"I will," Richard says. Then, aside to Michelle, "Let's not involve her any more than we have to. And no one else."

"Sorry," she says, feeling like a child. "I'm not used to this."

"Don't apologize. You'll soon get accustomed to it, believe me."

* * *

She gives Sigrun a little wave as she leaves the café, feeling like she's leaving a sanctuary.

"Right, let's go," Richard says as she clambers up into the large four-wheel drive he's collected from around the corner.

"Everything works so well here," he says, as he negotiates the snow-laden street. "Quick and efficient, that's what I like. Now we need a supermarket. This is going to be a long old haul, and there won't be many places along the way that are open in winter."

"Better stock up, then." She sounds a lot more stoical than she feels. It's a heck of a long journey and she doesn't travel well at the best of times.

"What will we do about money?" she says. Though she has some money in the bank, it's not much — not enough for this kind of journey, that's for sure. Anyway, she can't access it.

"I've brought cash, and I have a bank account in another name that we can use."

"But—" She's about to protest that she barely knows him, she doesn't want to rely on him — and she might not be able to repay him. But he cuts her short.

"Listen, Michelle. Money is the least of our worries. We need to get you out of here — now — and make sure you're safe. Your life is in danger, and you have to trust me. You have no choice."

She swallows, with difficulty. She feels as if she's swimming through mud. The sinking feeling that's bothered her ever since the moment Lars handed over the sample in the lift becomes a full-on rock in her stomach. Richard's right, she has no choice. She has to trust him.

"Where is the sample?" Richard says. "That's the first thing we need to do."

She explains where she's hidden it. In a few minutes, they're at the sculpture park. It's hardly recognizable as the same place, the snow now covering everything, smoothing off corners, concealing even the benches.

She undoes her seat belt, reaching for the door handle, but he stops her, his hand on her arm. "No, let me go," he says. "Can you point out the tree?"

She points, her hand quivering. In a moment, he's gone, a dark shape trudging through drifts up to his ankles. His footprints are the only ones on the path. If anyone's following them, it won't be hard to work out what's happening here, and Richard would be easy to waylay in this deserted space. But there's no evidence of a car drawing up behind them, no dark figures approaching. She loses sight of him, and for a second or two she debates whether to follow. Perhaps he can't find the right tree, perhaps the snow has confused him — but a second later he's back, kicking the snow off his boots on the rim of the car before he climbs in.

"Got it," he says. "Not a bad hiding place, especially in this weather."

Hurdle one has been crossed. They have the evidence, and they're getting out of Reykjavik.

CHAPTER TWENTY-THREE

Michelle

Heading north, away from the snow-covered capital, they're soon in the countryside, a monotone land of grey and white, relieved only by outcrops of speckled rock. Every so often the fog clears to reveal mountaintops, their sides striped with grey where the land falls away into steep gorges and ravines.

The snow continues to fall, though less heavily now, and visibility improves a little. Michelle finds herself lulled by the swish of the windscreen wipers, almost nodding off. When she'd offered to drive, Richard had said only: "I'm fine for the moment. If I get tired, you can take over for a bit so I can have a nap. But let's see how we get on."

In winter the Icelandic countryside is sparsely populated, the majority of people moving to the city until the weather eases. Small cabins are dotted around the lower mountain slopes, but few of them show signs of habitation. They're summerhouses, most likely shut up for the season. No cars outside, no smoke from the chimneys, blinds closed. The few villages they pass through, their names indecipherable through flurries of snow, are just a few buildings off the main road, a church. No sign of a café or a restaurant on the road, no hotels, nowhere to stop over. Around the halfway point they're due to pass through Akureyri, the town where Helga's partner lives and works. Michelle hopes she can last until then for a bathroom break. The idea of crouching in a blizzard, trousers down, is not appealing. Richard, though, stops a couple of times to stand by a fence or a tree.

Michelle doesn't much feel like talking, and after a few questions about the journey, she puts her head back and watches the whiteness go by in a daze. It's better to leave Richard to concentrate on the road, which is by turns slushy and icy. At times, when the clouds are low and heavy, the snow falls fast again and he slows the pace, picking his way along, guided by yellow stakes flanking the road.

At Akureyri they stop to use a public facility in a car park near the centre. They take it in turns to leave the car, rather than take the sample with them, watching for danger as the other one walks to the small brick building and back. As she waits for Richard, she feels the power of the small bottle of pills emanating from the locked glove compartment in front of her.

Akureyri is not a big place. It's positioned perfectly at the end of an enormous fjord, with mountains marching either side towards the sea. When they set off again, they're out of the town before they know it, travelling away from the coast to the east.

More awake now, Michelle's mind starts to work. Never in her life has she imagined being on the run. It sounds like an old movie: the desperate person on the run, the pursuers close behind.

"Richard, they're going to want to see my passport on the ferry, aren't they? We can't avoid that, surely."

"I've never taken this particular ferry before, though I've used ferries a lot," he says. "Some check your passport, some don't. If they do, there's not much we can do about it. We'll have to have our wits about us when we dock."

She's silent for a moment, letting this sink in. "So there might be trouble when we get to Denmark?"

He glances at her. "Look, I don't know. But it's as well to be prepared. Where we pick up the ferry, it's a fairly small place. The ferry doesn't carry that many people — they might not even bother. I doubt there are many dangerous criminals who use ferries, to be honest, so the checks will be less stringent, if they exist at all."

She sinks into a state of anxiety, not helped by the deteriorating weather. A stiff wind has turned into dangerous gusts, and the Land Rover creeps along, Richard struggling to keep it in the tracks made by other vehicles. Luckily there's barely another car on the road today, so keeping a straight line is less important. If this were any other time, Michelle would have refused to travel, as would any sensible person. But they have no choice.

* * *

She wakes with a start. She hadn't intended to drop off, feeling that she should support Richard by staying awake, keeping an eye on the road for him. But something has woken her. She straightens up in her seat, stretching her neck, stiff from an awkward sleeping position.

Ahead, the sky has cleared a little, even revealing a patch of blue. A shaft of sun illuminates a mountainside, the snow covering all but striations of black volcanic rock. Black clouds still threaten ahead, but for the moment the wind has dropped and only a few snowflakes land on the windscreen as they drive.

She looks across at Richard, noticing for the first time the set of his jaw, stubble appearing on his cheek. He drives confidently, both hands on the wheel, his eyes set straight ahead. But something's bothering him. He glances in the rear-view mirror, then the wing mirror. The car is travelling faster. It was the change in the tone of the engine that roused her.

"Are you okay?" she says, turning to see what's behind.

He shrugs. "I'm not sure. It's probably nothing, but there's a car behind. It's been with us for a fair few miles now. I'm just keeping an eye on it."

She starts to turn again, but he says, "Don't. Best not to let them know we've seen them." In the wing mirror, she can just make out some lights, a long way back. Her anxiety level rises a notch.

He glances at her. "Don't worry. There aren't many roads open, and this is the main one. Not many places to stop either, so it's not surprising if someone else is with us for a while."

"Should we let them pass? At least we could try to get a look at them."

"We could, but there's not an obvious place to stop. Let's leave it for a bit, see if anything happens. They could leave the road at any time."

Michelle has a sudden urge to call her son. Suppressing the urge makes her want to cry. "Can . . . can I ask you something?"

"Of course."

"My son, Toby — he's nineteen, at university. I haven't spoken to him for a while. Do you think it would be safe to call him? My phone's new, nobody has the number."

"What name did you use to buy it? Did you pay cash?"

"Yes, cash. They didn't ask my name."

He thinks for a moment. "Probably best not to. When we stop, you can use my burner phone. But if they know who you are, and they know you have the sample — there are lots of ifs in between as well — then they might monitor his phone. My feeling is they'll stop at nothing, especially as they know you're intending to blow the whistle."

"How would they know that?"

"You didn't hand the sample back. Why wouldn't you? And why aren't you in work? Your absence will be noted, and they know you were in contact with Andersson."

Another level of anxiety hits her. "Should I have called in sick? Should I call Helga, my flatmate? What if she worries

103

and calls the police? I didn't want to leave her a note in case they came to search the flat. I—"

"Woah." Richard makes a calming gesture with his hand, allowing it to fall onto her arm. "Michelle. It's only been a day. When we get to the ferry, we'll make some decisions. For now, let's just focus on getting there in one piece." His voice is firm, confident. It calms her for a moment.

But, staring out at the weather closing in and the pin-points of headlights behind, she wishes he hadn't said "in one piece".

CHAPTER TWENTY-FOUR

Lars

Lars hurries through Stockholm airport, his head down. Nothing happens to make him suspicious, nobody follows him. But he knows better than to relax. There are cameras everywhere, and if Kimia wants the footage, they'll get it.

At an internet café, he searches for somewhere to stay short term. He finds a small, private room-to-let arrangement with its own entrance, walks there and rings on the doorbell. His strategy works. The landlady is happy to take cash, the room is available and he can stay for a couple of days while he sorts himself out and plans what to do. Finds a way to disappear.

From the window of his tiny room, he checks for cameras in the street outside. He can't see any, but that doesn't mean there are none. He closes the blinds and sets up the burner phone, inputting one number — Richard Bamford's. Richard is probably the only journalist Lars would trust. He's been following him for years, reading his articles, watching him on social media. He has grown to respect Richard's careful analysis of malpractice — not only in the pharmaceutical sector but in government and other industries — and his refusal to be intimidated by the companies he exposes.

Some years ago they met by chance at an event and had an interesting discussion about investigative journalism. When they parted, Richard handed over his card. Lars kept it, not because he expected ever to have a story for Richard, but because he liked him and would enjoy meeting up again, perhaps at another of the many pharmaceutical conferences. As soon as Lars started to suspect there was something terribly wrong going on at Kimia, he'd searched out the card. He hopes fervently that Michelle Turner took his advice to contact Richard — if not, he may never find her again. Richard might be his only hope of exposing the company and getting his life back.

Venturing into the city, he buys scissors, a woolly hat, a hoodie and a warm scarf. He left Reykjavik with almost nothing. His coat will be good enough — it's anonymous enough to fade into a crowd. He stocks up on food and drink, paying for everything in cash. When he's finished, he finds another internet café.

There's nothing new on Kimia. The daily pharma news site follows them closely, but though there are rumours of a huge breakthrough, there are still no details. One of the more gossipy bloggers, however, speculates about an upcoming launch date. *Is this the one Kimia's been waiting for? Hints of a massive new drug that will astound the globe have been circulating for long enough. Perhaps we'll find out soon what it's all about . . .*

Lars knows for certain that Kimia will ignore his findings. They will have blocked his report, expunged all of the incriminating evidence. They'll go ahead with the launch regardless — if it's already scheduled, he has no doubt it will happen.

Any move on his part to try to stop them, to head off the catastrophe that will happen if PAN12 is released, will mean the end of his life, he's certain of it. His only hope is to disappear. If they think he's frightened enough — too frightened to blow the whistle — he may get away with it. If, for one moment, they think he'll tell the truth to the world, it will all be over. He must protect himself as best he can for the moment, play for time and hope that between them, he, Richard and Michelle can blow Kimia's wonder drug into the ether.

He sends a message to Richard. *Call me on this number . . .* It's a risk, but he'll give him the other number when they speak.

Back in his room, he spends some time altering his appearance. He chops his hair short and shaves the sides. He tries the hat with the hood up and a scarf over his mouth. Nobody would know him. It's cold outside and he won't look suspicious. Over the next few days, he'll let the stubble grow into a beard.

Now he must sit and wait for Richard to call.

CHAPTER TWENTY-FIVE

Michelle

As they drive further east, the weather at last changes, the snow on the road turning to slush, the wind dropping. To Michelle's relief, they seem to have lost the car that was behind them, at least for the moment. They stop by the side of the road to stretch their legs.

Sunlight pierces the clouds as she shivers in the icy breeze. In the field beside them, a small group of Icelandic horses gazes at them. They swish their long tails, blinking through shaggy manes. She takes long breaths of cold air, swinging her arms, stretching her back, forcing her stiffened legs to move. The journey is taking its toll. As she wanders over to the field, one of the horses breaks away, its eyes curious. It's a pretty mix of white and brown, with a mottled mane that reaches far down its neck beyond its shoulders. Michelle holds her hand out and it comes forward, hoping for some food.

"I'm sorry," she murmurs. "I don't have anything." But it lets her stroke its nose.

A whistle comes from behind. Richard's back at the car, beckoning her.

"Sorry, I've got to go," she says. As she turns away, the horse tosses its head and canters back to the group. She wishes she were that free. She longs for her home in England, where she felt confident, safe. But that's naive. She won't be safe there either.

"Cross your fingers," Richard says as she clambers into the passenger seat. "We're heading for a mountain pass. It's the only way into Seydisfjordur, so we've got to hope it's passable. Let's do it while the weather's clear."

"Are you okay with driving?" she says. "I'm not sure it's the best time for me to take over." These conditions frighten her, even on the flat ring road, and the thought of struggling up a mountain pass is not pleasant.

"Don't worry," he says. "You can drive when we get to Denmark. The roads'll be easier there."

When at last Seydisfjordur appears below them, she's surprised at how small it is. It's just a few houses dotted around a lake and a river, at the very end of a large fjord. Its name is announced Hollywood-style on a nearby mountainside. There's a typical church in the centre, and large low-rise industrial buildings close to the water — perhaps fish processing units.

"What time is our ferry?" she asks. There's no sign of a large boat anywhere.

"They go only once a week, depending on the weather. Let's hope we haven't just missed one."

"And the weather changes for the better. How long is the crossing?"

"I think about two days . . ." He glances over at her. "We'll go to a pharmacy, get some seasickness tablets before we go."

"How did you guess?" she says.

"You look a bit green already," he says with a smile.

* * *

There's a two-day wait for the ferry. They find rooms on the outskirts of the town and try not to draw attention to

109

themselves. As soon as they've dropped their bags, Richard suggests they find a coffee shop.

"We need to make some decisions," he says as they peel off their coats and hats. They sit at a table by the window, with a view over the water. Richard makes sure the door to the café is in his sightline. "First, text your flatmate in Reykjavik. Here, use my burner. You have her number?" Michelle nods. "Tell her you're safe, but you're not coming back for a while. You'll explain later."

Michelle types, her fingers clumsy. She looks back over the message, corrects a mistake and presses *send*. "Okay, done. And work? Kimia?"

"Don't worry about them. I imagine all traces of you will have been deleted by now. They'll have an 'official' story about your departure, no doubt."

She sighs, looking out over the grey water. "I'm sure they will. What about Toby?"

"Text him too. Tell him you're going on a trip, and you might be out of contact for a bit, but you're fine. He'll understand — you're in Iceland. You'll call him in a few days."

When she's finished, Richard seems lost in thought, gazing across at the mountains beyond the fjord. Clouds drift around, one moment concealing the upper parts, the next revealing peaks and valleys.

"So how did you come to be here?"

"I don't know really. I'm divorced and I didn't want to be on my own. I tried dating, but it was hopeless. I decided to have an adventure instead, and when the job came up — maternity leave — I jumped at it. I like Iceland, I'll be sorry to leave. I never imagined . . . this."

He laughs. "Why would you? It's the stuff of fiction. A massive drug that could change the world turns out to be a dud, but a wicked company decides to launch it anyway, even though people will die in their millions . . ."

In their millions. His words cut deep into her, and the scale of what she's fallen into shocks her all over again. She feels like a child, fearful and confused, in a world she doesn't understand.

Glancing at her face, he says, "I'm sorry, but we can't overestimate the potential of this. Imagine, if they launch this drug in its present form, it'll be the Holy Grail. A drug that reverses ageing? Everyone will want it — everyone in the 'civ-ilised' world —" he mimes the speech marks — "over the age of twenty-five. The price will rocket, supplies will dry up, people will fight over it . . . not just people, countries possibly. You can see how it would escalate. We have to stop it happening."

She cradles her coffee in both hands. "How, though? Have you ever dealt with anything this big?"

"Not as big, no. But just as dangerous. Big business is by its nature ruthless. It has one aim only, and that's profit. We're just pawns in the big chess game."

"How did you get into this side of journalism?"

"I saw what was happening with a particular company in the finance sector. It was fleecing its customers and getting away with it, posing as a caring organization. Its marketing was very clever, everyone believed it was solid. Except me. I decided it deserved to be brought down. That's the positive power of journalism, right there. I confess I got a thrill out of it."

"But what about your family? You're putting yourself in danger with all these exposures, surely?"

"Like you, I'm divorced. It was a long time ago, and we didn't have children. My parents passed away many years ago, and there's not much in the way of family left. So I'm well placed to do this work." He stretches. "I realize I can't do it for ever — it is stressful, that's for sure — and I was beginning to think of going back to a different kind of reporting. But this story . . ." He leans forward, his eyes widening. "This story, Michelle — it's a one-off. If I — we — can pull it off, we'll have almost literally saved the world. It will be the biggest scoop in history."

"What are the chances you can do this? And if you do, will I get my life back?"

He gives her a thoughtful look. His eyes, she notices for the first time, are dark blue, with deep laughter lines at the corners. His gaze is intelligent, probing. "I don't know, Michelle. Who knows what will happen? But if Andersson's right, then something catastrophic could happen and it looks like we're the only people who have a chance to stop it. I wish for your sake you weren't involved, but you are and they know it, and we can't change that now. All we can do is put the story out there and wait for Kimia to implode."

She knew in her heart that he couldn't tell her. How could he? Nobody can predict the future, and this future looks like it depends on the two of them in ways that she could never have imagined. She thinks back to that fateful meeting with Lars in the lift. If only the lift had left without her.

CHAPTER TWENTY-SIX

Michelle

When, much later, she thinks back to the ferry crossing, she feels sick to her stomach all over again.

At first, they stood on the upper deck to watch the spread of snow-covered mountains along the fjord, as the port disappeared rapidly behind the boat. But once they left the fjord and headed out into the open sea, nausea hit her like a hammer blow and didn't leave until she was back on dry land.

She retreated to her tiny cabin, where she lay for three days, with only the lashing rain and spray on the window to look at. She was dimly aware of the days turning into nights, but the rest of the trip was a blur: Richard coming and going, providing water and food that she couldn't eat, changing the bowl she'd vomited into, giving her a damp flannel to wipe her face and hands. Apart from that, the heaving of her stomach matched the heaving of the boat, and she'd never felt so ill in her life.

Finally, at last, the movement of the boat indicated their imminent arrival in Denmark, and with it her recovery. Weak with exhaustion and relief, she dressed and put together her possessions, peering out of the window at the first signs of land. Seabirds, smaller boats heading out, a drop in the wind. The water calmed as they inched into the harbour. When Richard knocked on her door, she was more than ready to go.

In the car and back on dry land, her stomach settles and her spirits lift, but it's only after they've left the port that she speaks. "I'm hungry," she says.

"Thought you might be," Richard says, guiding the car into a car park in the town. "Let's see what we can find."

A warm café, a mug of steaming coffee and a plate of food revive her and she begins to feel human again. Overcome by nausea, she'd forgotten their situation, the threat hanging over them, but now, her head clearing, it hits her again. She looks around the café and wonders how she got here. It's hard to believe her life is in danger, sitting here in an ordinary café, surrounded by ordinary people, drinking coffee. But then she reminds herself that she's in Denmark for a reason, and it hasn't gone away.

"Have I thanked you for looking after me on that hideous boat trip?" she asks, embarrassed to think that someone she barely knows has seen her in such a state. Cleaned up after her, dealt with the contents of her stomach.

He gives her a sympathetic smile. "You thanked me all the time and apologized constantly. I had to ask you to stop. It was the least I could do. You were in a terrible state."

She nods, not enjoying the memory. "Were you okay?"

"I developed sea legs a long time ago," he said. "But you weren't the only one. Most people disappeared downstairs and didn't reappear until we docked."

"Anything suspicious?"

"I'm not sure, to be honest. I kept myself to myself as far as possible. There was nothing obvious. Only—"

She gives him a quizzical look.

"It's probably nothing. But you know I thought we might have been followed? There was one car that rang an alarm bell when we boarded."

"You didn't mention it."

"No point in worrying you when I had no evidence of anything. And then you were rather indisposed."

She grimaces. "What specifically rang the alarm bell?"

"It wasn't anything specific. Just two blokes in a four-wheel drive. Didn't look like your normal travellers, that's all. I didn't see them again until we docked. Though I did stay out of the way most of the time."

"And when we disembarked?"

"They were ahead of us. Disappeared in the other direction."

She nods. Looking around the café, the normality of it suddenly seems alien to her. A dragging feeling pulls at her chest, a foreboding. An insight into her future, and it's not pleasant. "What happens when we get back to the UK? Am I going to have to go into hiding, change my identity, not see my family or friends? I'm not sure I can handle living like that—"

Richard makes a placating gesture with his hands. "You won't have to. Not for long, anyway. That's why I'm here, isn't it?"

"But what can you do? There's so much money at stake, and we know they're ruthless. They'll do anything to protect themselves."

"Hold on. I wanted to let you recover a little before we talked about this. I've had three whole days on the boat to think about it and little else to do but check on you every so often. It does no good thinking of the size of the problem — yes, it's huge, but if we break it down, it's easier to handle."

"Please go on. I'd love to be reassured."

"I'm not sure if I can do that — at least not straight away—" She opens her mouth to object but he silences her with a gesture. "But I have a short-term plan."

"Tell me, then."

"We should leave — we need to stay ahead of them if we can. In a nutshell, here's the plan. We're going to drive to Ostend and take the ferry from there. Let's go."

CHAPTER TWENTY-SEVEN

Michelle

Almost as soon as they're under way, Richard says, "We need to call Lars."

Startled, Michelle turns to look at him. "You know how to contact him?"

"He's been in touch. Wants me to call."

Lars's voice is loud and clear on the car's connection. "Hello, Richard?" He sounds uncertain, wary.

"Is this call secure?" Richard says without preamble.

"Here's the other number . . ." Lars enunciates each syllable carefully. Michelle writes the number on her hand.

"Call me back." Lars cuts the call.

Michelle punches in the number on Richard's phone as he drives. Lars picks up straight away. "Hello. Where are you?"

"On the way to Ostend. We took the ferry over to Denmark."

"Both of you? You went to Iceland?"

"Michelle needed help. Where are you?"

"Stockholm, holed up in a flat."

"Are you safe?"

"I doubt it. But I've done what I can to stay under the radar. What's your plan, Richard?"

"We're en route to England. We'll find somewhere safe, probably in London. Then I need to start working on this properly. What else can you give me?"

"You need to secure the evidence. In a bank or a safe deposit box. That's the first thing."

"Of course."

"I can give you names, dates, some of the data. I managed to keep some historical reports, but not much."

"Okay. I need to know precisely what you found, and what the implications are. We can't do it now, but let's talk as soon as we're there and have found a safe house. It's a twelve-hour journey to Ostend. I'll call you as soon as I can."

"Good."

"Look after yourself."

Lars snorts. "I'll do my best. You too. And Michelle — I'm sorry I've put you in this position. I had no choice."

"I know, Lars. I'm fine."

A click indicates the line has disconnected.

There's a short silence. "Will he survive this?" Michelle says at last, in a small voice.

"I'm going to do my damnedest to make sure he does," Richard says, his jaw set. And somehow, Michelle is convinced.

They swap seats at the next fuel stop, and Michelle takes the wheel as Richard sleeps. Though the car is unfamiliar, and she's not used to driving on the right, she soon gets the hang of it, though she's slower than Richard, taking extra care at junctions and traffic lights. At first, she watches the rear-view mirror like a hawk — and has to force herself to stop when her neck and shoulders start to seize up. She sees nothing unusual, but she doesn't know what she's looking for. A company like Kimia, with so much to lose, would be hiring the best to find her, she's certain. It's a frightening thought, and she tries to put it from her mind and focus on getting to London. The most important thing is to stay ahead of them.

Richard has mapped an unusual route through Europe. It's not the quickest, but he reasons that by taking the less popular roads, they'll have more chance of evading their pursuers. Although she's guided by the sat nav, at times she's convinced she's taken a wrong turn, because the route winds through narrow lanes and tiny villages. But the map shows they're moving in the right direction, so she learns to trust what she's told. She sits in silence, preferring not to have anything to distract her. Richard sleeps soundly beside her, as if nothing in the world is wrong.

As the hours tick by, she can't stop thinking about her situation. When will she see her son again? Will she ever feel safe? Where can she live in peace? What will happen if they release the story — and how long will that take? She's heard of journalists spending years uncovering the truth on major global stories. The thought is chilling. Years in hiding, looking over her shoulder, unable to be herself . . . she shakes her head to dispel the rising anxiety. She mustn't think like that. One thing at a time. Get to England, then deal with the next thing. That's what Richard said.

As they continue to drive through the fluctuating countryside of Europe, she begins to realize that this is it, right now. The first stage of the rest of her life has begun.

It feels like standing on the edge of a precipice in the wrong shoes.

* * *

Richard stirs as she pulls into a service station. His hair tousled, his eyes droopy, he has the look of a reluctant teenager woken for school.

"Sorry," she says. "I have to pee."

He pulls himself back into a sitting position, rubbing his neck. "Me too. We'll go in together. Park over there where we can keep an eye on the car."

They've reached the Netherlands, where for a brief period they're taking a main road. Traffic rumbles past and wind ruffles Michelle's hair as she walks towards the low-level building that houses the petrol station, café and shop. The toilets are towards the back of the shop, and as Richard holds the door open for her, she notices his head swivel, his forehead crinkling as a large four-wheel drive pulls into the service station, drawing to a stop away from the petrol pumps. Its windows are tinted, the driver invisible. Nobody gets out.

"Go ahead," Richard says. "We'll take it in turns. I'll wait for you in the shop."

She starts to ask a question, but he waves her on. Aware of the need for speed, she hurries to the ladies' room at the back, passing shelves of crisps and other snacks on her way. There are three cubicles, one of which seems occupied, though there's no sound from within. She wastes no time, emerging with a wary glance around as Richard nods and passes her on the way to the men's room. "Keep an eye on the black four-wheel drive on the left," he mutters as he passes her. "Don't let them see you."

She feels a tingling at the back of her neck, her palms suddenly damp. As she walks along the aisle, she keeps her head down, selecting a packet of nuts on her way to the checkout desk. Changing direction at the last minute brings her to the drinks cabinet, where she can see the dark shape to one side of the main area. She gathers a couple of bottles of water, keeping her face hidden from the outside.

Could this be it, the chase over already?

She waits, not daring to approach the counter without Richard, and tries to look relaxed, as if she's deciding what snacks to buy. She wanders slowly along the aisle, noting the camera overhead. She shakes her hair over her face, just in case. The assistant at the checkout is occupied with another customer, thankfully, and as she waits another car draws up at the pumps. An elderly woman climbs out. Good, that'll be another distraction. But where's Richard? He seems to be taking a long time. Too long. Or perhaps she's overreacting.

At the end of the aisle there's a carousel with a selection of hats. She tries on a peaked cap and pretends to study herself in the mirror. It gives her a good view of the black car, which still hasn't moved — but she can't make out anyone inside. The windows are too dark for her to see through at this distance.

She returns the hat to its carousel and edges towards the toilets. Her imagination starts to work overtime. Without Richard, she doesn't have a chance — they'll catch up with her for certain, and she'll have no defence against them. She'll disappear without trace. What should she do?

There's nobody nearby. She pushes open the door to the men's room a crack, looking away. "Richard?" she calls tentatively, but there's no reply. Now she's really concerned. She sticks her head around the door. The room's entirely empty, the door to the single cubicle open.

Richard has disappeared.

CHAPTER TWENTY-EIGHT

Michelle

Terror grips her, the blood rushing from her face. She starts to tremble. For what seems like an age, she stands transfixed, letting panic take over.

She's saved by a woman coming towards her, sympathetic eyes taking in her discomfort. She says something incomprehensible, and Michelle shakes her head. "Sorry," she whispers. Her throat seems to have narrowed, her voice lost in its depths.

"Are you all right?" the woman replies in perfect English.

Michelle takes a longer look. She hates herself for being suspicious, but there's nothing out of the ordinary, just a woman heading for the toilet. She takes a deep breath and with an enormous effort takes control. "I'm okay. Just needed a moment." She waves the water at the woman, who smiles and nods, turning towards the ladies' room.

At that moment, she feels a hand on her shoulder. She recoils, stumbling, almost falling against the shelves of sweets and snacks, the water and the nuts landing with a thump on the floor. Her mind races. She's about to be captured, taken somewhere remote and murdered, left to die alone. Or she could fight, run, decide to live, whatever the future might bring. It has to be fight for her life, run—

"Steady, Michelle," a familiar voice says. "I'm here. We need to go, now."

Richard retrieves the water and the nuts from the floor and places them back on a shelf. With his hand on the small of her back, her body moves as if under his control. Watched by the young man at the checkout desk, they keep their heads down. Richard steers her through the door before exiting himself, as if she's a small child. She daren't look at the black vehicle lurking by the wall as her feet put themselves one in front of the other.

At last they're inside the car and moving off. Light-headed from holding her breath, she releases it in one go. "I-I was terrified you'd been taken. Where were you?" she says at last, trying her best to keep the panic from her voice.

"Sorry. I found a back way out. Went to check on the Range Rover."

"Please don't do that again, I nearly fainted with fear."

"I won't. Sorry again."

"What did you find? Are they following us?" She cranes her neck to see in the wing mirror, but the road behind seems clear.

"There was definitely someone in there, I think on the phone. But I couldn't tell if they were there for us or not. Could have been completely innocent."

But from his tone of voice and the speed with which he leaves the petrol station, she can tell he doesn't believe this.

* * *

In silence they negotiate the unfamiliar countryside. Watching fields flash by, Michelle begins to feel sleepy, the adrenalin rush from the petrol station fading fast. Richard's face is set, unreadable as he focuses on the road ahead. He's probably working out their next move, assessing the options, the risks ahead of them.

That's what she should be doing too, but she can't keep herself awake. The sickness of the boat trip and the stress of the journey have exhausted her and she dozes, her head swaying when the car changes direction. From time to time she jerks awake, the panic returning, only to settle again, unable to resist.

Finally thirst wakes her, her tongue dry against the roof of her mouth. She probably snored, but just at this moment she doesn't care how she looks or what Richard thinks of her. When your life's in terrible danger, it certainly changes your perspective. Only a week ago, she'd have been mortified if someone had caught her snoring, her mouth slack.

She straightens up, reaching for the water bottle in the side pocket next to her. Ahead is more straight road. Richard drives fast but steadily as they pass other vehicles. There seem to be more trucks and vans than before.

"Where are we?" she says. "Are we getting close to the coast?"

He glances over at her. "Good you got some sleep. No, a hundred clicks yet. But we're in Belgium, homing in."

She decides not to put him right on the sleep issue. She may have dozed, but she feels like she hasn't slept for a week.

"Are we being followed?"

"Not that I'm aware of."

She wonders if it's possible they're being followed without knowing it, on a straight road with good visibility ahead and behind. They could be using a camera system, for all she knows, or some kind of tracker, or a drone. She sighs. All this is so far beyond her experience, she could conjecture for days and still not know what's possible. For a moment, she toys with asking Richard, but decides against it. In a way, she'd rather not know, for the moment at least.

"Where are we heading?"

"Calais. We could go via Ostend, but it's quite a lot further by water, and given the state of your sea legs, I think the shorter journey's preferable — and probably quicker." He grins at her.

"Thank you. I'm not relishing getting back on a boat, that's for sure." She pauses, quelling the memory of the crossing from Iceland to Denmark, the lurch in her stomach. "Richard?"

"I'm here."

She's uncertain of herself, not wanting to sound weak, but she needs to say what's on her mind. "Before, when you left the service station . . . when you weren't in the men's room, I completely panicked. What if you'd really disappeared — what would I have done? I felt utterly helpless. I mean, I know I'd have probably got back in the car and kept on driving, but then what? I think I need — we need — a Plan B, or some kind of back-up plan, at least. What if we get separated on the boat? We have to use the toilets separately, after all — we can't avoid that."

He nods, his eyes still on the road. His voice softens. "I'm sorry, Michelle, it was thoughtless of me. I know how terrifying this whole situation must be for you. Yes, I think it's a good idea to have some kind of fall-back position for you if I disappear. I'm going to do my damnedest not to let it happen, but it's as well to be prepared."

She manages a crooked smile. "What should I have done if you hadn't reappeared? I'm assuming run and keep on with the plan to get back to England with the sample."

"Yes, of course." He pauses. "And once you're there, hide as best you can. Do what we've been doing to keep yourself safe. Here—" he passes over his mobile — "put Lars Andersson's number in your phone. And Tom's — he's my research assistant. You'll meet him when we get to London."

As she types in the numbers, he continues. "Regarding the sample . . . I was thinking we have no option but to keep it with us, but I've changed my mind. We should get it somewhere safe in England, as soon as we can. Get it out of our hands. As it is, if they find us, they can just help themselves."

"But how?"

"I think the best way is the normal one, using Bpost. I've spent time in Belgium, and I know how it works. It's as reliable as any service would be, and we don't want to attract attention by making a fuss, using a secure service, or anything like that. It'll be like any other package. We'll stick it in a Jiffy bag and get it tracked."

"What, the normal post office? Isn't that a risk?"

"Everything's a risk. We don't want customs to open it and start asking questions, do we? But we must get it away from us, to somewhere safe, so it survives even if we don't."

Michelle flinches at this comment but pushes it away from her consciousness. This is disaster planning and they have to consider the worst.

"Can't we leave it here, in Belgium?"

"Not really. We'll need to go into hiding for a while when we get to London. But at some point we'll need it as evidence — particularly that report. There's no way we can ask someone else to collect it at some later date; anything might happen in the meantime."

She daren't ask what he's referring to.

"We'll have to make damn sure we're not being followed when we send it," Richard continues. "If someone spots what we're doing, they'll intercept it no problem and that will be it."

"So we'll send it via normal post. Then what? What if it takes longer than we do to get back to England?"

He shrugs. "It's going straight to a safe deposit box. We'll tell Tom, so if we go astray, he can get hold of the sample. I'll give him the name of another journalist who might take on the story."

Michelle stares out of the window, unseeing. This is so confusing. There are many ways this could go, and none of them sounds good.

"One thing at a time. First, let's get rid of the package."

She almost smiles. *The package.* It sounds like the kind of corny criminal-speak they use in cheap TV crime shows when they're describing a kidnapped person.

"Where will we send it?"

"Not sure yet. A bank, or a specialist centre. Probably in London, so it's near us. I need to make a couple of calls."

She nods. With so much at stake, nowhere is invulnerable. And nobody.

"Where do we stop?"

"Next big town. We need somewhere busy, so that we don't draw too much attention to ourselves." He glances at the sat nav. "Let's see. We're not far from Bruges — perfect. There'll be plenty of tourists there, even this time of year, and enough British people for us not to stand out. It's a detour, but not too far, and it's worth it."

She remembers Bruges from a brief trip with Geoff, when they were newly married and in love. Romantic, picturesque Bruges, with its historic buildings and waterways. They'd had a wonderful time, drinking Champagne, eating chocolate, wandering around the old town, taking pictures.

This visit, though, will be quite different.

She shivers, but not from the cold. "What if we're followed?"

"That we can't plan. But we've managed before and we'll manage again."

He sounds confident. But she's not reassured.

CHAPTER TWENTY-NINE

The problem is, the target isn't as easy as they made out. Lone woman, they said. British, they said, middle-aged. No history in the military or intelligence. Bad luck landed her in this position — she has no idea what she's carrying. Should be able to pick her off easy. A couple of days' work, at most. A doddle, I thought.

But they lied. They were wrong on all counts, and I was a fool to believe them. That was my first mistake, and it infuriates me. That compounded with the delay in getting me on board. That was one of their many mistakes. In their field, they're the very best in the business, top of the tree, earning billions, brains like planets. But they have absolutely no idea — zero, zilch — of what goes on in the real world. Let alone at my level.

The basest level you could imagine. Down where the cockroaches live.

I suppose they thought they acted quickly. But by the time the job landed in my inbox, she was gone. And she had the weather on her side. The one thing I can't control, even with all the money in the world at my disposal.

I couldn't reach Iceland. It was the worst snowstorm the country had seen for eight years. No one would take me there, not even Nobby, who'd flown helicopters through the worst war zones in the world, dodging all

127

kinds of flak. "Not on your Nelly," he said. "We'd be worse off than a butterfly in a typhoon. I'm not dying for you, mate, not even if you paid me a hundred million bucks."

So by the time I arrived in that god-forsaken country, the bird had flown. Not through the airports — I checked them out. The day she disappeared, most flights were cancelled. There was no record of her passing through — not CCTV, not mobile records, not credit card use, not facial recognition. Admittedly my contacts in Iceland were flaky, but I believed them. Iceland has sophisticated surveillance systems, and if they hadn't caught her, then she wasn't there. She could have holed up, for sure, but experience shows she can't do that for ever.

Unless she has help.

And there's mistake number one magnified by one hundred. She has help.

* * *

Who is it, helping her? It isn't the flatmate, because she's still at work. I'm instructed not to eliminate her. She's under surveillance in case the target gets in touch. It isn't any of her work colleagues — the client is clear on that one. They'd know if anyone else hadn't turned up for work.

The target left in a hurry, taking virtually nothing from the apartment. The wardrobe was full of clothes, her laptop lying on the table. She had what she was standing up in. There was no mobile that I could find, but I checked that out earlier. Unobtainable. She ditched it. How did she know to do that, and how did she disappear so effectively, so quickly?

Assuming she knows the importance of what she's been given, who would she turn to? She's an ordinary person doing an ordinary job. There's nothing in her background to suggest anything other than that — albeit she took a short-term contract in a foreign country. Either she's undercover, and damn good at it, or she's with a professional. This person knows what to do in a situation like this.

And I was too late to intercept them.

CHAPTER THIRTY

Michelle

By the time they reach the town, rain has set in, the sky low and threatening. The car splashes through standing water on the main road, turning to puddles at the roadside pavements as they near the centre.

She expects Richard to stop at the first post office they see, but when she points it out, he says, "Nowhere to park. We need to find one where we can leave the car in full view, so we can see each other. If we can't find another one, we'll come back to this one and park illegally if need be."

They drive on into the old town. Somehow all those beautiful historic buildings don't look quite as good in the rain. But nothing looks good to Michelle just at the moment. Knowing that you're being hunted and may not make it through the day focuses the mind rather effectively.

Richard finds a quiet square and stops the car. Michelle looks around in surprise: there's no post office here that she can see, just a couple of street cafés. "I'm going to ask someone," Richard says, leaping out of the driver's side. Startled, Michelle cranes her neck, but Richard doesn't go far. At the first café, its tables spilling onto the pavement, he stops and asks a man sitting on his own with a cup of coffee and a newspaper. The man nods his head and points, and Richard returns to the car. He pulls out his mobile and dials. "Mate, need an address urgently. Yes, safe deposit box, central London. As secure as it gets. Text it to me, in the next couple of minutes?" He cuts the call.

"Who did you call?"

"Tom. I'm going to brief him properly when I get the chance, get him started on the story. He's fast — and I trust him. He's solid gold."

"So, where's the post office, then?"

"Just around the next corner," he says, starting the engine. "Let's see what we have." He circles the square once, twice. "Just checking," he says, glancing in the rear-view mirror. It occurs to Michelle that checking might not be worth it. If there are CCTV cameras and their pursuers are onto them, a bribe will most probably do the trick.

"Let's just do it," she says, as Richard's mobile pings.

"Yep," Richard replies. "Let's hope they sell envelopes."

As they turn the next corner, it becomes apparent that the Bpost building is in a large pedestrian area. Cars are not allowed, although at the second pass Richard finds a street on the opposite side of the square that has a view of the imposing frontage. It's not a proper parking space, so there's a risk Michelle will be moved on, but they agree that if that happens, she'll drive slowly around the block and hover close by until he returns. "It's the best we can do, I reckon," he says, opening the door. "Lock the doors, keep your eyes peeled."

And he's gone, walking confidently towards the large redbrick edifice. Michelle bites her lip. She can almost not bear to look — or to wait. Her heart beats fast, her hands turn clammy. She inspects every figure in the square and decides to count them to keep herself occupied. But people move too much and she loses track as they mill around. She changes tack and focuses on the ones who look suspicious, even while she knows that danger could come in any form, even the most innocent. Richard has disappeared into the maw of the building now, and she feels even more vulnerable, sitting on her own in a car that's parked illegally, in a place she doesn't know. She sinks as low as she can in her seat while still being able to see the doors of the post office and the space in front of it.

She's startled out of her skin when there's a knock at the window. Inches from her face is a young man in uniform, an official-looking badge on his chest. She opens the window a crack, and he says something incomprehensible.

"English?" Her voice shakes with fear.

"Parking not possible here," he says, his face deadpan.

"Sorry," she says, closing the window. Though she knows she must mistrust everyone, he seems genuine. She scoots over to the driver's side and starts the car. Dammit, now she's got to drive around, which means she'll lose sight of the building. She heads back to the square with the café where Richard asked for directions, and circles it slowly. She checks the time. She'll hover for five minutes at a time, then return to the forbidden spot. Then repeat — if she has to.

But after twenty minutes, there's no sign of Richard.

* * *

Cursing, she returns to the first square, stops the car, and turns the engine off. They didn't have a plan for this — why didn't they? Anything could have happened on a long scale from ordinary to catastrophic. It could be a simple problem, like a queue. Or he could be dead. Michelle drops her head to the steering wheel. How on earth is she to cope with this? All her instincts tell her to refuse to accept the situation, to opt out. It's an illusion, she's imagining it all, she should just go home, call Toby and get on with her life.

But logic kicks in. If she does what her instincts tell her, she'll be dead in a flash. And many other people will die, not just from the effects of the drug, but from the wider implications it carries with it. She must carry on; she has to find Richard. She sends another text. This is the fourth — it's pointless when he hasn't answered the first, but she can't think of anything else to do, and she has to do something.

If Richard's been captured, can they track her down from the texts? If she calls, will they home in on her? Can they intercept a call from a burner phone? If only she were more tech-savvy. She knows so little about what's possible.

But how long should she wait? An hour? Two hours? Surely she'll start to look suspicious if she hangs around for longer. Even an hour is too long, though she decides that's her limit. It's unlikely he'd queue for longer than that — he would surely return to the car and they'd try to find a different branch of the Bpost.

The minutes tick by. She keeps her eyes out for the traffic warden, takes another tour around the streets behind the square, getting snarled up behind a delivery man for a few endless moments. Time has never passed so slowly. She returns to her lookout post. Still no sign — no sign of Richard, nor of anything suspicious.

Should she follow him in? But that would mean leaving the car, risking everything. It has to be a last resort. The longer he's gone, the more likely it is that something bad has happened, and the more danger she'll be in. But if she drives away and by some miracle he escapes their clutches, only to find that she's gone, she'll never forgive herself.

And, oh God, if he's been captured, the likelihood is that the drug and the damning report will have been taken too, so it will all have been for nothing. That can't happen.

She braces her shoulders, sets her jaw and starts the engine. If she's going to go down, it won't be without a fight — and she won't desert Richard. It may be for nothing, but she'll do her damnedest to help him. As she drives slowly towards the main square, it feels as if she's going into battle.

CHAPTER THIRTY-ONE

Michelle

She's still in the side street when things start to happen. People start to run like confused ants across the open square, without any obvious target. Women pulling small children by the hand or struggling to run with buggies, men striding out, coats flying. But then she realizes they're not running towards something, they're running away — from the Bpost building. People race down the steps, some jumping from top to bottom in their haste, and more people swarm away from the doors as she watches. Surely this is no coincidence. Richard's in trouble.

She reverses the car back into its space, leaving the engine running. Something's happening in that building. People start to gather a distance away, watching the entrance as a police van draws up. A few stragglers bring up the rear of the stampede — a woman holding the hand of a small child, a couple of men.

One of them has a familiar, confident gait.

She almost faints with relief as he strides towards the car. He comes straight to the driver's side and opens the door, his

133

jaw tight, his mouth clamped shut. She scrambles over to the passenger seat with difficulty, but she doesn't care because Richard's back.

He maintains silence, taking a complicated, circuitous route through the centre of Bruges, backtracking sometimes, circling roundabouts until Michelle feels dizzy, glancing behind and in the wing mirrors every few seconds. Michelle keeps quiet, letting him focus on their getaway, gripping the door handle to steady herself at every unexpected turn. When she takes a peek in the wing mirror on her side, she sees nothing to indicate they're being followed. But she'd rather be safe and carsick than sorry and in danger.

At last they're in the outskirts of the city. He releases a breath and glances over at her. "Sorry," he says. "Just needed to make sure we were properly away. And sorry to take so long — you must have wondered where I'd got to."

"I was about to mount a rescue operation," she says with a feeble effort at humour. "Tell me."

"There was a queue when I went in, but it didn't look too bad. Then the woman in front of me seemed to take an age — every time I thought she'd finished, she produced something else she wanted to send. But everything seemed normal, nothing to raise my antenna. Then after about fifteen minutes, I got to the front of the queue, handed over my package and paid. That's when something happened. A couple, perfectly ordinary looking people, came forward and flashed some kind of ID at me and at the guy at the window."

"Oh, my goodness, were they—?"

"I wasn't going to hang about to find out."

"What did you do?"

He chuckles. "I didn't hesitate — I pointed at the man, yelled 'GUN!' and ran for the door. There was a shocked silence. A woman squealed, everyone panicked and started to run. It was chaos — which was what I wanted — people screaming and shouting and tripping over each other to get out. A couple of security men appeared from nowhere, but I kept going and didn't look back."

"Wow. That was quick thinking. I'm impressed."

He looks sheepish for a moment. "Saw it in a film."

She starts to laugh, and then she can't stop herself. This ridiculous, terrifying situation they find themselves in has just got so much more ridiculous. Richard looks startled, then starts to chuckle himself.

But when she's calmed down and wiped the tears from her eyes, the tension returns. She gulps. "So they know you're with me, and they know where we are, and they must know the car—"

"Hang on a minute, we don't know any of that, not for sure. But I agree on one thing — we should ditch the car."

"What do you mean?"

"Change it for something less recognizable. We don't need a big four-wheel drive anymore. We'll drop in at a car hire place and get something less distinctive."

"Do you think it was them?"

"If it wasn't, it was a big coincidence. The first time we stop to do something other than pee or buy food, something strange happens. Those two were definitely focused on me. It may have been a case of mistaken identity, but I doubt it."

"So they weren't police?"

"I certainly wasn't stopping to check their ID. I'm pretty sure they weren't. But . . ." He stops there, leaving her wondering if he has any more bad news.

"But what?"

"But you'd have loved the look on their faces when I shouted 'GUN!'"

Sometimes, reading news of war and famine, disease and corruption, she allows her imagination to picture Armageddon, and she wonders if she'd have the ability to survive.

Right now, she knows who she'd want by her side.

* * *

The new car is small, white and nondescript. It's easy to pretend they're an ordinary couple. As they head towards Calais,

135

Michelle begins to feel a little more relaxed. They've had some scrapes, but they've made it this far. Surely there's a good chance they'll reach London now.

But Richard thinks otherwise. "Now we're getting close to the Channel, I'm wondering if we should use Calais after all," he says. "If there's any sign we're being followed, we should change tack. Maybe change car again. The last thing we want is to board a ferry with the guys who want us dead. Too many opportunities for a strange watery mishap."

A strange watery mishap. The thought is enough for the bile to rise in Michelle's throat. She swallows hard, trying not to think about the last time they crossed the water. To distract herself from the memory, she says the first thing that comes into her head. "It feels like we're caught in some weird spy drama. There's so much I don't know or understand. The people who are chasing us, presumably someone hired by Kimia — a private detective, or their own security people — do they know about you? If they do, how did they find out? Are they using some kind of technology to track us?"

"Such as?"

For a moment, she's embarrassed, but her need to know is more important than losing face. "Well, at home I watch a lot of thrillers, TV dramas, crime series — where they're able to track pretty much anyone using CCTV, drones, satellites . . ."

Far from laughing at her, Richard looks serious. "I know. The same has occurred to me. I have no idea how far they could go, given they'd be willing to pay any amount to stop us. I don't even know if they've identified me yet. I'm assuming they know you're with someone, but do they know who?"

"I haven't told anyone. I haven't spoken to a soul since the girl in the café in Reykjavik. No, I tell a lie, there was a woman at the service station who asked if I was okay." She pauses for a moment. "You don't think—"

"We can't rule anything out. But there are other ways they could trace me. Facial recognition technology perhaps, but who uses it apart from the police and the secret services?

And could they — would they bribe them?" He shrugs. "We just don't know."

Michelle stares out of the window, biting her lip. She can't make sense of any of this. The tension in her forehead is beginning to turn into a headache, or it could be the start of a migraine. She's started to suffer from these in recent years. She's exhausted, overstressed and hungry — all trigger points for a nasty migraine.

Richard seems to sense her despair. "Listen, I don't believe they've clocked me yet. They almost certainly know someone is helping you, but I keep a very low profile online — I have to, for my work. Very low indeed. I never post on social media — I'm not even registered — and my photo doesn't appear anywhere in the public domain. I keep a very close eye on it. Which means it's going to be extra hard for them to work out who I am, even if they've managed to get a photo of my face. But the fact we've got this far with only one major incident is good. Perhaps they're not the best in the business, or perhaps they weren't expecting you to escape so quickly, if at all. They certainly won't expect you to know not to use your mobile or credit cards, or to be able to exist without them. It'll be hard for them to keep track. So far, so good. We're ahead of them, and we're going to stay that way."

"I hope so."

Something in her voice makes Richard turn to look at her. "You look shattered," he says. She closes her eyes, because tears have begun to form and she doesn't want him to see.

"I-I have a bit of a headache."

"Right, we're going to stop for something to eat," he says. "Just here." He indicates a small service station on the right and eases the car off the road.

CHAPTER THIRTY-TWO

Michelle

Richard sends a long text to his researcher. "He can get started now," he says. She wants to ask how long it will take, but bites back the question. It depends on so many things.

They buy bottles of water and headache tablets, though the pain in her forehead has receded now she has eaten. They decide to push on to Calais, since they seem to be ahead of their pursuers, and take their chances with the ferry to Dover.

"We'll have to show our passports, won't we?"

"Yes, we can't avoid that now," Richard says. "We haven't booked tickets though, so they can't check ahead if we're aiming for a particular ferry."

"How are we going to do this without drawing attention to ourselves?"

"The same way as everyone else. We're going to join the queue and follow the leader. But before we do that, we need to change the way we look. We'll stop off in town, get new clothes, change our hair — nothing too radical." Michelle gives him a sideways look. "We don't want to attract attention, but if they're looking out for a long black coat, let's go for a short blue jacket. Maybe a hat, or a pair of glasses, or a hoody . . ."

"I get it." She wonders how she can change her look. Her coat, in particular, is designed for an Icelandic climate, not a temperate English winter. She needs to find something more appropriate. But she's not trying to look good, just ordinary. That makes a change from trying to look attractive. Or youthful. After this — if there is an "after" — she'll give up trying to look youthful. How shallow that all seems now, now that her very survival is at stake.

Reflexively, she raises a hand to her head. "Should I cut my hair?" She hopes he'll demur, because it's her best feature.

"It would be best."

She grimaces. She can't help herself.

"But if you clipped it up, it would be good enough."

She turns to smile at him. "I'm beginning to like you, Richard."

* * *

Her new clothes feel stiff and unfamiliar as they inch towards the ferry. Their stop-off in Calais town centre was short but effective. Richard looks quite different in a hoody and jogging trousers, with a baseball cap to complete the outfit. It doesn't seem appropriate for the situation they're in, but it's hard to know what would be. Michelle has scraped her hair back into a ponytail and exchanged contact lenses for her glasses. The heavy down-filled coat has been replaced with a lightweight navy jacket. It's not flattering but she doesn't care.

This is another "pinch point" on their journey, where they could easily be in danger. Richard goes alone to buy tickets, without incident. The woman at the counter barely glances at him, working fast as the line of passengers grows by the minute. Waiting in the car, slumped low in her seat, Michelle watches in the wing mirror, alert for anyone who looks like they might approach. But everyone around them seems focused on reaching the ramp and getting on board. The ferry must be full today, she reckons — the car park's packed and still they keep coming, filling a second waiting area.

At last they're able to board. They leave the car below deck and aim for a lounge area, choosing a corner space where they can keep an eye on the room around them. Richard puts his bag down on the bench seat next to Michelle. "I'm going to watch from the deck while the rest of the cars embark," he says. "Stay here. I won't be far away. As soon as we get going, I'll be back." She nods, watching his back disappear through the double doors to the outside.

Sitting there alone, she feels jumpy, vulnerable, and at the same time angry with herself for showing weakness. She has to remind herself all the time that in this situation, she can be forgiven pretty much any reaction — it doesn't mean she's a powerless woman, or any less capable of looking after herself.

When he returns, Richard brings two large cups of coffee. "Just what I need," she says as he sits next to her, his eyes scanning the room. Children wriggle and squirm on uncomfortable seats, people come and go to the small café area in the centre, the door to the deck constantly swinging. Nothing seems out of the ordinary as the ferry drifts out of the port, its engines filling the space with sound, the floor vibrating.

"Anything?" she says.

"Maybe. At the last minute, a motorbike boarded with two guys. Could be completely innocent but I'm going to watch out for them. They were in full leathers, so it's going to be hard to identify them."

Michelle feels her shoulders tense. "I don't know how you do what you do," she says. "Is it always this stressful, being in your job?"

He chuckles. "Most of it's desk research," he says. "Pretty unexciting stuff. But I know what you mean. This situation — it's more dramatic than most. I've never done a runner across Europe before. But then the stakes have never been this high

140

before, with so many lives at risk." He thinks for a moment. "Or with people who are quite so . . . criminally ruthless."

Michelle feels a powerful need to be distracted.

"Tell me about some of the other stories you've worked on."

"There are so many. Some more interesting than others." A family gathers around the table next to them and he drops his head, hiding his face. "Maybe some other time. I'm going to take a quick tour of the room, maybe check out the deck again."

Michelle glances through the rain-speckled window. It's drizzling outside, grey skies turning darker on the horizon. Her stomach lurches. She takes deep breaths to steady herself, holding the inside of one wrist with her fingers. Someone told her — she can't remember who — that it helps stop travel sickness, though it didn't work for her last time. But as the French coast shrinks behind the boat, the water seems calm, a gentle rocking the only sign that they're out at sea now.

Richard returns with a shrug. "Nothing that I can see," he says. "Just be alert — we might need to move in a hurry. Feeling queasy?" He indicates her wrist.

"Not really. It's probably just the memory of the last time." She grimaces. "I need to take my mind off it."

"Shall I tell you some jokes?" he says, smiling. "Not that I'm very good at remembering them."

"Tell me about yourself," she says. She knows so little about him, though they've been in each other's company constantly for the last few days.

"It's not very interesting," he says.

"Try me. Think of it as first aid. Better than having me throw up in your lap."

He chuckles. "You're very persuasive."

"Go on, then. I don't even know where you're from. You have free rein."

They sit side by side as he talks, both still scanning the room. But soon she finds herself focused on his face, soothed by his voice, as the buzz and rumble of the engines fade into the background. What he thinks of as "not interesting" is fascinating.

* * *

As soon as the cliffs of Dover appear in the distance, they grab their bags and head for the stairs to the vehicle deck. People start to gather behind them as the ferry chugs slowly into port.

Richard's eyes scan the lines of cars. "Just trying to spot that bike," he says, but there's no sign of any motorbikes when the queue begins to move. Directed by men in orange jackets, the lines of vehicles take their turns to disembark. Slowly at first, the vast area empties, and soon they're back on dry land, driving through the outskirts of Dover. After a few minutes, a roaring comes from behind and a group of motorbikes overtakes them one by one. They flash by, the riders dark shapes in full leathers. It's hard to distinguish one from the next.

"Looks like they're travelling together."

"Could be," Richard says. She can tell he's still on the lookout for the one he saw earlier.

"Scenic route?" she says as they pass the line of cars waiting to join the motorway to London.

"It's safer."

"Where are we heading?"

"Central London, at least for the moment. It's the easiest place to hide."

"Where will we stay?" She longs for her comfortable flat, with her things around her. And a warm bed.

"For the moment, we'll find a short let. Earl's Court, maybe. Tom's on the case — he'll have something set up before we get there. Then we'll see."

Michelle's heart sinks. Earl's Court, full of B&Bs and bedsits, where people squeeze into flats and rooms to save money, where travellers head with their backpacks. You never get to know the neighbours, not even by sight, in an area like

142

that. Is this what she has to look forward to? She longs for her old life, a quiet routine with no adventures. With Toby. His smile flashes into her mind, and she feels tears threaten. God, she misses him — now more than ever, because she can't see him. Or even speak to him. What if he's not okay? What if he's trying to contact her, because something's gone wrong, or he's unwell? What if Kimia's on to him too, and he's in danger? Her instincts as a mother kick in at the memory of his smile. It seems like years since she last saw him or spoke to him.

She blurts out: "I must talk to Toby."

Something in her tone alerts Richard to her agitation. "It's okay, Michelle," he says, reaching for her hand. He gives it a comforting squeeze. "We're going to work this out, I promise you. Once we're settled somewhere I'm going to get straight on to it. Talk to Lars, rope in a few contacts, start to drill down into this story. And we'll find a way for you to talk to Toby. I promise."

"Thank you," she says, oddly distracted by the touch of his hand. "I'm worried they might be after him — get to me by threatening him." She daren't say more because of the lump in her throat.

"It's possible. Though it's only a couple of days since we left. They'll be more interested in finding you and the sample. I imagine they think it'll be easy. We have that on our side, remember."

"But if they take Toby hostage, I couldn't . . ." She swallows. "I need to talk to him." She knows she sounds like a recalcitrant child, digging her heels in to get what she wants. But the instinct is too great to resist.

"You will, Michelle. We're going to stop and get new burner phones as soon as we can. You can text him the new number and ask him to call you."

"Thanks. Should he get a burner phone too?"

"Yes, straight away. Text him now. Tell him you'll pay. He should get it as soon as possible and only use it to contact

143

you. When you speak to him, be very clear — he mustn't mention this to anyone, or he'll be putting himself, and you, in danger. And tell him to keep an eye out for anything unusual or suspicious."

She nods.

"Is he in a hall of residence, or a flat share in the city?"

"Hall of residence, in the city centre. It's relatively secure, but I'm sure if someone wanted to get in, they could."

Richard is quiet for a couple of minutes. "You need to give Toby some story about why he should be on his guard. I'm trying to think what you can say."

"I could say I'm being stalked, perhaps?"

Richard nods. "Yeah, not bad."

"Someone I dated for a bit? Toby knows I've been on dating sites . . . Someone could have turned out to be a bit creepy, turning up all over the place — perhaps he knows where Toby is? I don't want to frighten him, or get him too worried about me, but I have to warn him."

"It's good enough, for the moment. Tell him to mention it to the caretaker, or whoever looks out for the students in that building. And whoever's responsible for pastoral care. Oh, and get your profile off those dating sites."

"Don't worry, I did that a long time ago." When she finally realized how humiliating it all was.

"What about social media? Facebook?"

"I have an account, though I don't use it much . . ."

"Cancel it, and everything else you can think where personal information might be held."

"But how can I do that without using the internet?"

"When we get there, wherever 'there' might be, Tom will set us up so it's hard to trace us. It won't be one hundred per cent, but they won't expect you to have that kind of skill."

CHAPTER THIRTY-THREE

Lars

Lars is trapped alone in the unfamiliar apartment, waiting for news of Richard and Michelle. He's altered his appearance as far as he can and stocked up for a few days so he doesn't have to go out.

Now would be a good time to find further information on PAN12 for Richard. He's buried everything related to Kimia under false file names that only he knows, with complex passwords and added security software. Like many scientists, he has a good grasp of technology, and with a bit of effort he can solve most problems. In another life, he'd have made a good hacker. As it turns out, that might have been the safer option.

He sets up his new smartphone and spends an hour or so accessing the files he needs, copying them into another secure account and renaming them. These are the results of early testing on the drug, the tests that ensured it was passed for clinical trials — trials on humans. This was before his time at Kimia, carried out by a small team of people with similar skills to his own, but who have since moved on to other projects. Surely there must have been anomalies in those initial tests? But if there were, the data isn't showing them. What's left of the data is clean, and PAN12 appears to have been one hundred per cent safe for testing on humans.

Lars takes a break to fetch a coffee. There's not much more he can do with the information he has — and it's not enough. It won't help Richard break the story. He wonders what will, and what else he can do to stop the launch of the drug.

It's possible Kimia will delay the launch, of course. Perhaps the fact that they've lost a sample and the incriminating data related to it will slow them down. Perhaps they'll wait until Michelle and Lars himself are eliminated. Richard too, if they find him. It would be the most logical thing to do. But in his heart Lars is doubtful. It's not that he doubts they'll be ruthless in hunting down the sample and disposing of the three people who know the truth about it — no, they'll go ahead with that. But postpone the launch, even by a few weeks? Extremely unlikely.

The launch is crucial to the future of the company. Its directors have committed everything to it — their reputations, their company's future, even their own lives, if what he suspects is true. Eye-watering amounts of money are involved. Lars wouldn't be at all surprised if, were the launch to be delayed, the company would collapse. If the truth comes out and the drug is cancelled, it'll be catastrophic for everyone even remotely related to it. And that includes some very powerful investors — leaders of global companies, politicians, heads of state. It couldn't go any higher.

No, three nobodies that have got away with one tiny sample — that's not going to stop the movers and shakers at Kimia. Their ambitions are set so far into the stratosphere they'll stop at nothing.

He logs into the pharma news site and searches for Kimia. There's no big news, only the speculation he's already seen about the launch of a ground-breaking drug. He checks the bloggers, then the other pharmaceutical press. One of the more esoteric journalists has written a piece about the top echelons at the new breed of biochemical companies: not the people who founded them, who often fall away once the company reaches a certain size, but the people who lead them to global domination. Powerful, intelligent people with the vision, the determination, the sheer ruthlessness, to push through all the regulations and the red tape, the politics, the line of failures trailing behind them, the lost billions, the disappointments and the setbacks, to lead their companies through everything, beating their competitors to a position of incredible power and wealth.

In this piece, which runs to several pages, Kimia gets a couple of mentions: for its ultra-secretiveness and for the rumours of a breakthrough. Nobody at the company would agree to speak to the journalist, but she mentions something that makes Lars sit up. She mentions that the CEO is never photographed and rarely interviewed — on the rare occasions he's heard outside the organization, it's over a phone line. She describes the board of directors as "disarmingly youthful". No assumptions are made about the cause, but the writer seems impressed that they're in such senior positions when they look like last year's graduates from university.

The directors are taking PAN12, of course they are. And of course they look youthful. They know PAN12 works; it reverses the effects of ageing. But they also know the drug's potential long-term effects.

They're taking it, knowing it might kill them.

Why would they do that? Because it's worth it, of course — the stakes are that high. They've calculated the odds. Perhaps one or two of them will die, but the others will live on and benefit from the huge proceeds of the launch of their flawed drug. All they have to do then is disappear. They probably have it all planned out already.

He finds the journalist quite easily. She's a freelancer, writing for a variety of publications in the pharmaceutical sector. She has to make her contact details available for the sake of future work. No contact details, no work.

Should he call her, or use some other method? He decides to use one of his burner phones. This woman, Petra Valkovitch, might know something useful. For a moment, he wonders if he should wait for Richard, check with him whether this is a good idea or not. But he decides to save Richard some time and contact her himself. He'll have to find a good pretext, for sure, but he feels pretty certain he can pull it off.

CHAPTER THIRTY-FOUR

I don't know who employs me. It might seem strange, working for people you've never met, or even spoken to, but you get used to it — particularly when the money starts to come in. I get my instructions by email usually, sometimes an encrypted message. I do the job, get paid. Simple as that. It works for me.

Let's call them the Agency, for want of a better handle. The Agency gets the contracts, not me. That way the Client — the one who decides the job needs doing, and pays — doesn't need to know my name, what I look like or where I live. They don't even know how I do it. Squeaky clean for them — and for me too. The fewer people who know, the better.

I get to decide how I do it. Usually I work to a deadline: complete the job by X date or Y time. Sometimes, like now, I don't have a deadline — but the job's urgent. Generous bonus for a successful outcome within a week. I've already lost two days and that's not like me. Must be getting sloppy.

But I have to rely on the information I've been given, and for this job it's sketchy to say the least. I know her name, I know some of her background. I know she has something she shouldn't have — a sample of some drug, and a report — and could choose to upset some very powerful people if she decides to use it against them. But that's about it. I don't bother trying to find out why it's so important. That's not my job.

* * *

Mistake number two was subbing the job to the wrong people. I tracked the target down as soon as I got the instruction. She was still in Iceland, heading for the ferry to Denmark — not a bad idea, I have to concede, and probably the only way out in that weather. My contacts were good, but they weren't the right people to do the rest of the job. Anyway, finishing her off in Iceland would have been tricky — too obvious. For a country with such a small population, a professional assassination would have made the front pages. I suppose you could argue that hiding the body would have been easy — in the snow, the mountains — but by the time I got there, it was too late for anything.

I have contacts across many continents — Europe, Russia, Africa. Some in Asia too, though less solid. Their expertise varies, of course, and some have skills that others don't, so I'm careful who I choose to do a job. The mistake I made in Belgium was not being there myself to complete the task. My guys tracked the target down to Bruges, where she stopped to send the item on somewhere. But the idiots lost both the item and the target. There was a diversion, and my guys weren't bright enough to spot it. Careless of them, and I'm kicking myself for not being there. But I wasn't even in the country. I had another job to finish off, and I couldn't be in two places at once. I'm smart, but even I can't manage that.

Now I'm on my own, in the UK, and I'm not going to miss the target this time. It's been messy, but I'm going to clear it up once and for all.

CHAPTER THIRTY-FIVE

Michelle

From the outside, it looks like an office block. There's no lobby to speak of, no sign on the door. The stairs are scuffed and grubby.

Tom has found a "caretaker" rental arrangement. The owner of a large building waiting for planning permission has decided to convert it into temporary accommodation while its future is settled. People take rooms on a short-term basis and "look after" the building — preventing squatters or vandalism — in the meantime. The rooms are former offices, pretty much unchanged, with multiple electrical points and phone connections, dusty slatted window blinds and stained carpets. A makeshift shower has been added to a large women's toilet area and the shared kitchen is tiny. In the fridge, which Michelle opens with trepidation, items are labelled: *Carmen, JJ,* and *Mike's milk: please don't use.*

She can't keep the dismay from her face.

"It's not for long, I promise," Richard says. He opens the doors to two large rooms, both big enough to house a small company. In the centre of each is a pile of assorted furniture, all looking as if it's seen better days. A mattress leans against one wall. "These two rooms are ours. You take that one—" he indicates the smaller of the two rooms — "I'm going to set up an office in this one straight away, and it'll double as my bedroom."

Michelle takes a deep breath. She has no choice, so she might as well get on with it. She only hopes her mattress is relatively new.

Her room looks out on a neglected courtyard choked with weeds, surrounded by uniform windows, some with identical blinds, some — the inhabited rooms, she supposes — framed with curtains. It's a pretty bleak outlook. She sighs and contemplates the furniture, taking a close look at the mattress. It's obviously used and a little stained, but the fact is, she'll be sleeping in her clothes for at least a few days, so it doesn't matter too much. The pillow, at least, seems new. That's one small comfort. If she's got to stay here, then the bed's the most important thing.

She heads back to Richard's room, closing the door behind her. He's set up a table, a chair and some bookshelves, a laptop open on the table, surrounded by notebooks and papers.

"Where did all that come from?" she says.

"Tom got it delivered — it's my mobile office, always ready to go."

"This Tom sounds like the perfect Person Friday. Will I meet him?"

"Sure. He's the other person you'll see for a while. You'll like him. I couldn't do my job without him."

"Will he make tea?" she says. It's a weak joke, but she's exhausted and not a little despondent.

"He's at the supermarket as we speak," Richard says. "He'll get us supplies for a few days."

She sinks onto the faded mattress, which he's placed by the wall. "How long will all this take, Richard? Are we here for days or weeks? Please don't say months . . ."

He turns to her with a sympathetic look. "Look, 'I don't know' is the honest answer — I'm sorry. But the longer we delay getting the story out, the more dangerous it's going to get for us. Hopefully it'll be a matter of days — a couple of weeks at most. Tom and I are going to spend every hour we can putting the evidence together. In the meantime, I'm afraid, we have no choice but to lie low."

Even a few days here sounds like an age, a couple of weeks like an endless stretch. "Can I help? I've got nothing else to do, and I can't just lie about in my room for days on end."

"Of course, we need all the help we can get." Richard grins at her. "There's a mountain of work to be done. We need to follow up every lead, research every mention, dig out all the dirt we can find. We have to be meticulous or the story could fail — and we can't let that happen. Tom will get you a laptop and secure access, and we'll all work together in my room."

"Okay, where do I start?"

"We need the table from your room in here, and probably the bookshelf as well. Don't do it now, we'll leave it to Tom tomorrow. We're a team now, you, me and Tom. My room is centre of operations." He makes a sweeping gesture at the sterile space around them.

"Huh," she says. "In which case, I need food and drink."

Fortunately it's not long before Tom, the mysterious researcher, arrives, bringing a sense of normality to their strange set-up. He's laden with supermarket bags, sweating profusely. He dumps them unceremoniously on the floor of Richard's room. "Stuff that'll keep," he says shortly. "I've found a second-hand fridge. I'll bring it tomorrow."

"Thanks, Tom. Meet Michelle."

"Nice to meet you, Michelle." He wipes a large paw on his trousers, grins and engulfs her hand in a clammy grasp. He looks like a student — bearded, with dark curly hair falling to his shoulders and over his eyes. He's tall and slim, dressed in faded jeans, trainers and an oversized check shirt. His eyes are brown, deep-set and intelligent, with a hint of steel.

"You too." She removes her hand, resisting the urge to rub it on her jumper.

"See you tomorrow." With that, he's gone.

* * *

Finally she gets to talk to Toby on his new burner phone. His reaction to the story of the stalker is amusement, then excitement. She worries she's underplayed it. "Please take this seriously, Toby," she says. "It's not a game, really. I need to know you're okay."

"Just kidding, Mum. I will, don't worry, please. I'm hardly ever on my own, and strangers here would stick out like a sore thumb."

"I know that. But he's clever, and he uses tricks to get to people. Just be vigilant, won't you?"

"I will. Be careful yourself, won't you?"

"I'll be fine. I'm here in a safe place for a few days — best you don't know where."

"It's like a spy movie!"

"No, it's not—"

"Only joking, Mum."

"I hope so. It's not a joking matter, honestly. I need you to text me every day, so I know you're okay."

"Every day? How am I going to remember to do that?" He sounds incredulous.

"Is that so hard? Set an alarm, say five o'clock every day. You only need to type two letters: *OK*. Though obviously if there's more to say, say it. Got it? I'm serious, Toby. And look after that phone. Only use it to contact me, please, and don't give anyone else the number."

"Yes, Mum. I heard you the first time. I'll look after it. Safe as houses. Gotta go now. Love you, Mum!"

"You too. Stay safe."

She's left feeling both alarmed and reassured. It was so good to hear his voice, but it felt surreal, like something from a past life. All she wants is to reconnect. To sit in comfortable silence with him, eating or watching a film. To know he's there with her and is safe.

CHAPTER THIRTY-SIX

Michelle

A strange half-life unfolds. She sleeps badly the first night, though she's exhausted with travelling and the constant threat of discovery. Unfamiliar noises wake her and she imagines the door bursting open in the dark, terrifying figures dragging her away. When the light creeps into her room at last, she wakes with a headache and a twist in her stomach.

Tom's already in Richard's room when Michelle knocks. Answering the door, he says "Aha, the team is complete. Come in, Michelle, I'm making tea. My role in this set-up — delivering food and making tea."

"It's a lot more than that, from what I hear," she says. "But thank you, tea would be great."

"Help yourself to breakfast," Richard says with an expansive gesture at a row of food items set out on the floor by the wall. "It's simple, but it's edible. Michelle, can Tom get the other table from your room, please? We need to get down to it today."

Half an hour later, the room is beginning to shape up. They each have a table, a chair and a laptop. Tom is in the process of setting up online security for the team.

"Let's draw up a plan of attack," Richard says. "Did I see a whiteboard somewhere?"

"Where do we start?" Michelle helps herself to a notebook and pen from a pile of office supplies on the floor.

"Kimia." Richard writes the name on the whiteboard, underlines it twice. "Facts, background, people, media coverage, reports, anything we can find online. We need to make a note of anyone who's ever written about them, with contact details — we'll need to talk to them. Can you get started on them, please? Where's the company registered? Who set it up? Investors — who or what are they? Who's on the board of directors? Anyone who's left the company — what's happened to them? Flag up any negative news stories, anything at all. Also find out everything they're working on. Drugs launched, projects announced, everything and anything . . ." Michelle can barely keep up. When he's finished, there's a long to-do list.

"Michelle, can I suggest you take the tasks you're most comfortable with, and I'll take the rest?" Tom says. "I'm not making any suggestions about your competence, just there's some stuff here that's familiar for me, but it may not be for you."

Michelle waves him away. "Of course. I'm not an experienced researcher, but I'll do my best. I'll do the factual stuff — the list of drugs and projects, the company background. For starters, anyway."

Richard writes *Lars Andersson* next to *Kimia* and underlines it. "I'm going to check Lars out. Then I'm going to call him. We need to interview him as soon as we possibly can. We don't know what kind of danger he's in."

His meaning isn't lost on Michelle. The scientist who stole the sample must be in grave danger, and he's alone, as far as they know. Thank God he had the presence of mind to give her Richard's card. Without Richard, she wouldn't have lasted more than five minutes.

As for Lars, alone with the power of Kimia threatening him, he may not be around for much longer.

* * *

Not long after, Richard calls Lars, but the line is engaged. "What the fuck?" he says, half to himself. Michelle feels her stomach clench. "He can't talk to anyone else on this number, it's supposed to be the secure one." He tries again.

Tom looks up. "Think he's been compromised?"

"Who knows?" Richard calls the number again, concern creasing his forehead.

"Who else would he be talking to?" Michelle says to Tom as Richard paces the room. "He must know the dangers."

"He should." Tom shrugs. "But remember, he's a scientist. They're strange creatures. Who knows what he'll be thinking. If we get hold of him before they do, we'll make sure he understands."

Richard punches a message into his mobile. "Hope we're not too late," he says, grimacing, before sitting at his computer again. "We really need him to stay alive. He's our biggest asset."

His grim statement makes Michelle shudder. What might happen to Lars, now or imminently, doesn't bear thinking about. Their job will be even harder if he's out of the picture, there's little doubt about that. She's aware of a tightening in her throat, a ringing in her ears.

But a few minutes later, Richard's mobile buzzes and he strides to the end of the room, talking in muffled tones.

"Lars?" she mouths at Tom.

He shrugs again, focusing on his screen. "Right, almost there," he says. "Just waiting for it to finish loading and we're good to go. We're as secure as we can be. But don't send any emails yet, I'm setting up the software so we can't be traced. I'll let you know when it's safe — won't be long."

Glad of something to focus on, Michelle makes a start. Kimia's background, the list of their projects, the drugs they've launched. It's the tip of the iceberg, but they have to start somewhere.

CHAPTER THIRTY-SEVEN

Lars

Petra Valkovitch answers the call with her name. Traffic noises blur her voice, and from her breathing Lars deduces that she's walking.

Without introducing himself, he says, "Is this a secure line?"

"No," comes the answer. "I'll call you back."

He waits a few moments. When she calls, the traffic sounds have gone. "Are you on your own?"

"Yes. Who is this?"

"I'm a scientist, a biochemist. I worked for Kimia."

There's a pause. "Kimia?"

"Yes. You've written about them."

"Yes, I have, but . . ." Her tone is wary. "I can't talk about . . . them, I'm sorry."

"Don't hang up, please."

"What do you want?"

"I'd like to talk to you about the piece you wrote."

"But if it involves . . . the company you mentioned just now, I really can't talk to you."

"Why not? Are they threatening you?"

"I have to go."

"No, please. Just two minutes of your time. You can answer yes or no — or not answer at all, if you prefer."

She hesitates. He can hear her breathing again, the click of an earring against the handset. "Two minutes. But we haven't spoken, do you understand? And I don't want to know your name."

"I understand. I've never spoken to you." He thinks for a moment. He needs to ask the right questions. "Did you speak to the CEO?"

"No. He doesn't—"

"I know. Have you ever seen a picture of him?"

"No."

"Why do you think that is?"

"I don't—"

"But you know he's over sixty, right?"

"Yes . . ." Good. She sounds intrigued.

"And the rest of the board — you described them as 'disarmingly youthful'. Did you wonder why they're so young? Correction — why they look so young?"

There's a sharp intake of breath. "Do you mean what I think you mean?"

"I'm just putting it to you as a possibility."

"I have to go. You've had your two minutes."

"Wait—"

But the line goes dead. With clumsy fingers, Lars redials. Number unobtainable. He tries again and again, and each time the long tone echoes in his ear.

* * *

She's been silenced. Kimia's not the kind of company to enjoy speculation of the kind she made in her article, even if it was innocent. They will have got to her already, threatened her — maybe her family — and paid her off.

He doesn't blame her. She's just a journalist doing her job — and while she writes opinion pieces, she's not in the business of antagonizing the companies she's paid to report on. But she is someone who might be useful to Richard Bamford, who'll no doubt be more persuasive in getting her to talk.

Why hasn't Richard called him? He stares at his mobile. Richard's message yells at him. *CALL ME NOW.*

Lars dials.

"Who were you talking to?" Richard's voice is harsh.

"I . . . a journalist, someone you should contact. Her name is—"

"This phone is for contacting me and nobody else. Don't you realize the danger you're in?"

Lars is taken aback. "Yes, of course. But listen, there's something else going on."

"Get yourself a new burner phone. Get three. Now, as soon as we're finished. You're going to need them. Disguise yourself as far as you can and only go to one shop. Buy more food while you're out if you need it, stuff that'll keep. Make sure you're not followed and be as quick as you can. Don't speak to anyone unless you absolutely have to. Do you understand? Call me when you get back. You can tell me about it when you have a new phone."

"But—"

"For your own sake, go now, and call me as soon as it's done."

The line goes dead.

Lars stares at the screen, nonplussed. Surely one call from a burner phone wouldn't put him in danger? But he can't risk it. He respects Richard, who's far more streetwise than he is. Lars is an innocent by comparison. Suddenly he feels deeply vulnerable. All his brainpower has gone into his work as a biochemist. He knows he's clever, he knows it takes a certain level of intellect to do what he does. But because of that, his understanding of the world outside the sterile bubble of biochemistry is sketchy, to say the least. It's a place he'll never understand, where people happily put thousands of lives at risk in the pursuit of power and money. Where innocents like him die because they've never needed to survive in the outside world.

And he doesn't want to die.

CHAPTER THIRTY-EIGHT

Michelle

A burst of expletives at the other end of the room shatters her concentration. She and Tom glance up at the same time. Richard's body oozes tension as he walks back to his desk, his jaw set. Two sets of eyes follow him to his chair, where he pauses for a moment before turning.

"Sorry about the language."

Tom nods, gets back to his computer. Michelle opens her mouth to ask what's going on but closes it again. Perhaps it's best to leave Richard to decide what and when to tell them. She returns to her screen.

It's easy enough to get the formal background on Kimia. Its annual report is professional, providing the kind of information that it's required to and nothing more. The company registration is straightforward, and though Michelle isn't familiar with the regulations in Iceland, she's pretty sure there'll be no mistakes, either in that country or elsewhere in the world. Everything looks completely above board. Taxes paid, profits announced, shareholder payouts detailed. But then this company wouldn't make mistakes of an official nature. No, the real truth, the secrets, will all be below the surface, where they can't be seen. Where only the determined or the reckless would venture.

Are they being reckless? Probably, but they have no choice. They've got everything to lose if they don't go through with this. It's a chilling thought.

She turns to Tom. "Okay if I set up a filing system online so we don't duplicate? We're going to need to keep track of who's done what, and store the information logically."

Tom stretches and nods. "Yeah, good idea. Let me show you how I've done it in the past."

When Richard's phone buzzes again, they all look up. He nods to them as he takes the call. "Good. That's good. Don't set up the other phones yet. Okay, what's up?"

* * *

Richard puts his mobile on speakerphone and turns the volume up, placing it on his desk so they can all hear. There's no other sound in the building to distract them, and Lars's voice is loud and clear.

"I know what the board of Kimia is doing, and it's incredible — shocking. Illegal, and despicable."

"Start at the beginning, Lars. Michelle's here and we're listening. Take your time."

"Okay. I worked on this project as soon as I joined Kimia, and nothing else. A tech billionaire — I don't know who — invested massive amounts of money in developing this drug. It's top secret. We work — worked — in a high-security area, everything was checked. We weren't allowed phones or private possessions in our area. We signed the most stringent non-disclosure agreements, and were told not to share details of the project with anyone else in the organization, except for a handful of directors. I was thrilled to be involved and I threw myself into my work, as did the others — a select few — on the project. The code name for the drug is PAN12. It's

163

rumoured they intend to launch it in a matter of months. All the industry knows is that it's supposed to be ground-breaking, life-changing and huge for Kimia. Probably the biggest thing to happen in pharma for decades — maybe ever."

"Go on," Richard says.

Lars sighs. "I was analysing the results of a set of clinical trials, but the data didn't add up. Not at all. It just seemed completely wrong. These were trials of PAN12 on actual people, held in our own medical facility. It's rare for anything to go wrong at this stage, let alone badly wrong, because the drug will have passed so many stages of testing already. I ran the data ten, twenty, thirty times — it took days. But the results were always the same. I checked the software, tried a different method, and still the data looked disastrous. The drug had failed. It was a catastrophe.

"It was well beyond my pay grade, so I took the results to my boss. To cut a long story short, he shut me down. Took the report, told me to delete it everywhere, said I was off the project and shouldn't discuss it with anyone, ever. End of story."

"What did you do then?"

"I was devastated — I'd dedicated years of my life to this programme, only to have it taken from me. But it wasn't the impact on me personally that shocked me, it was the damage it could do. What the results showed, well, it was shocking. Some rare, catastrophic diseases were implicated. The drug seemed to revert — to do the opposite of what it was supposed to do — in a proportion of the people tested. Quite a large proportion, by scientific standards. The drug that's supposed to be a miracle, reversing ageing, was actually killing people in the most terrible way."

Michelle looks at Richard in horror. All the colour has drained from Tom's face.

"What's worse is, I think they're going to go ahead with it. They've already tested it on humans. I can only think they did that without revealing what they already knew — the drug does work, but in some people, it only works for a time. Then it fails dramatically. Not in everyone, but in a significant number. When you extrapolate that proportion to country populations, you have a catastrophe. It's criminal. They can't test a drug on humans if they know it can cause damage — there are stringent rules about that. That alone would shut them down if it were to get out."

"Of course. How did you get hold of the sample?"

"As soon as I realized, I went over to the medical centre and collected the remaining sample and the report before they had the chance to cancel my pass. That's what I gave to you, Michelle, in the elevator. For which I'm sorry."

"It's okay," Michelle says. "I guess I was your only chance. I'm glad I got the sample out for you."

"Don't tell me where it is — it's best I don't know. Anyway, to continue: I was summoned upstairs, accompanied by security. I couldn't escape. At Kimia, nobody gets summoned upstairs, so I knew I was out of the company, and in big trouble. How could they let me go, knowing what I'd found out? But they did let me go, and somehow, I managed to get out of the country. They probably wanted me out so they couldn't be implicated in whatever happened to me next. Otherwise, why am I still alive? I know what they do, I'm not completely unrealistic. I know how much is at stake. Vast amounts of money, global reputations."

Richard nods at Michelle and Tom, his eyes wide with anticipation. She can almost see his mind working on his editorial, his fingers itching to start writing.

"Lars, you said there was something else?"

"It's clear to me that Kimia's directors are taking the drug. The journalist I spoke to commented on how youthful they look. I think they're taking a calculated risk. We need to find out if any of them has died in the last few years."

CHAPTER THIRTY-NINE

Michelle

"What?" Richard's voice rises, a look of incredulity on his face. "Say that again?"

Lars clears his throat. When he speaks, his voice is hoarse, as if he's finding it hard to get the words out. "Their average age is mid-forties. They all look about twenty-five, with the exception of the CEO, but he doesn't look much older. In real life, they look even younger than the pictures on the website. Of course, pictures can be enhanced — but in their case, they actually look more youthful in real life, rather than the other way around. What I didn't understand at first was why they'd be taking PAN12 themselves, knowing it could kill them."

"Perhaps they didn't know about the dangers when they started taking it?"

Lars hesitates. "At first, I thought the same. But the project has taken more than twenty years. I joined Kimia towards the end of PAN12's development. Clinical trials started at about the same time, three years ago, but I wasn't involved in the initial results, and the scientist who was has since left the company — unsurprisingly, as it turns out. That's a line for you to follow up."

Richard nods at Tom, who makes a note.

"Do you have a name?" Tom says.

"No, it wasn't in the file. I searched for the details of those early clinical trials," Lars continues, "but I was denied access, even though I was working on later trials of the same drug. Normally I'd have had access to all the data, to compare it over time, but they withheld the early results. It's entirely contrary to normal working practices. I queried it with my boss, but he told me I didn't need the earlier data. When I pushed him, he revealed, reluctantly, that he himself didn't have access, and he didn't know why. He's an associate director, which is pretty senior, but even he wasn't allowed to see those results. Why would that be? Because they had been quashed at the most senior level. They knew PAN12 didn't work. They knew, all right."

"Wow," Richard says, scribbling furiously on a notepad. "Going back to them taking PAN12 . . ."

"According to my data, if they've been taking the drug — the one that's about to be released — for at least two years, there's a strong chance that for at least one of them, it will already be breaking down in their bodies. Rare cancers will be occurring, strange respiratory inhibitions, heart failure. Not one of the directors is ill, to my knowledge, and they all look as if they've just stepped out of college. It's one of the reasons you never see their photos in the media. Or at least, you only see the ones they're prepared to put on their website. There are no ages mentioned anywhere, nor any birth dates, but if you dig deep, look into their education, past employment histories, you'll find they're much older than they look."

"And what precisely does your data show, from the clinical trials?"

"I was running data from a test group that's been involved from the start, so we're in year three of them taking the drug. They all show definitive — remarkable — external and internal signs of rejuvenation. It's pretty dramatic, and very obvious from their photos. The excitement around the development of this drug is certainly warranted. If it worked, it could set the world on fire."

"But?"

"Their internal organs are similar to those of people at least ten years younger, sometimes more, than they actually are. However, a small but significant sample of the test group has developed unusual and alarming symptoms. These symptoms indicate extremely rare diseases. Most of the subjects are still outwardly healthy, but there are early signs of the kind of damage to internal organs that indicates shutdown unless those organs are removed. Some would have fatal consequences. All within a matter of months, not years."

"My God." The words burst from Michelle's mouth. "Oh my God. Those poor people. Do they know yet?"

"I don't know. I doubt it. I'm not on the front line, so I don't know what they're told."

Richard takes a breath and opens his mouth to ask another question, but a sudden realization causes Michelle to break in. "Wait a minute — my flatmate, Helga. She's a senior manager at the medical centre. She's running the team doing the testing." She gazes at Richard with wide eyes. "She can help us."

Richard raises a hand. "That's great, good idea. Add her to the list."

The mobile looks small and insignificant on the table. But the information it's communicating is world-shattering, momentous. The situation, their surroundings, the events of the last few days, Lars's revelations, are almost unbelievable. Michelle is finding it hard to stay grounded. They're sitting on cheap IKEA chairs, talking to a rather old-fashioned communications device in a run-down room in a former office. It feels surreal.

Richard says, "So we're ninety-nine point nine per cent certain that the board knows about the failure of PAN12. If they do . . ." He thinks for a moment. "And if they're still taking the drug — which we can't confirm, of course — then why?" He pauses again. "Lars, say the drug worked — without any of these terrible consequences — and a person were to stop taking it, what happens then? Do they suddenly age? Do their bodies revert to their original timescale, so to speak, and would they resume normal life as an old person?"

"We don't know for certain, because as far as I know, nobody's stopped taking it yet. But it looks pretty certain that they'd revert to their original timeframe, so to speak. So if a person whose physical age had reduced to perhaps thirty, and their real age was sixty or seventy, say — if they stopped taking the drug, then within a short space of time, their body would start showing signs of rapid ageing until their actual age was reached. Doing that would inflict a certain amount of stress on the body, but there's no reason why, if there are no life-threatening diseases present, they shouldn't then live to a healthy old age."

Tom makes a sudden movement. "Wait a minute!" His eyes are fixed on his computer screen. "There was another director. There's not much on him; he died about a year ago. They've obviously tried to suppress the information, but it looks pretty innocuous at first glance. A heart attack, apparently."

"He could have been an early casualty of the drug, then." Richard frowns. "Is that possible, Lars?"

"Certainly it's possible. Deterioration in the body can be devastatingly quick."

Richard carries on. "Goddammit, this is huge!" He can hardly contain his excitement.

Michelle's confused. "But if one of them has already died, why would they carry on taking the drug?"

"The stakes are astronomical," Richard says. "And besides, people like them have no scruples. I bet they all agreed that the sacrifice was worth it. Maybe one or two would die but the rest would live on and reap the rewards of their wonder drug. They'll have looked after the family of the dead guy. Paid millions to keep a lid on it."

Tom whistles. All three of them sit back in their chairs, wide-eyed.

There's so much to take in, Michelle feels as if she's losing hold of reality. Drained, exhausted by the scale of the story. "But why not keep refining the drug until they find a way around the problem? They have the money, surely?"

There's a snort from Lars at the other end of the line. "They have the money, but time isn't on their side. Competitors on their tail, investors looking for a return — and they've put a marker down to release the drug this year. They'll lose a huge amount of face if they delay, particularly if it's for years. Not to mention losing billions of dollars. And there's the risk of one of their competitors launching ahead of them."

Michelle writes, *Track competitors.* "Lars, do we know who those competitors are and how close they are to releasing the same type of drug?"

"I don't know exactly . . ."

"An educated guess?" Tom asks.

"Look at the industry press and the bloggers — rumours have been circulating for a while. There are a number of possibilities." He mentions four names in particular, being careful to spell them out. Michelle recognizes none of them, despite her background, but she's not surprised: in the pharma sector, new companies are launched all the time, often sub-brands belonging to major names, but separated by complex legal set-ups.

Lars adds, "Look for the ones with the powerful investors, the big names in industry and technology, and any chief executive who's boasting about developing a life-changing drug. They have huge egos; some of them can't resist."

"How much influence would the investors have on the timing of the release of a drug like this?" Richard says.

"Huge. A big investor like one of the high-tech US companies — Amazon, Google, Apple, Tesla, Meta — they'd be in the driving seat. Of course they want the drug to succeed, to pass all the regulatory requirements, to be passed for distribution all around the globe, but the pressure on Kimia to get it out quickly will be phenomenal."

170

CHAPTER FORTY

Michelle

There's a stunned silence after the conversation with Lars. Richard's head is in his hands, Tom doodles in a notebook as if his life depends on it. Michelle stares out of the window, unseeing, unbelieving.

She's bewildered. This is evil incarnate. For someone to release a flawed "wonder drug" into an unsuspecting world, knowing people everywhere will welcome it with open arms, believing it to be safe — that is simply obscene. The victims would be people like her, perhaps a little fragile, unconfident. People who only want to look better, to live longer, to be healthy grandparents or even great-grandparents, to find someone who loves them . . . *Knowing* the drug could kill people in the most horrible way, but launching it regardless — it's like every villain in a child's fairy story rolled into one. The evil witch, the cruel king, the bad wolf, pretending to be kind and generous, but turning out to be conniving, selfish and murderous.

"Are you okay, Michelle?" Tom's anxious eyes meet hers. "You look a bit pale."

She shakes her head. "It's the most hideous thing I've ever heard. I know I'm the innocent one here, but . . . there aren't the words."

"We're all shocked," Tom says. "But maybe Richard and I are a little more used to the evils of mankind." He grins. "I think a cup of tea is called for."

Michelle manages a weak smile. "You know just what to say, Tom."

But as she sips her tea and tries to make sense of what she's just heard, a kernel of fury begins to grow within her. She would have been the perfect target for a drug like this. Not so long ago, she longed to look younger — no, to *be* younger — to be attractive, to be the envy of her friends, to have men desire her, want her, adore her. What on earth was she thinking? How shallow could she be?

That Michelle, thankfully, has gone. This Michelle wants to tell everyone, especially women, that other things matter far more. Kindness, self-esteem, generosity, love. Family and friends.

But the fury is not so much aimed at herself. It's aimed at a world where money matters over everything else. Over the natural environment, over the future of animals, plants, the seas, the entire ecosystem. Over humanity. That's what's making her angry.

But amid the anger she also feels utterly small and helpless. How in the name of God are they going to stop this happening?

* * *

"Are you going to get in touch with your flatmate?"

Richard's question startles her. She's embroiled in what seems like a never-ending rabbit warren of information about potential competitors to Kimia, trying to decipher the formal, sometimes inscrutable, language on their websites and in their published documentation. It seems to her that they're trying their best to be obtuse; they don't want people to know what they're up to, so they hide behind technical jargon and regulation.

She'd almost forgotten about Helga.

"She's an important contact," Richard says. "We need to talk to anyone who was on the clinical trials. She could help us with that — and also, if she'll talk to us, she might be able to shed some light on how they've managed to cover up the bad results."

"Of course. Sorry, I wasn't prioritizing."

"No problem." Richard smiles. "We're grateful for any kind of help."

"Why wouldn't I help?" she says, bridling a little. "We have to stop this happening. It's up to us, isn't it?"

Richard nods, turning back to his desk. "Remember — don't text, don't leave a voice message. Don't stay on the line too long. Suggest she gets a burner phone and calls you back."

Michelle looks up Helga's mobile number immediately, cross with herself for not calling her straight away.

But a knock interrupts her. They freeze, their eyes locked on the door.

"Any idea?" Tom whispers.

"I'll do it," Richard says. He moves around Tom and steps over to the door, his trainers making no sound on the worn carpet. He listens for a moment, then goes down on all fours and peers underneath. He straightens up and gently turns the handle, opening the door only a few inches.

"Hello?" they hear him say as he steps into the hallway, closing the door behind him.

A woman's voice responds, a young, high-pitched voice that echoes in the corridor. But they can't distinguish the words. Richard's low tones respond and after a few moments he's back, edging round the door so he doesn't have to open it fully.

He puts a finger to his mouth and returns to his desk, typing furiously. A moment later a message pings on the other computers. Michelle opens a WhatsApp message. *Friendly neighbour, but I can't be sure. I've put her off for the moment. We need to get a spy hole in the door. Tom, can I leave you with that, please?*

Tom glances over at Richard, gives him a thumbs-up. "On it," he mouths.

A few minutes later, Richard checks the corridor. "All clear," he says, closing the door again. "But I think our phones should be on vibrate and we need to keep our voices down. I'm going to do an experiment. I'll shut the door, and you two have a conversation — normal voices, please."

"How's that company research going?" Tom says as the door closes on Richard.

"All squeaky clean," Michelle replies. "I've been through all the official registration information, every source I can find. So far no evidence of anything going on. How are you getting on?"

"What, with finding a bullet-proof door?"

"No, with the rest of it all . . ."

Richard reappears in the room. "A faint rumble of voices, but I can't hear what's said. We need to keep a close eye. If they know we're here, they'll listen in. Let's use messaging for sensitive stuff, try not to mention names or places in conversation. I know it's awkward, but . . ." He leaves the sentence hanging. Michelle can imagine how he might have finished it and she'd rather not know.

A sense of urgency overtakes her. She dials Helga's number with trembling fingers.

CHAPTER FORTY-ONE

Lars

Bamford's reaction to him contacting Petra Valkovitch took Lars by surprise. His first thought was that it was an overreaction. But now he's overwhelmed with fear, struck by the force of his words.

He follows Bamford's instructions to the letter. *Get yourself a burner phone . . . get three . . . disguise yourself . . . don't speak to anyone . . .* He leaves the apartment with his coat collar up, his hat pulled down over his eyes. After he's bought the burner phones, he walks round a supermarket, collecting tins and packets of food, keeping his eyes down. He checks around him at every turn, then decides it looks too obvious, and possibly weird, so sticks to monitoring every aisle he turns into for signs of danger.

But what does danger look like? They're dealing with a ruthless, powerful group of people, prepared to stop at nothing. If they had to, they'd kill their own grandmothers to protect their precious drug. They wouldn't think twice.

So whoever is hired to follow him — or murder him — could look completely normal. Indeed, the more harmless they look, the better, Lars supposes. It's hopeless trying to outwit them, he doesn't stand a chance. He chucks a box of hair dye into his trolley. He's a natural blonde, like many Swedes. Changing his hair colour will make him look at least a bit different. Then he wavers, wondering what to do about his beard, the one that's already beginning to grow. He can't have dark hair and a blonde beard, or even stubble. But a beard is a good disguise, isn't it? He panics for a moment, then sees the women's beauty section. Don't women dye their eyelashes? Perhaps there's some special product that will help him out. It'll be a chore to keep it up, but if it saves his life, what's a bit of extra time spent on his appearance? Time isn't going to be a problem for him — in his current situation, he'll have far too much time on his hands. He leaves the shop laden with dye for his hair, his eyebrows and hopefully his beard, as well as food stocks for at least a couple of weeks. He also has a new scarf, a baseball cap and a box of surgical masks.

Instead of returning to the flat directly, he diverts across the city, turning into alleyways, retracing his steps, taking a purposeless bus journey to shake off an unseen follower. By the time he gets back, he's exhausted.

* * *

Lars is fully aware of his importance to this story. Without him, they have the sample and the report, but none of the background and none of the contacts. They might, in time, gather all the information they need. But there is no time. Kimia's aim will be to stop them at all costs, as soon as possible, silently and discreetly. So the more he can give to Richard, right now, the better. He'll dedicate everything to helping him, and then maybe, just maybe, he might live a little longer.

The phone call with Bamford is long and stressful. The journalist is holed up somewhere with Michelle and someone else — another journalist, perhaps. Lars is relieved that Michelle has made it to safety, at least for the moment, and that she has Bamford to help her. Involving her was a spur-of-the-moment decision that was his only option, but he feels bad for her.

He runs through everything that's happened in the last few days, speaking fast. The shocking revelation from running the data. The strange meeting with his boss, collecting the sample just in time, the terrible summons to the top floor. The feelings of injustice, betrayal, helplessness and fear. Being marched from the building, his colleagues' shocked faces . . .

When the call is over, he sits for a while, scouring his mind for details he might have missed that might help Bamford's story. He writes a list of possible leads, including some of the names he's already mentioned, in a WhatsApp message to Bamford, giving contact details where he can.

He stands to one side of the window, only too aware that danger could come from anywhere, and gazes over a sterile cityscape, a labyrinth of streets and office blocks. Down below, cars line up at a junction, their lights bright in the dim light of late afternoon. Figures in dark coats hurry along windy pavements, hunched against the chill. Bicycles weave in and out of the traffic — people taking their lives in their hands, disobeying the traffic signals, oblivious to the fragility of their existence. Shopfronts gleam with artificial light, drawing shoppers in with colourful displays. Everything looks so normal.

Here, in this claustrophobic apartment, alone, Lars is horribly aware that normality is something he can only dream of — something he once had but has lost for ever. The reality of his situation hardly bears thinking about. That way lies despair.

He squares his shoulders and grabs the boxes of dye. Anything to take his mind off things for a while.

An hour later, he puts the hairdryer down and gazes at the new man in the mirror. It's not an improvement, he reckons, but he does look different. His blue eyes are somehow dulled by the darkening of his hair. He forces himself to forget that he's looking at his own reflection — he needs to gauge whether the new look is convincing or not. With an effort he sees himself as a stranger. He decides it's not a bad disguise, and when the beard has grown, he'll look even less like Lars Andersson, the biochemist. More like an ageing student, perhaps, but that's not a bad thing.

CHAPTER FORTY-TWO

Michelle

Michelle stabs a finger at her mobile and dials. It diverts to voicemail. "Shit," she says, cutting the call.

"What's up?" Richard asks, his eyes still on his screen.

"Helga's phone's off." She has another try, with the same result. Her stomach clenches. "I could try her at work — would that be safe?"

Richard shakes his head. "They'll be monitoring all calls in to her."

"I doubt she's allowed to take calls anyway. She said they leave their mobiles in lockers when they start their shifts."

"You'll have to try again later."

"How about I leave her a message?"

"Again, not a good idea. Just try again, every hour perhaps."

It's so frustrating. And worrying. "What if she's in trouble? She said even knowing I had the sample could be a problem for her. I'd hate her to lose her job because of me."

"If she does, it won't be your fault," Richard says. "Do you have any other way of contacting her? Her family, friends maybe?"

179

Michelle's imagination starts to run wild. Helga falling into a trap, being kidnapped, raped, tortured for information about Michelle and where she's gone. She'd never forgive herself if—

"Michelle?"

"Ah, yes — actually, no. Dammit, I've forgotten her boyfriend's last name. Magnus. Magnus . . . what was it?" She gives herself a mental shake. *Buck up, Michelle.*

"It's the stress," Tom says. "Don't beat yourself up. It'll come to you."

"Hang on, there's a way to find out . . ."

She's surprised at how many restaurants there are in Akureyri. But as soon as she sees it, she remembers. Beck's — no problem with that pronunciation. "I've found her boyfriend's restaurant. I can call them and get his number."

"Okay, but don't leave a name."

She pretends to be a friend who's lost Helga's number, and within a few minutes a member of staff has given her Magnus's contact details. They have no reason not to — Iceland is normally such a safe place, and they'd have no reason to be suspicious of her. Or anyone else, she reminds herself, thinking of who they're dealing with.

She sends a quick WhatsApp from her laptop to Magnus, saying she's a friend from Reykjavik and has lost Helga's mobile number. Within a few minutes she gets a response — Helga has a new number. She calls straight away, but there's no answer.

"I'll keep trying," she says. "I don't know what shift she's on, so she could finish at any time."

"Hm," Richard says, frowning. "Why would she have a new mobile?"

"Well . . . she knew I had a drug sample at home, and how I came by it. It's forbidden, and she said it could mean trouble for her as well as me. Also, I've disappeared, haven't I? Maybe she's being cautious."

"True. But be extra careful, make sure she gets a burner phone before you talk to her."

Michelle feels her eyes widening. Have they got to Helga already? She'd never forgive herself if something happened to her. Is she putting her friend in even more danger by involving her in all this?

She glances up to see Richard watching her face. "It's okay," he says. "If she's able to help us, she'll be saving lives. Don't forget that. She's already involved — you told her what happened with Lars. We'll give her the best advice for keeping safe."

"What are you going to say?"

"That we need her help to publish this story and stop Kimia releasing PAN12. We have to find people who were on the clinical trials, or evidence that the results were covered up. That information will be hugely valuable — it'll give us the evidence to prove our story. If she's prepared to do that, she should leave Kimia, and Reykjavik, straight away."

"What if she's not willing to help? It's a huge ask. She might be too scared of the consequences, and I wouldn't blame her. She's young, she's got plans for her life."

"If she's not—" he shrugs — "we'll have to find another way, and she can carry on working there if she chooses to. But if we're successful, it won't be long before it all collapses anyway, and she'll be out of a job."

A sudden realization. A jolt runs through her like an electric shock. "Oh no. No, no . . ." She gasps, fumbling with her mobile. Tom and Richard both stare at her in surprise.

"Toby. He's supposed to text every day at five o'clock. It's five thirty."

CHAPTER FORTY-THREE

Michelle

"Let's not panic yet," Richard says. "He's forgotten, he's in a lecture, his battery's flat — could be any one of a hundred reasons. Call him now."

Michelle paces as she waits for the call to connect. When she hears Toby's voice, she almost faints with relief. But relief turns to panic as she realizes it's only a voice message. *Can't pick up right now — call you back.*

She texts, *URGENT — call me NOW*. Then she dials and redials. The same message plays straight away, every time.

"You're getting an answering message?"

She looks up, nods.

"So his phone's not disabled — you wouldn't get that message if it was."

It's a small comfort. She bites her lip. She doesn't trust herself to say anything. Standing in the middle of the echoing room, a feeling of utter helplessness creeps over her. Everything, everyone she knows and loves, is in jeopardy.

Nothing seems safe. Tears drip onto her shirt and she sways. Her legs feel like they're giving way.

Richard comes over and wraps his arms around her without a word. "It's okay, Michelle. It will all be okay."

After a moment or two, she feels more grounded. The panic ebbs away and she raises her head. "Thanks, Richard."

"Sometimes a hug is all you need." He releases her and returns to his seat. "Try Toby again now."

But before she can dial, the burner phone in her hand buzzes. "It's him."

"Mum, it's me."

She almost passes out with relief. She has to put a hand on the wall to steady herself.

"Sorry, I forgot to text — I was on the phone to Gail. She's panicking about you. She was about to call the police."

For a moment her mind goes blank. Then his words sink in. "Gail. Has something happened?" Amid all the chaos, she's forgotten to contact her best friend.

"She's been trying to call you, but she's been getting 'number unobtainable' and getting more and more worried. She tried your flatmate — her phone's unobtainable too, and then she called your work number. They told her you didn't exist! Mum, what's going on?"

"Are you okay? Nothing strange going on at your end?"

"No, everything's fine here. But this doesn't make sense. What's going on?"

"I told you, this man—"

"No, Mum, it's more than that, isn't it? Why have you suddenly left your job — and you're not in Iceland, are you?"

"Ah, hang on a second, Toby, I need to check something. Don't go away . . ."

"But Mum—"

"Just wait a second." She covers the mouthpiece and turns to Richard. "He's okay, but we need to tell him." She explains about Gail.

183

Richard nods. "Tell him you'll call him back. We need to work out some way of keeping him safe, and decide what to tell him."

***

She deals with the problem of Gail first, sending her a text to say she's fine, but she's on a "special project" and will be out of touch for a while. Once Gail is reassured, she won't let Michelle down.

It takes some time to decide what to do about Toby. It isn't easy, because every option seems fraught with danger: they risk giving away their hiding place, or putting Toby at greater risk if they move him. But it turns out the academic calendar is on their side. It's only a few days until the Easter break, when Toby has three weeks' holiday. Normally he'd come home, but even if that were safe, her home in London is occupied by tenants. They toy with the idea of sending him away with friends, but decide that might put him in even greater danger. They discuss getting him a full-time security guard, but Michelle can't imagine that working. How would he manage with a permanent shadow? He'd want to be out socializing, meeting friends. No nineteen-year-old would want a permanent chaperone, whatever the risks. Toby's patience would be tried to the limit. He'd do his best to shake the guard off, however much they warned him.

Abduction is what Michelle fears the most. If Toby were taken because of all this, she'd cave in, no question. She'd find the PAN12 sample for them, go to the ends of the earth if they demanded it.

All the other options are equally risky, so they decide to bring him to their lair in London. Somehow they'll have to transport him from the north of England and smuggle him in without compromising either his security or theirs. Tom is working on it now.

It won't be easy, and he may not like it, but Michelle wants him close by. He can help the team — he might even

184

enjoy it. By way of work experience, it could be the best he can hope for, there are so few jobs around for students looking for temporary work, even in London. At Christmas all he managed was a few nights' bar work and a stint at a local garden centre, watering plants. Not much of a challenge for a bright student studying for a physics degree.

Richard thinks he could be useful to them. "A physics degree, is it? Great! An enquiring mind, analytical skills — just what we need."

"But what if this goes on for months? He won't want to miss great chunks of his course."

"We'll cross that bridge when we come to it. Hopefully it won't take that long — and let's face it, if it does, it's best he's safe. He can always defer. Special circumstances."

Special circumstances, indeed.

CHAPTER FORTY-FOUR

Michelle

A second night sleeping in a huge office. Or rather, not sleeping. Alone on the tatty mattress in the bare room, the windows covered with dusty blinds, she can't keep her mind steady, and the list of things to worry about seems to get longer every minute. Not only Helga and Toby, but herself, Richard and Tom. They're all in danger. Where are their pursuers now? Are they in England yet? Or London? They could find them at any moment. Death could be tonight, tomorrow, a week or a month away. She hasn't felt so vulnerable in her life.

Does Kimia know that she's joined forces with Richard? If they know who he is, they'll understand immediately his interest in helping her. A story in the media could threaten their very existence. They'll stop at nothing.

They can't go to their homes, use their bank accounts, leave the building or make a phone call safely. The only person who can come and go is Tom — and if he gets spotted, they'll have to move like lightning to get away. She can only hope it doesn't happen before Toby joins them.

He's due to arrive tomorrow, transported via some kind of secure method conjured up by Tom and Richard. She trusts their decisions — she's too anxious to think straight, and if they think it's safe then she has to believe it is. But what if something goes wrong? What if Toby dies because of all this? She tries not to think about it, but it keeps coming back.

What if they can't get the story finished in time to stop Kimia launching PAN12? What if everything's for nothing, and there's an international rush to buy the drug? People will die in their millions. That's an enormous responsibility and one she can barely think about.

What if it all takes months, even years? How will they survive? How will she bear it? The thought is almost worse than being too late to stop Kimia.

She throws off the covers in a fit of nervous energy and dresses without caring what she's putting on. It's the middle of the night and there's no sound from within the building. She steps quietly into the corridor. All the windows around the quadrangle are dark, but there's a light under Richard's door. She knocks quietly, the code they've agreed, and the door opens. The lights are on, he's fully dressed. His face is drawn, a dark shadow of stubble on his chin.

"It's hopeless," she says. "There's no way I'm going to get any sleep tonight. If there's something useful I can do, I might as well just carry on."

"Be my guest," he says. "Coffee's on."

She pours herself a cup, breathing in the strong aroma. It seems to give her a little more strength. "Are we getting anywhere, Richard?"

He nods. "We are. We're gathering the information that'll be needed to back up the story, contacting people who can help us. We're closing in. I'm thinking about how to release the story, who to give it to for maximum impact. The story will take off, wherever it starts, but I'm thinking big on this one."

"The BBC? One of the broadsheets?"

"Something like that — but it needs to have global reach. It's a complex story and it needs plenty of space, so I'm think-ing probably an influential newspaper with multiple media attached — web presence, broadcast. A Murdoch paper, for instance. The global media will pick it up from them, also the news agencies — it'll go viral on social media, and boom! It'll spread like wildfire."

"How soon? Sorry to ask again . . ."

"Could be days, could be a couple of weeks. If it's months, then we'll have failed. Sorry, can't be more specific than that." Richard turns back to his computer. "The sample's safe, anyway."

The sample. She'd almost forgotten about it. "Has it arrived in the UK?"

He nods.

"Where is it now?"

"Best you don't know."

"Will you get it analysed? Or tested somehow?"

"Tom's looking for somewhere that can take on this kind of thing. The sample won't help us much, I'm afraid. But the data — the results of all the testing, over time — that's what we need to verify our story."

"Is Lars the only person who can help with that?"

"For the moment, maybe. But if we release the story and it's convincing enough for the regulators to go in, Kimia will have to release the data."

"Give me something to do. I need to take my mind off all the disaster scenarios it's running through."

Richard gives her a crooked smile. "Try to imagine what happens after the story. When we've stopped them. Much healthier."

"I wish I could . . ."

"I understand, Michelle, I really do. It's terrifying, and stressful — the most stressful thing possible, because your life is at risk. It's worse for you than it is for us, by a long way; we're more used to it than you. Believe me, I'm terrified too."

"You seem so calm. So matter-of-fact."

"It's my job. Underneath, I'm a mess, same as you."

He's being kind, but she's pretty sure he's nowhere near as big a mess as she is.

"Let's find something for you to focus on," he goes on. "How about you check the list of pharma blogs for the latest on Kimia? We need to check any announcements re PAN12 — find out how long we've got. Oh, and check today's media sites, globally, for any mention."

She opens her laptop, glancing at the time. It's pitch-black outside, not that there's much to see from here. The room's large windows with their inadequate blinds gaze out onto the blank facade of the building opposite. There's not a light to be seen, just an orange glow from the street lamps down below. It's gone three in the morning and theirs is the only illuminated window. It feels like the whole world is asleep except for them.

* * *

Michelle's sharp intake of breath startles Richard. He swings around in his chair to face her. "What is it?"

She lifts horrified eyes to his. "A date," she says. "They've set a date for launching PAN12." She pauses, peering at the screen. "April the first. Really?" It's hard to believe that even Kimia is cynical enough to set the launch for April Fool's Day.

"Show me." He strides over. The blog has only a small following, but the writer specializes in following the biotech industry. They've mentioned the rumoured launch of a "wonder drug" a number of times before.

"Could be speculation," Richard says. "What do the other blogs have?"

She clicks on more links, scans the text quickly. "Nothing as yet. But this was posted just now. They may catch up later. I'll keep a close eye."

"April Fool's Day. Marked by many countries, all around the world. Are they mad?"

"Arrogant, cynical bastards, more like. How can they possibly think that's funny?"

"We don't know it's true though. Let's see later on. But if it is true, we've only got three weeks to crack this story."

Richard's forehead crinkles. He looks pale and drawn in the glare of the fluorescent lights. "We'll have to get moving even more quickly now."

"What would happen if we — you — release the story as speculation, without the proper back-up?"

"The problem isn't releasing the story — it's getting it published in credible media. They have to check the veracity of their story or risk the might of Kimia on their backs. Kimia would hit the publishers with everything they have. Top lawyers, libel suits, you name it; they wouldn't stop until they'd destroyed whoever took the story, and the journalist who wrote it. It's a risk for publishers. The stakes are massive, so they'll want to have every weapon in their armoury lined up to counter any accusation of false or inaccurate reporting."

"Obviously you know what you're doing, and I don't, but couldn't we speculate anonymously, set the story rolling, get other journalists interested? There must be a way of doing it."

"It's possible, but dangerous. Companies at the top of the global tree . . . well, let's say they have ways and means of finding things out — and shutting things down." He rubs the fingers of his right hand together. "It's all to do with money. That's why we're holed up here for as long as it takes. It's why we're ready to move out at any moment, if we have to. And it's why I'm not well known. What I do is risky, and I don't want to be famous for the wrong reasons."

"Are we ready to move out at any moment?"

Richard nods. "Tom's got a fall-back safe place already set up. Don't get too settled in." He turns back to his computer.

"Not much chance of that," Michelle mutters, thinking of her bare office bedroom, her meagre possessions in a pile on the floor. She shivers. Outside, rain spatters the dark windows of the building, the wind whistling around its concrete corners. There's no sign of life anywhere else in the building, and nothing to make it feel like home.

But today, if nothing goes wrong, Toby will arrive. When he does, she'll feel a lot better. If he doesn't . . . she can't bear the thought.

CHAPTER FORTY-FIVE

Michelle

Richard has started writing. For the past hour his eyes haven't moved from the screen. The gentle rattle of his fingers on the keyboard lulls Michelle into a state of half-sleep, her eyes drooping.

A knock on the door startles her. It's their code, and it can only be Tom. She crosses the room to turn the lock, recoiling as Tom strides into the room, barely managing to save the door from smashing back into the wall. In that moment, the energy in the room changes, the air strangely charged. She can almost smell the fear on him.

"We need to move." He keeps his voice low and steady but he's breathing hard.

"Right." Richard is on his feet, his laptop already closed. He gathers papers together.

It takes a second or two for Michelle to register what's happening. She feels the blood drain from her face. "But what about Toby?"

"Don't worry about Toby," Tom says, stuffing his laptop into a bag along with the rest of the items on the desk. "He'll join us at the new place."

191

There follows a silent, tense scramble to gather essential items from the two rooms they've called home for only a few days. Tom leads them to a back staircase and they follow him down to the street. At the door, Tom checks both ways.

"Let's get a cab," he says, striding towards a busy street at the junction. "We'll be less obvious then."

A couple of minutes later they're clambering into a black cab, its engine growling as it waits for them to settle. Tom shows a slip of paper to the driver and closes the window between him and the back seats. His eyes flicker to and fro, checking pavements, other cars as they wait at traffic lights, motorbikes. He keeps his eyes moving, ever vigilant.

Michelle breathes a little easier. "What happened, Tom?"

"I came round the corner. There was a car — nothing unusual about it, except it had tinted windows. That got my antenna up. It was hovering outside the building. I ducked back into a side street and kept an eye on it. It moved on, but a few minutes later it was back. It parked in a bay, but the engine was running. The driver had his laptop open. He kept glancing up at the windows. There was something about him. Could have been nothing, but . . ."

The cab stops in a busy street and they all get out. Tom pays the driver. "We have to split up. Michelle, come with me. Richard, you go separately. Here's the address." He hands the slip of paper to Richard. "Don't go there directly. When you get there, text me. We'll do the same. Come on, Michelle."

Richard nods at Michelle. "Tom has a good antenna. I'm sure this is the right thing to do. Nothing wrong with keeping moving. You okay, Michelle?"

"As long as Toby's safe, I'm fine."

In the next cab, she sits back, closes her eyes and wonders if she'll ever be fine again. She's so tired of all this. Her body sways against the seat belt as the taxi barrels through the grey streets of London.

* * *

Helga's voice is wary, distant. "Who is this?"

"It's me, Michelle."

"Oh, Michelle, I've been so worried about you! Are you okay? Where are you?"

"I'm okay, but I'm . . . in danger. It's all to do with . . . what that scientist gave me. Can you get a burner phone — do you know what that is? Good. Text me on this number — text, don't call. Then I'll call you back. I must talk to you."

She hears Helga's breathing, her mouth close to the handset. She imagines her reaction. Surprise, concern, fear.

"Okay, I can do that."

"Quickly, Helga — as soon as you can."

"Yes."

Michelle cuts the call. Richard says, "Ditch that phone as soon as you have her number, okay?"

"Right."

The new place is remarkably like the last one — offices occupied temporarily by guardians, though it seems half empty. Grubby carpet on the stairs, hurriedly converted showers, old nameplates still on the doors. Little sign of the other occupants.

Their new workspace, though, is huge. Desk-shaped marks pit the carpet. From the look of it, there must have been upwards of twenty people working here. The only furniture in the vast space is three tables and three chairs, organized by Tom in advance. They're well used and marked, but they'll do the job. Two rooms are partitioned off at each end, presumably once meeting rooms. These are their new bedrooms, where they tried to sleep last night. More old mattresses for beds.

Michelle has set up her workstation by a window that's overshadowed by a huge plane tree, its new leaves about to appear. She longs to be outside in the fresh air, free, unnoticed. But she'll only be able to do that once they've done their job — if they can do their job. She sighs and opens her laptop. Richard is already typing furiously. Tom talks quietly on his mobile on the other side of the room.

Her mobile pings. Helga's as good as her word. She inputs the number on a second burner phone, removes the SIM card from the first, cuts it in half and throws it in a plastic bag where they're collecting their rubbish.

Helga answers immediately. "Michelle, what's happened? Where did you go? I've been so worried . . ."

There's no sound in the background. "Are you alone? Is it safe to talk?"

"Yes — why, where are you?"

Michelle ignores the question. "Listen, we can't talk for long. It's all to do with that sample — PAN12. The truth is, the drug is horribly flawed, Helga. They know it, and they're hiding the evidence. They mustn't release it. Can you — will you help us?"

"I-I don't know. What do you mean, flawed? How do you know this?"

"The scientist — that's why he had to leave the company. He found serious discrepancies in the data. It showed the drug breaks down in a significant number of people. It kills people, Helga, and they're still planning to release it!"

The pause at the other end of the line is so long, she wonders for a moment if Helga is still there. "That can't be true. It must be a mistake, or they wouldn't be releasing it. They've set the date, it's only a few—"

"It's not a mistake, Helga. I know they've set the date. So it's urgent, and we need more evidence to stop them releasing it. Time's running out. Can you help us?"

"Who is 'us'?"

"It doesn't matter. Can you help?"

"What are you planning to do? Please don't put yourself in danger, Michelle. You must return the sample. I'm sure it'll be okay if you do . . ."

This is all taking too long. Michelle's aware of Richard in the background, hovering, frowning. "Don't worry about me. Really, there's no time to explain. What's important is that we stop Kimia. Can you help us?"

A long pause. Michelle imagines the dilemma she's putting Helga in. "What do you need?"

"Names and contact details of the subjects in the latest clinical trials. That would be the first thing. And if you can, we need the data on PAN12 — as much as you can get."

There's a sharp intake of breath as Michelle speaks.

"I can't do that, Michelle," Helga says. "You know I can't — I'll lose my job. I'll be breaking my contract. If they find out, they'll get the lawyers on to me, or worse. They're ruthless, they don't hold back if someone breaks their contract—"

Michelle closes her eyes. She hates doing this to her. "I know, I know. So if you help us, you'll have to get away, leave immediately. But you'll be saving many lives, Helga." She holds her breath.

Helga lets out a long breath. "I don't know, Michelle. It's too much to ask."

"It's a huge thing to ask, and I'm really sorry." The words sound hollow, flimsy, though she speaks from the heart. "But Kimia's launching a drug that will literally kill thousands of people — perhaps millions. What they're proposing to do is inhuman. It's the worst crime imaginable. And you have a chance to help stop them."

"If you're right, that's terrible. But, I don't know . . . Is there nobody else you can ask?"

Helga's plea is like a stab in the chest. But Michelle must get her agreement. "If there was, I wouldn't be asking you, I promise. We have a chance here to save millions of lives. We have so little time. We have to stop them."

There's a touch of frost in Helga's voice when she replies. "I know what you're saying, but where's the proof? You're asking me to ruin my life for something I don't even know is true."

"I know, I'm sorry . . . But I promise you, it's a massive fraud. The scientist's report proves it. Please, Helga — it's the right thing to do."

"I don't know, Michelle. I wish you hadn't asked me."

"So . . ."

"I can't give you an answer right now."

Michelle's heart leaps. "Of course you must think about it, Helga. But you mustn't talk to anyone about this. Do you understand? Nobody — not even Magnus."

"Okay, okay. I'm not promising anything, Michelle. The answer will almost certainly be no."

Michelle closes her eyes. She keeps her voice steady — she doesn't want to spook Helga. They need her too much. "Think about it. But remember, we don't have much time before the PAN12 launch. If you can help us, please tell us soon — today if you can. And if you need to talk, text me first and I'll call you back."

Helga cuts the call abruptly. Michelle's not surprised. She's just landed her friend with a terrible dilemma. Helga will be taking an enormous risk if she decides to help. The burden of guilt on her shoulders almost overwhelms her.

"Everything okay, Michelle?" Richard is right beside her before she's conscious that her head is in her hands.

"Was that too long? It was such a hard thing to ask her to do."

Richard nods at the mobile in Michelle's hand. "Ditch it. It was long, but you had no choice. She's one of the only people who might be able to get us what we need. Will she help?"

"She wants to think about it. She wasn't at all happy, but I think she realizes . . ."

"That's all we can hope for. Give her a couple of hours, then text her. Good job, Michelle. We're getting closer all the time."

A sound in the street below startles Michelle, reminding her that if they're getting closer, their pursuers might well be doing the same.

CHAPTER FORTY-SIX

Michelle

Another sleepless night passes. She barely gets any rest on the makeshift bed, tossing and turning and worrying through the small hours, longing for sleep. She feels drained, grubby, and taut with anxiety.

But seeing Toby's face pop round the door is a huge boost. She runs to him, crushing his slender body in her arms, tears welling.

"Whoa, Mum, let me breathe!" He laughs, kissing her on both cheeks.

"Sorry, it's just . . ." She can't speak for the lump in her throat.

"I know," he says, giving her a squeeze.

Toby was always a bright kid. He sailed through school, getting the highest grades at every level. Though he never seemed to put a lot of effort in, he absorbed everything like a sponge. He had an enquiring mind, joining in discussion groups, the debating society, showing an interest in history and politics, forming opinions of his own. By the time he left for university he was ready for the challenge, and she knew he'd throw himself into student life — the social side, for sure, but also the opportunity to expand his horizons, try new things, tap into experts in many fields. He'll be a valuable member of the team.

It's not long before he starts to make a positive contribution. For a couple of days, he shares a table with Tom, who sets him up with a laptop and disappears, returning with another laptop, some new burner phones and more supplies. Michelle wonders briefly where the money's coming from. But that's the least of their worries. If they end up broke and living in this strange place for ever, it'll be bad, but a million times better than allowing Kimia to kill people.

Toby understands what they need in moments. "We need to hack into their systems," he says, his eyes flashing with excitement.

"If only," Tom says. "Their systems are among the most sophisticated in the world. Security is their middle name. We don't have a hope."

"There's always a way," Toby says.

Tom shrugs. "I love the enthusiasm of the young."

But Richard raises his eyebrows. "Do you know something about hacking?"

"I'm doing cybersecurity as an option," Toby says. "So yes, I do. A bit."

Michelle's surprised — she didn't know that. But she should have known. He's always been good at problem solving, always worked things out for himself. As a child, he took to technology as if it were second nature.

"Do you want me to have a look at it?" Toby says, his eyes flicking from Richard to Tom to Michelle.

Richard grins. "You could turn out to be the perfect addition to our team."

"It's probably not legal."

Richard scoffs. "Who cares? The stakes are high here. If we need to break the rules, it's for the best reasons. Just be careful. Make sure you — or rather we — can't be traced."

It's Toby's turn to grin. "Great. What do we need?"

"Er, wait a minute." Michelle frowns. "Is Toby going to break the law here? Because I'm not sure how I feel about that. Of all of us, he's the one with the most to lose. What protection does he have? If he's caught, he could ruin his career — not to mention end up with a prison sentence."

"Mum . . ." Toby rolls his eyes.

"It's okay, Toby," Richard says. "Your mum's right to question this — it's not something to be taken lightly." Michelle nods, relieved. "But what I do, what we're doing here, is in the interests of everyone. There's protection in law for the anonymity of a journalist's sources, of which Toby will be one."

"On the other hand, the Computer Misuse Act 1990 criminalizes computer hacking," Toby says, not looking at Michelle.

Richard raises an eyebrow at Michelle. She nods and shrugs. Her son isn't to be underestimated.

Richard bangs a hand on the table, startling them all. "This is without doubt, one hundred per cent, in the public interest. No question about it."

There's no arguing with that. But it leaves Michelle uneasy. Now, not only is she putting Toby in danger by involving him, she's condoning him breaking the law.

Where will this all end?

* * *

"What am I looking for?" Toby's eyes are already glued to his screen, his fingers tapping furiously.

Richard draws a chair closer. "First of all, we need more evidence that the drug fails — the results of the clinical trials. Those results will have been buried deep somewhere in the company. They've probably been deleted, which means we may never find them, unless we find a way to retrieve them. We can only hope that if the authorities have enough evidence to go in to Kimia, they'll have a way of finding deleted information.

199

"Second, crucially, we need proof that the board of Kimia *knows* that PAN12 fails. Lars has told them himself, but we also need written evidence that they know.

"The data from the clinical trials will have been held at the medical centre, where they were conducted. Also, there will be names and contact details of the test subjects — the people who took PAN12 in clinical trials. We have to hope the information still exists. We need those, and we're hoping Helga can help."

"Helga?"

Michelle explains to Toby how her flatmate is involved. "We've asked her, but it's a big thing — if she's found out, she'll lose her job, her career will be ruined, and she'll be in serious danger."

"So will she help us?"

"We don't know yet — I'm waiting for her to get back to me. But I wouldn't be surprised if she says no."

Toby thinks for a while. "Probably all I'd need is entry to the system via the medical centre. If she can get that without being suspected, it might be all we need from her. Does the drug have a codename, other than PAN12?"

"It will have been given a code in the clinical trials, so that nobody would know what it was," Richard says. "Lars can help us with that."

"If all she has to do is give us a way into the computer system, she might be more likely to help," Michelle says. "And I'd feel a lot better about asking her."

"She may only have low-level security clearance," Tom says. "If so, you could get stuck behind a massive firewall and not get any further into the system."

Toby shrugs. "It's worth a try, surely? I've got a couple of mates who could tell me how to do it — they're better than me — and I needn't tell them why I'm asking. It could easily be theoretical . . ." He looks hopefully at Richard.

"Do it," Richard says. "Be careful involving your mates though. Remember, no contact numbers. Use one of these."

He chucks a box across to Toby. "Under no circumstances tell them what you're investigating."

"Don't worry, they won't ask. They're nerds, they're only interested in the problem." Toby grins. "For them, it's a bit of fun."

But not for us, Michelle thinks grimly. And by the sound of it, not for the rest of the human race.

CHAPTER FORTY-SEVEN

Michelle

"Helga, it's me."

"I haven't had the chance . . ." Helga's voice is cold, distant. It's immediately apparent to Michelle that she's hardened her stance since they last spoke a few days ago. She's relieved that they're asking less of her now.

"Listen, all we need is a way into the system at the medical centre. Can you do that?"

There's a pause. The sound of a car in the background, Helga's footsteps crunching through snow. She's breathing hard, as if she's rushing. "I can give you my security code — it'll get you into the computer system, where I record the results of clinical tests. But after that, I can't help you. I'm sorry, Michelle. It's too much to ask."

"I understand. Text me the code. I promise I won't bother you again."

Michelle cuts the call and lets a long breath go. "I feel such a heel."

"I know," Richard says. They're together on the other side of the room from the desks, leaning against the wall. A long line of windows stretches along the rest of the wall, revealing an empty car park and a row of Victorian houses. Litter dances in the wind. A line of green rubbish bins, graffiti scrawled along it, squats against the wall. Beyond are seventies high-rise blocks, windows like eyes scouring the horizon. It's a bleak outlook, so different from the huge skies and glorious views of Iceland. It seems months ago that she was there, innocent of all this.

"But listen, if she helps us and we bring Kimia down, she'll understand why you had to ask her."

"I know, but it doesn't help how I feel."

The mobile in Michelle's hand vibrates. "It's Helga's code," she says, showing the screen to Richard.

"Perfect. Give it to Toby."

Michelle stares through the grubby window without seeing. There's no sense of achievement in forcing her friend to betray the people she works for, however ruthless they are. Richard follows her gaze. "Depressing view, isn't it?" he says.

"In more ways than one," Michelle says.

Richard gives her a sideways look. "Listen, Michelle, when this is all over . . . we—"

"What?"

He sighs, turns away. "Not now. When this is all over, we can say and do what we like. For the moment, we must get on with it."

* * *

The room turns cold as the weather outside worsens. For days, a storm rages outside, a brutal wind whistling around the half-empty building, creeping under doors, round ill-fitting windows. Rain spatters. The sky turns dark with storm clouds. Overhead lights cast grim shadows across the room and the desk lamps turn their faces into ghoulish masks as they work. Inside, as they toil over their makeshift desks, it's freezing.

Michelle shivers. She has so few clothes with her, and she's already wearing most of them. Noticing, Tom disappears into one of the side rooms, reappearing with a small fan heater. "Put this under your table," he says. "It won't do much for the room, but at least your feet will be warm."

"So kind, thank you." She feels a surge of gratitude. There's no heater for him. He's already wearing a woolly hat, while Toby's face is in shadow beneath a hood.

Meanwhile, Richard strides around the room, engrossed in a call with Lars. He keeps his voice down, so Michelle can't hear the conversation, but from time to time he returns to his desk, scribbling notes onto a pad, checking his laptop screen. It's the longest call any of them has made so far, and Michelle can't help wondering about the risk.

On the shared desk next to Michelle, Tom works through a list of contacts provided by Lars. Judging by the sighs of frustration and whispered curses coming from his direction, he's not having much success. Michelle's job for the next few hours involves monitoring all the news sites, blogs and websites that might be reporting on Kimia. Boring but important. There's been a pause since the speculation regarding the launch date of Kimia's new "wonder drug", and she's keeping her eye on further developments.

Suddenly she sits up, her attention caught by a headline. *Something Is Afoot in Iceland — and It's Not a Troll.* A blog that follows Big Pharma — the top movers and shakers in pharmaceuticals — has the same news. She scans the piece. It confirms the rumour: an important new drug from Kimia is set for release on 1 April. It can only be PAN12. She checks the other regulars: all of them report the date. Comments on what exactly is to be released vary from the mundane to the outrageous, some commentators believing that Kimia's publicity machine is "bigging up" a re-release of one of its older drugs, some speculating that their new drug will change the face of pharmaceuticals for ever. She almost laughs at the irony of that one.

"Looks like April the first is indeed the big day," she announces to the room. "Pretty much all the pundits are reporting it, though nobody has anything concrete on what's actually being released."

"Have you checked the pharma job sites? Sometimes you can get clues from recruitment activity," Tom says.

"That's next," she says, returning her gaze to the screen. She's dimly aware of Richard finishing his call and going back to his seat, but in that moment there's a sound from below. A low boom, followed by a crackling sound. For a moment, they all freeze.

"What was that?" Toby whispers, his eyes wide. Michelle shakes her head.

Tom's the first to move. He lopes towards the window, keeping his head low, aiming towards the side of the building where the sound came from. He peers out, turning his head carefully so his body's not exposed. "I can't see anything," he says in a low voice. "Stay there, all of you. Get down, on the floor. I'm going to check the corridor." The double doors at the entrance to the room have small, reinforced glass rectangles cut into them. Tom cranes his neck, then gently, slowly, opens a door a crack. He hesitates a moment, then his tall body is gone, slinking through the crack, smooth as a snake.

Michelle's paralysed with fear. Toby crawls over to her, his arm around her as they crouch, waiting. "What if he doesn't come back?" he says.

"Tom always comes back." She sounds much more certain than she is.

After what seems like an age but is probably only a few minutes, Tom returns, his face grim. "There's a smell of burning," he says. "Could be kids, but . . ."

"Right," Richard says, scrambling from the floor. "We're moving."

"Again?" Michelle says. She feels the small amount of energy she has left draining away.

"Right now," Richard replies, already packing his bag. "Come on, Toby, get your kit together. To the other door. Right behind me, please."

At the other end of the room is an identical set of swing doors. Michelle can't help wondering if they're being drawn into a trap — a diversion being set on one side of the building to flush them out on the other. "Do you think it's safe this way? They might be waiting for us," she whispers to Tom as they pause, bags on shoulders, on the inside of the double doors.

He shrugs. "I'd rather head away from a fire than towards it, that's all I know," he says. "Don't worry, I've checked the building out."

As they creep into the dim corridor, Michelle can only hope he has.

CHAPTER FORTY-EIGHT

Michelle

Tom leads them to some back stairs. Cigarette ends, sweet papers and crisp packets litter the steps. The banister is sticky from contact with many hands. They pass the ground floor and head towards the basement, where the acrid smell of urine greets them in the stairwell. Michelle can only hope Tom knows what he's doing as he heads along a service corridor. Huge, filthy pipes line the low ceilings, lit only by dim emergency lights and exit signs. At last they reach an outside door, where Tom pauses, listening. He puts a finger to his lips and they strain to hear. There's nothing. He presses the security bar, wincing as it grinds and clicks, and glances through the opening as fresh air rushes in. There's a distinctive smell of rain mixed with diesel fumes — and something else. Memories of an abandoned car on waste ground where she used to hang out as a teenager come flooding back. Burning rubber.

"Mum!" Toby grabs Michelle's arm. He's peering down the dim corridor behind them. She whips round. Something's moving at the opposite end, coming fast towards them — a tall figure, dressed in black.

"Run!" Michelle shouts.

They pile out of the door. Outside is an empty parking area flanked on three sides by brick walls, barbed wire curling along the top. Tom leads them to the only exit, then stops abruptly. Richard, Toby and Michelle bump up behind him.

"Go! Go!" Richard says, glancing over his shoulder at the closing door.

"Wait!" Tom puts out an arm as a large black car blocks the exit, its engine running, windows blacked out.

"We have to go!" Richard insists, grabbing Michelle's arm. "Stay low! Run! To the back of the car . . ."

Later, she remembers thinking, *If they have guns, we're finished.* In that instant, the driver's window winds down and a black-gloved hand appears. A gun points directly at her.

Instinct takes over. Shielding her head with her bag, she races towards the rear of the car, Toby's footsteps pounding directly behind her. There's a muffled bang. Something hits her with enormous force, tearing her bag from her arms, forcing it away as she runs. Behind her there's a strangled shout, the crunch of a car door. They round a corner and she almost crashes into a woman with a shopping trolley. "Sorry, sorry," she mutters without breaking her stride. The woman gestures angrily.

"Mum, I'm here," Toby says, his breath coming in great gasps.

"Thank God," Michelle says, slipping her arm into his, propelling him along, trying to slow down so as not to attract attention. They're on a busy street, vehicles slowing for traffic lights at one end. Pedestrians walk around as if it's a normal day. She glances behind them but there's no sign of anyone. She can almost imagine what normality feels like.

"I'm fine. My God, Mum, that was pretty full-on."

"My bag — I lost it."

"I think it saved you. They shot at you." There's a break in his voice.

She feels the blood drain from her face, bile rising in her throat, even while her legs keep moving. She can barely process what's happening.

But they're not out of danger yet. She glances at her son, walking stiffly beside her. He looks grey with shock, the hand that pushes back his hair shaking. Michelle feels a visceral stab at her heart. She's put her own son in terrible danger.

"I'm so sorry to drag you into this, Toby. It's the last thing I wanted to do."

"You had no choice, Mum, remember? And I'm an adult. I chose to help. I'll be okay."

With a shock of realization, she looks around. "Hold on — where's Richard? And Tom?"

"I don't know, they were behind us. But let's keep walking. We can call them when we're safe."

Michelle stops suddenly. Toby almost trips over her. "Wait, what if one of them's been shot?" she whispers. "We have to go back—"

"No! Don't stop, Mum, you have to stay safe. That's what this is all about."

"But—"

Toby pulls her into an alley, breathing hard. He glances around the corner.

"Are we being followed?"

"I don't think so. But listen, Mum, you're the key to all this — you, Richard and Lars. What I saw back there . . ." He hesitates.

"What? What did you see?" Michelle closes her eyes, expecting the worst.

"Tom — when the gun went off, he threw his bag at the car window. I was still running, but I caught a glimpse. Tom opened the door and was grappling with someone."

"Where's the other guy though, the one following us in the corridor? What if Richard's been caught?"

Toby shakes his head. "I don't know. What do we do now, Mum?"

"Just give me a minute. We'll think of something."

But what? Things have just got a whole lot worse.

* * *

209

As she stands there, her feet wanting to go one way, her heart the other, a black cab draws up beside them. They step back, ready to run. A door opens and a hand gestures, inviting them in.

"Get in, you two, quickly . . ." It's Richard. Relief flooding through her, Michelle scrambles into the cab, Toby on her heels.

Richard barks an instruction at the driver. A pulse in Michelle's temple beats so hard it hurts. The man glances in his rear-view mirror and gives a thumbs-up.

"Are you all right?" Richard turns concerned eyes on Michelle, then Toby.

"We're physically intact, if that's what you mean," Michelle says. "Emotionally and mentally, not so much."

"For a moment there, I thought you'd been shot."

"It was a close thing. The gun . . ." She swallows, the realization of how close she was to being shot beginning to dawn. Her hands start to shake. She folds them in her lap to hide them from Toby. "The gun was pointing directly at me, but somehow I got away with it. Toby thinks it hit my bag."

"Was your laptop in it?"

She nods. "That's what saved me, probably. I doubt it's much use now."

"Where are we going? Where's Tom?" Toby asks.

"I don't know the answer to either of those questions," Richard says. "Tom can handle himself. But—"

"But what?"

"The last I saw, he was wrestling with the shooter. I didn't stop to check what happened." He hesitates for a moment. "But I only heard one bullet being fired. Did either of you hear another shot?"

They shake their heads in unison.

"Should we go back, try to find him?" Michelle hates the idea they may have abandoned Tom to his fate. Perhaps he's lying there injured, or maybe their attackers have bundled him into the car and taken him away. Perhaps they're interrogating him, torturing him for information, hurting him. A memory

210

of a war film, where Germans carried out terrible physical abuse on prisoners, flashes behind her eyes. That film gave her nightmares.

Her imagination isn't helping.

Richard puts his mobile to his ear. "Trying him now . . ." But after a moment or two he gives up, cutting the call, and removes the SIM card. "Not connecting. We'll have to wait for him to find us."

"But how will he do that? Does he have another way of communicating with us?" Toby voices Michelle's thoughts.

"We have a couple of ways. Codes, if you like. If he can, he'll find me."

Toby seems reassured. But Michelle doesn't like the way Richard puts it. *If he can* . . . What if he can't — does that mean he's in trouble? If so, how can they help him? She realizes how little she knows about the enigmatic Tom. All the normal small talk, finding out about people's lives, has been put on hold in their little group; they've been so focused on Kimia and the story.

"Will he — can he go home? I don't even know where he lives," she says to Richard.

"He hasn't been back to his flat for the last week," Richard says. "I don't know where he lives, but obviously he's been extra careful about throwing them off the scent. He's very good at that."

"Does he have a family?" Now Michelle wants to ask all the questions that she hasn't asked since Tom started working with them.

There's a note of irritation in Richard's voice. "I have no idea. Let's worry about where we're going next, shall we? Tom will be okay, I'm sure of it."

Michelle bites her lip. He's right, of course. The story has to be their focus. But she wasn't prepared for all the collateral damage. Toby facing trauma, delaying his studies; Helga putting herself in danger by helping them, risking her life plans; Tom, who could be injured, dead or captured. This story, if it ever gets released, has a lot to answer for.

CHAPTER FORTY-NINE

I have a theory that once things start going wrong, you've had it. The job's contaminated, that's all I can say. It never gets back on track. And for once in my life, I'm surprised. A feeling I'm not used to.

I've never felt fury like it.

I went back upstairs and broke the place to bits. Kicking and cursing and ripping away at that room until there was only dust and detritus and garbage and everything was ruined. It took only a few minutes. Then I got out.

Emotion doesn't come into my assignments. I'm cold and calculating. It's the only way to be in this line of work. I like to think I'm a consummate professional. I'm taken on to do a job and I do it. It's nothing to do with me as a person, so my feelings don't come into it. Unless you count my pride in my work. I've never failed. So how the fuck did this happen?

There's another one.

Another me, another assassin, another professional with the same target.

I didn't believe it at first. I wondered if the police were on to it for some reason, though it didn't seem likely, given what I'd been asked to do.

*I was ready to go in. It wasn't hard to find out where they were —
you can get all the information you need when you have a wodge of cash in your hand. All I had to do was ensure it was a clean hit. That is,*

212

taking all of them out, because by now I had two others to deal with. It was getting messy, and I hate mess.

The one thing I hadn't expected was to find someone else on the job.

It was all working out nicely. I was closing in. I had them in my sights. But then it all went pear-shaped. The targets split, someone fired a weapon, I had to pull back. I was caught napping, and that never happens to me.

Nobody treats me like this. Nobody second-guesses me. Never, in my life, has a client had to bring in someone else because I'm not doing a good job. My blood runs cold, my mind goes into hard calculation. I'm going to get them all. Target, back-up asset, client. Nobody will escape.

CHAPTER FIFTY

Lars

Lars needs to move on, and it needs to be today. He knew it was on the cards, but he was hoping he could stay just a little longer in this small space that has become a home. But Richard was adamant. Lars sourced the place online, and even though he gave a false name, that makes him vulnerable. They'll be on his tail, for sure.

Everything is uncertain now, his future unpredictable — if he has a future at all. He's a person who likes certainty. Lars is a scientist, after all. Scientists work with a theory, test it, test and test again. It works or it doesn't. He deals in facts. He's had one purpose in life until now. His work, his status as a biochemist, has defined his adult years, nothing else. But now everything's changed, and without his work, he feels useless.

The only thing that's important to him now is stopping Kimia. Otherwise his life is worth nothing. But to see it through, he has to stay alive a little longer. He must help Richard and Michelle bring Kimia down.

It's easy enough to get his stuff together — there's not that much of it. Once his bag is packed, he sits for a moment, wondering where to go, how best to hide. In the modern age, disappearing is harder than ever. Phones can be tracked. There's CCTV in every street, almost every shop. A person has to show ID at every turn. Credit cards can be tracked, cash withdrawals monitored. Luckily he still has some cash, enough to take a train or a bus out of the country.

Or maybe a boat. Stockholm offers that too. He decides that's the best way. He'll try for a ferry, perhaps head for the Baltics, where it might be easier to disappear. He has visited Estonia more than once and has distant relatives there. Maybe he can look them up.

Or maybe not. He can't put them in danger too. Not for the first time, he wonders if he should call it a day now. End it before it's ended for him. He's not scared to die, and everything he's lived for is gone, so there's no reason for him to stay. But the method of dying — that does scare him. As a chemist, he knows how to drift away, with no pain. He can't bear the thought of a long, drawn-out, physically agonizing ordeal. He's just not made that way. He's not brave, and he doesn't trust himself not to break down and say anything in order to stop the pain.

But here he is, and he's obliged to keep going for the short term. Estonia it will be. He glances at his watch, sniffs his armpit. Time for a final shower; he may not get another chance for a while.

* * *

He freezes, the towel on his shoulders slipping soundlessly to the floor.

There's no window to the bathroom — what he heard came from next door, or perhaps the corridor. It was a strange noise, a single thump, like someone dropping a heavy cushion on a carpet. He lets a couple of minutes tick by.

Everything's quiet, only the distant burr of traffic and a seagull's soft cry in the distance.

215

He reaches for his trousers. If he's going to investigate, he'd rather not do it naked. His feet are bare, but at least they'll be quiet on the hard floors of the apartment.

He creeps into the living room, his ears taut with the intensity of listening. At the door, he risks a glance through the eyehole. Nothing, no movement at all, just the solid blank grey wall opposite. He's imagining things.

But of course there's nothing. They wouldn't be so amateurish. If they want to confront him directly, they'll knock on the door or ring the bell.

Or perhaps not. Of course not. They'll bash it in, annihilate it, shoot the lock to smithereens. He's such a fool — a complete innocent. He recoils from the door, backing to the other side of the room, his right hand flying unbidden to his neck.

A look of mild surprise crosses his face as a warm liquid oozes through his fingers. The next minute he's lying face down on the carpet, his mind saying, *No, no, no,* over and over. Or perhaps he's actually saying it, out loud. His body is completely relaxed; he can't move a muscle. Nor does he wish to. He's comforted by the warmth of the underfloor heating, content to lie there for ever if needs be. But his eyes are open, still able to identify the table legs, the corner of the sofa. As he watches and waits for the inevitable, a pair of shoes steps into view. They look expensive, polished to a high shine. Black, like the trousers above them. They pause for a moment, and he knows they're the last things he'll ever see.

CHAPTER FIFTY-ONE

Michelle

They find a busy café and take a table right at the back. Music plays, some kind of bland pop, barely audible through the buzz of conversation. People come and go at the counter, ordering coffees and food.

"Let's regroup," Richard says. "I'll get the drinks in."

"What do we do now?" Toby says, watching as Richard weaves through the tables.

"He has to get the story finished," Michelle says. "That's the most important thing, it's our only way out of this mess. We need to find somewhere he can work. Somewhere we can carry on." She's surprised at the firmness of her own voice. Inside, her emotions are churning. Nothing seems to be going well for them. They have nowhere to stay, they've lost a member of the team, and now her few possessions are gone. Clothes, wash bag, underwear. Forget expensive face creams, she hasn't a toothbrush or a comb to her name. It's trivial given the circumstances but the loss of her bag seems like the last straw, and it's a struggle to stop the panic rising.

Helga's in danger. Lars too, even more so. They've been shot at — Toby could have been hit. And Tom's disappeared.

It really couldn't be much worse. Suddenly she can't breathe. "Toby, could you get me some water, please — now?" She blurts it out, holding on to the table, which sways and bends under her fingers. The walls of the café undulate, chairs start to rise upwards . . .

"Mum? Mum, can you hear me?"

Toby's anxious face is inches from hers. She's lying on her side on the bench seat with Toby beside her, Richard crouching down, his eyes at her level, holding a glass of water. Luckily, nobody else is nearby. No one seems to have noticed what's going on at the back of the café.

"What happened?" she says, pushing herself into a sitting position. She's relieved to see that the walls are back to normal, the table solid beneath her hand, though she still feels a little wobbly.

"Steady," Richard says. "Looks like you fainted. I've brought sandwiches and drinks. Try to eat."

She can't remember the last time they ate anything, but she's not hungry. She sips at the water for a few minutes, breathes deeply.

"Better?" Toby says.

"Yes, better. Eat, Toby, don't wait for me."

"Mum, you fainted. You must get something inside you." He unwraps a sandwich, puts it on a plate for her and tucks into his own. "Cheese. Nice and bland."

She eyes the sandwich warily. "Thanks, Toby — sorry to scare you. It's all getting on top of me."

"It's not surprising," Richard says. "Don't beat yourself up. We all need to eat and drink. When we've done that, we'll put a plan together."

With every mouthful, Michelle feels better. They're alive and nobody's injured, and that's something she can hold on to. When they've finished, she says, "We must get this story done, Richard. Where can we go now?"

"I'm going to make a phone call. There's one place I know we'll be safe. A journalist mate who's always travelling. She'll let us stay at her place."

"How long before you're ready to send the story?" Toby says.

"A couple more days, with a bit of luck. If you can get me details of those test subjects, and we can talk to some of them, we should have enough."

"I'm on it, almost there. What about the info Tom was researching?"

"Don't worry, I have access to his work. And yours too, Michelle — it hasn't been wasted, though you've lost your laptop. We'll get you another one."

"And some underwear? Toothbrush?" she says tentatively, not wanting to appear frivolous. The story must take precedence.

"Yes, we'll get those now, while we're out. Best not to have them delivered. We'll stock up on food too." He looks towards the busy street outside. "Look, you two can nip across the road now while I make this call. I'll stay on the pavement outside. Toby, be your mum's eyes and ears. Stay close to her, watch the entrances and exits and look out for anything strange. Let's keep it as short as possible."

* * *

This time they're in a proper home, a stark contrast to the grim office spaces where they've been holed up in recent days. It's a spacious flat high up in a Georgian terrace, four floors and many steps above the ground. The front door opens into a light-filled living room and kitchen, with three bedrooms off to the sides, one with a luxurious en suite. The latter is clearly the owner's bedroom, with clothes in the wardrobe, a robe lying on the bed. She's also an investigative journalist, according to Richard, and happy to help a friend and colleague in need. Richard and Toby lay claim to a second bedroom with twin beds, leaving Michelle to take a rather beautiful spare room with a double bed. She doesn't object — it's wonderful to have somewhere comfortable to sleep.

"I think I'll just lie down for a bit," she says. "I feel a bit fragile."

219

"No worries, Michelle. It'll be good for you to get some rest. Toby and I will probably be here all night," Richard says. Toby responds to his look with a grin. For him, it's still a thrilling situation, despite all the drama of the last few hours. Michelle can't decide if this is a good or a bad experience for him. One thing is certain: it's never going to happen again. Her taste for adventure will be well and truly satisfied when — if — they come out of this alive.

Michelle closes the bedroom door with a sigh of relief, dumping the bag of shopping on the floor for later. She'll have a shower when she wakes up, freshen up properly, put on her new clothes. The bed is deliciously comfortable after sleeping on old mattresses on the floor. She kicks off her shoes and waits for sleep to come.

CHAPTER FIFTY-TWO

One lead takes you to another. It doesn't take long to find out who it is, through my network of contacts. You need to know the competition. We're not friends — it doesn't work like that — but we cross paths in our line of work, and it's worth knowing what your competitors are up to, so you don't step on each other's toes.

I laugh out loud when I find out who it is. For once, my employers have lost the plot. This guy has nothing like my credentials, not even close. He's almost an amateur compared with me. But then, of course, I am the best. It's just this particular job that's turned sour.

Was it even them who took him on? It's so out of character. They're professionals, like me. They know from experience that two hitmen on the same job means trouble of the worst kind. So I shouldn't jump to conclusions. It's possible the client has hired him in frustration, because the hit hasn't happened as soon as they'd like. That makes sense. No wonder it's a mess.

He'll lead me to them. I'll catch them — and him — all together.

All I have to do is track, watch and wait. That's what I'm good at, apart from the obvious. I'm a patient man and I play by the rules, like it's a game of chess. If X goes to Y, then Z happens. It's not hard, but you have to think straight and be patient. Some quick thinking at the end could be called for, and I'm not bad at that either.

Once I know where they are, all I have to do is hunker down and bide my time.

When I realize there are three of them in the flat — there were four in the last place — I offer myself a small wager. One of them has gone rogue, I'll bet on it. With the kind of money this client's throwing around, that's pretty predictable. It won't be the woman, and it won't be her son. They're just not the type. It won't be the hack — too righteous by far. They all are. Think they can stand in judgement on just about everyone. My view is, that's their choice, and they can live in a hovel for the rest of their lives while I watch the sun go down in paradise. No, it'll be the helper. The fewer the better, as far as I'm concerned. In and out in a flash.

It won't be long now before I hang up my gun. Or rather, guns, knives and other killing paraphernalia. Mustn't forget the garrottes. I'll miss them.

Time I got out. It's not my age, it's the law of averages. The more success I have, the more likely it is that I'll fail. And as I said, I don't fail. I'm the best, and I'm going to quit while I'm ahead.

This job landed in my lap at just the right time. It would have taken another ten years of hard graft, high-risk work, to earn what they're paying me for this one. This is my swan song, my testimonial, and nobody's going to take it away from me. Nobody.

Which brings me back to Hitman Number Two.

He's one of the new breed. Young, keen, physically at the top of his game, for sure. Clever, in the sense that he can hack a computer, analyse the data, cut corners with the latest tech. He'll be quick too, laser sharp. But not street clever, not experienced. He hasn't seen what I've seen, done the things I've done. I can outsmart him. And that's exactly what I'm going to do here.

Paradise, here I come.

222

CHAPTER FIFTY-THREE

Michelle

Richard frowns. "This isn't good. I can't get Lars."

Michelle, searching on Toby's laptop, stops abruptly. Toby looks up from his phone. A look passes between them. They've always known how much danger Lars has put himself in. He's crucial to the story — the lynchpin, the one who started the whole thing, and Kimia won't forgive him for that. It would be tragic if he can't see the story through, watch the axe fall on the corporate neck.

For Michelle, it would be a terrible blow. In her heart, she's doing this for him.

"He'll have changed his mobile, won't he?" Toby says.

"He will have done, but he's supposed to let me know each time, as soon as he's done it." Richard redials, his fingers jabbing at the keys. "Shit. Definitely not in use."

"What can we do?" Michelle feels her stomach knot.

"Nothing. We'll just have to wait and hope it doesn't mean anything bad."

"Didn't you suggest he should move to a different place? Perhaps he's on his way, and that's why he's out of contact . . ."

Richard moves his head in a kind of "maybe" gesture. But he's not convinced. "It's possible. There's nothing we can do but wait. I need to get cracking on the story. Let me know if there's anything important, otherwise I'm going to need a few hours without interruptions. I'll work in the bedroom, you two stay here."

"Right, we'll leave you to it."

"We'll keep the coffee coming."

"Thanks." Richard nods and leaves the room. Michelle can't help noticing how grey he looks, how the frown is deepening, his eyes sinking into their sockets. She's tired, having slept very little in the few days they've been at the flat, but he's hardly stopped. He must be close to exhaustion. But there's nothing she can do to help, except keep monitoring, do what she can to replace Tom in supporting him. Where is Tom? Every hour that passes, the hope that he'll reappear fades.

"Mum, I need the laptop. I need to crack the Kimia system and get those contacts for Richard."

"Okay — just let me finish a couple of things first, then you can take over." She wants to check up on Helga, for her own peace of mind. She scribbles down the number for Kimia, then searches again for Beck's, Magnus's family restaurant in Akureyri.

But she can't find it — the website has disappeared and it's delisted from all the restaurant review sites. It's as if it never existed. But how can that have happened? Helga said Magnus would inherit it after his parents had retired. It was doing really well, she said, and there were great plans for expansion of the brand. She checks the local Akureyri paper, types in "Beck's" in the search box. A reference comes up immediately, but what she reads makes her heart sink.

TOP RESTAURANT BECK'S CLOSES:
FAMILY LEAVES ICELAND FOR GOOD
Restauranteur Karl Beck surprised the local community and fans of his popular eponymous restaurant in Akureyri by

closing down suddenly last week. He was unavailable for comment, and appears to have left the country with his family. Friends and customers were bemused and upset. "We had no warning of the restaurant being closed, or that the Becks were leaving Iceland," a neighbour said. "We're shocked and saddened — we loved that place, and we thought we were friends." The premises have been put up for sale through a local law firm.

Michelle can't believe it. As far as she knew, the business was doing well and Magnus was preparing to take over. What's happened, and where's Helga in all this? A sense of foreboding overtakes her. First Lars, now Helga. She hands the laptop over to Toby without a word and takes her mobile to the bedroom.

Dialling Kimia's number sets her heart racing again. It's a big risk, but she must know what's happened to Helga.

* * *

"Helga Jonsdottir, please." She doesn't bother to disguise her voice. She's never been any good at accents — her best option is to keep it short.

"One moment, please," the receptionist says and the line goes quiet for a moment. "We have no one of that name listed."

She feels a rush of blood to her scalp. She cuts the call and throws the mobile onto the bed as if it's scalded her fingers. What the hell does this mean? Is Helga dead or kidnapped — or has she decided to flee, along with Magnus and his family? The fact that Kimia has no listing for anyone called Helga means they've deleted her, closed her down. Did they discover she'd betrayed them, and if so, how?

Perhaps she's simply resigned, gone to join Magnus. It's possible she's too scared to stay at Kimia, having helped Michelle. But would they delete her name from the database if she'd resigned? Wouldn't they simply say she'd left the company? Perhaps Michelle should have asked to be put through to the medical centre, asked for Helga there. They might have revealed a little more. But she daren't call back. Any calls for Helga, if she's under suspicion, would be noted. It's too risky. She doesn't know what to think.

There's something very strange going on here. Helga's gone, her presence at Kimia erased. It's not a coincidence. It must be related to the PAN12 story.

Either Helga's dead, or something's happened to make her disappear off the face of the earth.

CHAPTER FIFTY-FOUR

Michelle

Toby sticks his head around the door. "Mum, guess what?"

She sighs. She's a long way past guessing games. "I'm really tired, Toby. What is it?"

He grins, punches the air. "We've cracked Kimia's system!"

A piece of good news at last. She can't remember the last time she smiled. "Great work, Toby! Was it Helga's code?"

"No, actually, it wasn't much use in the end, which was weird . . . But my mates sorted me out — it took us a while, but we did it!"

Michelle can only guess what Toby's friends are like. "You told them to keep quiet, didn't you?"

"Mum . . ." He gives her a sideways look.

"Sorry. Of course you did. Can you access those names and contacts now?"

"I'm downloading them as we speak."

"And it's secure? Are you sure you can't be traced?" Her knowledge of computer technology is more than vague — she barely has the right vocabulary, but she must be certain.

"Mum, *of course* I'm sure. As sure as anyone who's been advised by the maestro hacker, Drumkit! Actually, you didn't hear that."

Sometimes she wonders if she speaks a different language from Toby. "Drumkit?"

"His handle, obviously, not his real name. Is this worth interrupting Richard for?"

"It sure is — knock first though, just in case."

"Oh, and by the way, you owe me." Toby's eyes are dancing.

"News to me. What do I owe you?"

"I never got my trip to Iceland, did I?"

"Quite right, you didn't. I definitely owe you that. Don't worry, when this is over, we can go wherever you want. We're going to need a holiday."

* * *

All the greyness lifts from Richard's face at the news. "That's the best news, Toby!" he says, clapping him on the back. "Michelle, could you make the calls to the test patients please?"

"Of course . . ." She needs to take her mind off Helga. And Lars, and Tom.

"Here's what you need to say." He hands her a sheet of paper with a list of questions. "It's important you get their agreement to be quoted, and to be interviewed by the authorities. Obviously, we're looking for at least one person — preferably two — who had an adverse reaction, during or after the trial. And anything else they can tell us about the drug."

"I understand. Any sign of Tom?"

Richard shakes his head. "Nothing."

"Aren't you worried about him? I mean, that he's gone so quiet? Don't you think we should check the hospitals, try to find out what happened? I hate to think of him injured and on his own."

"I am worried, though he's pretty resourceful. But we can't risk being traced again, we just have to hope he's okay.

Listen, I'm very close to finishing my piece: I just need the last few bits of evidence, and I can submit it. I have to focus on that."

Michelle's heart leaps. "So it might all be over soon? Oh, Richard . . ." She can hardly contain the rush of joy. She has an overwhelming urge to hug him. But he makes a calming gesture with his hands.

"Maybe. The problem is, we're missing a key person if we can't find Lars — and we don't have nearly as much evidence as I'd like. There's so little time."

"What would happen if we released the story now, without Lars, and without all the evidence?"

"We may be able to spark an investigation right away. That would stop the launch of PAN12 and put some big question marks over the future of the drug — and the company. But if the media can't get it through the lawyers because there's not enough evidence, we risk Kimia putting up a whole load of barriers to publication, covering up the evidence, resisting an investigation by the authorities, releasing the drug and threatening lives. They can delay the story, slap injunctions on the media, tie everybody up in lengthy court cases . . ."

Michelle feels another surge of excitement. They're so close, and she can't bear to live like this for much longer. "Richard, let's do it!" she says. "If there's even a slim chance it'll stop them, it's worth the risk. Surely the media will take it on, do their own research? Big stories take on a life of their own these days, surely, with the internet, social media — and the regulatory bodies won't be able to ignore it. If we push it, we could even make sure the police sit up and take notice."

Richard rubs his forehead, his long fingers easing out the deep lines that track into his hairline. "That's true," he says. "But even once the story's published, there's a long way to go. We have ten days until the beginning of April. Only ten. We have to move fast to get the media on board, and the authorities will have to move fast too. That's not in their psyche. It'll take a hell of a lot of persuading, even once the story's out.

We'll still be looking for more evidence, and more, and tying up loose ends."

"But we'll be safe, won't we? Once the police get on to it, surely?"

"Certainly we'll be safer than we are now." He sighs. "Look, I need to get back to it. And you need to get on with those calls." He turns towards his bedroom.

"Before you go . . . I tried to contact Helga—"

Richard turns back, his eyes sympathetic. "I know you feel guilty about her, but there are more important things . . ."

She shakes her head. "No, I realize that — but listen, Richard, she's disappeared. There's nobody of that name at Kimia, and her boyfriend's family restaurant has closed down suddenly. The family's gone. Left the country without a word, according to the local paper. It's weird, isn't it? I mean, she had plans to go north to join him — but not for a couple of years. What do you think?"

Richard shakes his head slowly. "I'm afraid . . . sorry, Michelle, but it sounds very much like they've got to her. They've probably given her a shedload of money in return for information about us — about you. So much money she's been able to emigrate with her boyfriend's family, leave the business behind and start a new life on the other side of the world."

She thought by now she'd be unshockable. But she is deeply shocked — and hurt. She shakes her head. "No, not Helga, surely?" That beautiful, open face, the honesty shining through. It's horrible.

"I'm sorry, Michelle. It's cynical, but everyone has their price, and huge amounts of money are very persuasive. It could be how they found us so quickly at the last place. I'm not saying it was her, but—"

She sinks onto a chair. "Oh no. Really?"

"Really. I wouldn't be surprised. She had everything to gain by betraying us."

* * *

Toby goes quiet for a while, typing manically, his fingers a blur. Michelle bites her lip, does her best not to pace the room while he works.

At last he sits up. "Boom!" he says. "Got it!"

"The test subjects?"

"Yep. Go me!" He scribbles a couple of names and numbers onto a scrap of paper. "Here, you can start with these. I'll get some more while you get calling."

Michelle retreats to the bedroom, composing herself. She's always better making calls without an audience, and the weight of this responsibility makes her nervous. Without solid evidence, the story could fail, and PAN12 will be released. With it, and with some witnesses to back it up, the story could avert a global catastrophe. If that isn't nerve-wracking, she doesn't know what is.

The first two calls don't go too well. Though she reaches the right people, neither is prepared to talk about their experiences. "I signed a non-disclosure agreement," says one. "I'm not prepared to break that contract." The other simply hung up on her once she'd explained what she needed. Back to Toby for more names, and she steels herself to carry on. After another thirteen calls, her nerves are frazzled and she's no further forward. The fourteenth, too, brings no joy. The man swears at her and cuts the call as she's mid-sentence. None of this is doing her anxiety levels any good.

She stands and goes to the window, opening it wide. Standing in the cool draught, she takes long, deep breaths into her belly, savouring the tang of diesel from below. The sound and smell of London traffic has always calmed her, providing a background hum indicating life around her. Leaving the window open, she returns to her list.

Perhaps it's the lift she's got from the air, perhaps it's a boost in confidence from breathing deep, but this time the experience is entirely different. "I'm so glad you asked about this," the woman says. Her name alone indicates she's Icelandic, and her accent is strong. But her English is good.

"I was suspicious from the start about the drug. I had a very strange reaction. They didn't seem interested in the details; they just took me off the trial. There were no apologies, no notes. There was no monitoring of my condition, though I felt ill for some time afterwards."

Once the woman starts, there's no stopping her, and Michelle struggles to keep up with her notes. She has to keep asking her to pause while she catches up. They talk for over an hour. By the time they finish, Michelle is triumphant. The woman agrees to testify to both the media and the authorities if they need her, and to put her signature on Michelle's report of their conversation.

She stands, stretching her stiff shoulders for a moment or two before leaving the room to tell Richard the good news.

CHAPTER FIFTY-FIVE

Michelle

The buzz of the entry phone is loud, insistent, like the wings of a giant mosquito searching for prey. Someone is downstairs on the street, and they badly want to come in.

They freeze. Michelle, mid-sentence, looks at Richard with wide eyes. He puts a finger to his lips, rising from his chair and ushering her silently into the living room, where Toby sits, his body rigid with fear.

The buzzing continues. There's no camera on the entry phone, so there's no knowing who might be there. It could be completely innocent: a man with a delivery, a neighbour, a friend of the owner, but somehow they all know it's not.

Richard moves towards the door, taking care to approach at an angle. "Stay away from the windows, keep low," he whispers, gesturing to them to keep down.

He puts an ear to the doorjamb. "Nothing," he mouths, indicating to Toby. "Here, push the sofa up against the door."

On the soft carpet the sofa makes a dragging noise, not loud, though to Michelle it's deafening. They wait a few more minutes. Nothing.

"What do you think?" Michelle whispers. A flashback to the last time they escaped, the crack of gunfire, sets her heart racing. Her mouth goes dry, her breath rasping.

Richard shrugs. "I don't—"

He's interrupted by a soft knock on the door to the flat. They all flinch, Richard stepping back to flatten himself against the wall, the others crouching low to the floor.

"Richard, it's me, Tom." His words are barely audible, but it's definitely him. Michelle closes her eyes and exhales. Thank God, Tom's alive.

But Richard holds up a hand. "Tom, is that you?" he calls through the door.

"Yes, it's me. Are you going to let me in or not?"

"Are you on your own?"

"Of course. Let me in."

Richard nods, satisfied. "Here, help me with the sofa, Toby."

"Come in, Tom, good to see you," Richard says, holding the door open as Michelle and Toby stand to welcome Tom back. But there's a strange look on his face as he steps through the doorway. He looks haunted, his movements stiff, his eyes sliding away from theirs.

It's then that she realizes Richard hasn't closed the door, and there's a second person pushing through into the room.

* * *

He's tall and rangy, in a black suit over a black T-shirt. He looks pleasant enough. There's even a smile on his face. But in their heightened state of suspicion, they all react the same way, as if someone has yelled *Danger!* and the word is reverberating off the walls, the ceiling, the floor.

It's as if someone's flicked a switch. All three move in different directions. Richard slams the door on the intruder, shoving his shoulder into the door. But instead the man makes a deft move to his left and the door slams, shutting them all in. Michelle, already backing away, turns to flee, without thought of where to go, expecting Toby to follow her.

234

But Toby has other ideas. He catapults his body across the floor and grabs the closest thing to a weapon — a bronze figurine of a cat sitting on a low shelf. It's big and heavy, and Toby lurches as he flings it towards the intruder, who's taken by surprise. The figurine hits his chest, causing little damage before it falls to the floor — but the element of surprise is just long enough for Richard to make his move. He darts towards the bedroom, where his computer sits open on a table.

"Stop right there." The man's voice is level, almost friendly. But there's no doubting what he means. Michelle turns slowly. Her worst fears are confirmed. In his hand, solid and black, is a gun.

She's aware of Richard turning too, slowly registering what's happening, while Toby stands frozen on the spot. She puts a hand out towards him. *Steady.*

"That's better," the intruder says with a grim smile. "Now, please, let's all calm down and take a seat." He flicks the gun at them, indicating the sofa. They sit gingerly, in a reluctant line. Richard's leg touches Michelle's, and through the fabric of his jeans she can almost feel the fury in his veins. Every part of his body seems to radiate with barely controlled energy. On her other side, Toby's doing his best to meld with the furniture, all bravado gone at the sight of the weapon.

The intruder moves forward to stand beside Tom, a look of amusement on his face. "So this is the rogue unit, is it?" he says, contempt dripping from every word. "My, what a powerful force you are. An ageing hack, a middle-aged nobody and a skinny boy. I'm terrified." He tuts. Despite her fear, Michelle feels a stab of irritation. *A middle-aged nobody?*

Richard ignores the man. "Tom, what's going on? What are you doing?" His voice has dropped an octave. Michelle can't help glancing at his face, where she sees the anger barely suppressed.

Tom, too, looks different now. The haunted look has left his face now. In its wake there's an expression close to triumph. Excitement, even, as if he's feeling a sense of achievement.

"You never asked," he says, fixing Richard with a stony glare. "You know nothing about me. I've worked with — for

235

you for years, been your servant, your factotum, your rock. I've saved you from ignominy. You could never have finished those stories without me. You're happy enough to take the credit, but you never gave me one iota of thanks."

Richard looks as if he's been hit in the face. The shock of Tom's words has erased the anger in one swipe. Michelle understands: she always felt that Richard's relationship with Tom was akin to father and son. But that's not what Tom is saying, not at all.

"I can see it in your face — I'm right, aren't I? You never even thought to ask me how I was, what was going on in my life. Did you? Well, let me tell you. I look after my ageing mother — and her twin sister, also ageing and very ill. I have no income, other than the small amount you pay me and a pittance of a carer's allowance. I have no place of my own. I'm a drudge, and when I work for you I have to pay someone to help with my mum and aunt. So the money's even tighter. You have no idea." He takes a deep breath. "So when someone comes along and offers me not just a bit of money, but more money than I could earn in a bloody lifetime — well, that's hard to refuse. Somehow I don't care if they thank me for helping them find you. Nobody's ever thanked me before, I'm used to it. I'm used to it, and now I'm rich, and I'll be wealthy for the rest of my life. Guess why I led him to you, Richard? Any thoughts?"

Richard says nothing. But Michelle, indignant on Richard's behalf, can't hold back. "Hang on a minute, Tom! Richard trusted you. You were friends, and you've betrayed him in the worst possible way. I—"

"Shut up!" The tall man's voice cuts through hers like a knife. Richard makes a small movement next to her. His hand, down by his side, searches for hers and finds it. She closes her mouth with a snap.

The man turns to Tom. "And you — shut the fuck up. We're wasting time here."

Tom nods, the muscles in his jaw twitching. The gun moves slowly from Richard to Michelle, to Toby and back again.

236

"Where is it?" The man looks pointedly at Richard.

"In the back bedroom." Richard's voice has turned to a growl.

"All of it?"

Richard nods.

"Do it," the man says to Tom. "Get the computer, the papers, notes, files, memory sticks. All of it, mind. Make sure there's nothing hidden. This too." He indicates the laptop lying abandoned on the floor, where Toby left it when they moved the sofa. "All their mobiles. Tear the place apart if you have to. We have plenty of time." He smiles and sits opposite them in an armchair. "We'll make ourselves comfortable while you search. Don't even think about trying anything clever." He gives Toby a piercing look. Toby drops his eyes to his lap.

CHAPTER FIFTY-SIX

As it turns out, the "track" part of it is simple. Obviously, Hitman Number Two is in London, as he's already made contact with the target, though he failed that time, the loser. He'll be out to get them now; he won't make the same mistake twice.

Neither will I.

He's nearby, I know it. A handful of red folding notes to the right person and I get the CCTV of the cock-up at the last place. The cops were all over it, though they got nowhere. That's where the journo's helper got caught. I was a fraction too late, but I wouldn't have caused such a public spectacle. My plan would have worked if it hadn't been for him. It was a beaut. Silent but deadly, that's what I like. No CCTV, no hostages, no mess. I'd have cleared up and got out, with the information I needed.

Anyway, after a few hours of ducking and diving, I've got what I need. I know where they are now. Now the "watch" part starts. Anyone in this trade has had to learn infinite patience. It's true, the old saying: Good things come to those who wait. I can wait. I've spent all my life waiting and watching. It's worth a few empty hours, a bit of discomfort, when you know the outcome will bring you paradise.

I have a particular skill in relation to waiting. I can keep part of my mind alert, super prepared, ready to move in a nanosecond, while another part of my brain does other things — makes plans, prepares for the next job, paints paradise in my head.

The building's easy enough to find. The flat is at the top. That doesn't pose any problem. The good thing about apartments is that they usually only have one front door — back doors being superfluous as the ground is a long way down. I suppose apartment buildings in New York might be different, but in London a fire escape is rare, especially on these poncy historic buildings. I've never understood the appeal myself. Doric columns, moulded ceilings, Regency fireplaces: not my bag. I'm going to have the best fuck-off contemporary glass box anyone's ever built, views that make you weep, in paradise.

Over the road, a tatty stationer's is only too pleased to let me up to the roof. Could be because I handed over more than they make in an entire year. Once I'm up there, it's not hard to spot them with my high-powered binoculars. Heavy but effective. The first one I see is the woman. She won't be a problem, nor her skinny boy. The hack stays mostly out of sight, but I glimpse him in the background now and then. I'm not planning to shoot them from here, though I could do one, easily. Too messy to get them all. I'll swoop in as soon as Number Two arrives, get them all in one go. It'll be simple.

I settle down to watch and wait. Shouldn't be too long now.

CHAPTER FIFTY-SEVEN

Michelle

They're sitting in a line opposite a hitman. At first she's too frightened to look directly at him, her gaze travelling from the floor to her hands to the figure opposite, though she looks away quickly. The man's eyes travel across his three hostages and back in a lazy, insulting way, a contemptuous smile flickering around his mouth. She wonders how long they're going to have to sit there, motionless, while he studies them. She finds it hard to keep her eyes from the gun.

When his glance drifts away from her, she allows her eyes to slide around the room, looking for something, anything that might be able to help them. There's nothing. In the background, Tom gathers things in Richard's bedroom. There's a rustling of papers, a commotion as a search goes on, then a few moments of silence.

"What's going on?" The hitman keeps his eyes steady as he shouts over his shoulder to Tom.

"I need to check it's all here on the computer," Tom calls back.

"Do it later," the man says. "We need to get going."

There's a muffled snap as the laptop closes. Tom reappears in the doorway, a bag over his shoulder, the strap cutting a groove in his jacket.

"Get this one and the phones," the man says, indicating the other laptop. Tom collects the laptop and the two mobiles sitting on the table.

"Any more?" he says. They shake their heads in unison.

"Search them."

Tom hesitates for a moment, then indicates for them to stand. "Put your hands up and turn round." They comply. Michelle finds her own anger rising as Tom's hands touch her hips, sliding down her legs to her ankles. Tom, who she thought was a friend, invading her space, treating her like an object. He finds nothing, but before they're allowed to sit down, he searches the sofa, throwing cushions around the room.

"That's it," he says to the gunman. The gun flicks, indicating for them to sit down.

"It had better be," he says. "Now, we need to return what was stolen."

Tom nods, turns to Richard. "Where's the sample?"

"You know where it is," Richard says. "And you also know I'm the only one who can access it."

"Then you'll have to get it for us," the gunman sneers. "He's coming with us," he says to Tom.

Michelle feels the tension change in Richard's body. At the same time, Toby shifts his weight. She risks a glance at him, gives him a tiny shake of the head. He mustn't try anything on, not with a gun in their faces.

But her mind's racing. If they take Richard with them to get the sample, what happens to her and Toby? Her entire body shakes. They won't risk leaving them alive, why would they? Kimia's ruthless; they'll stop at nothing. She and Toby have no value for them now.

Will they shoot them here or take them somewhere else, where they can be disposed of more discreetly? Is there any chance at all that they'll just tie them up and leave them? In her heart, she knows there isn't. But this is her son, sitting right next to her, and he's only nineteen. She has to protect him, plead for his life. The words start to rise in her throat—

Richard coughs, a signal he's about to speak. At once the gun focuses on his chest.

"It's too late." His voice is deep and flat. Michelle and Toby forget themselves, their heads swivelling towards him in surprise.

"What do you mean, it's too late?" Shock registers on Tom's face, while a look of intense fury flashes over the face of the gunman. He leans forward, the gun poised.

Richard pauses, stretches his legs out in front of him, sighs. It's such an unexpected gesture they all watch, transfixed, for a moment too surprised to say anything.

The hitman leaps to his feet, pointing the gun at Richard's face now. Michelle and Toby recoil in shock, tucking their legs towards each other, away from the weapon. Michelle's arm snakes around Toby's thin shoulders.

"Fuck's sake!" the man yells, the gun waving. "What's too late?"

"You. You're too late. I've sent the story," Richard says, his voice steady, his eyes challenging the gunman.

For the second time in a matter of minutes, everything happens at once. The gunman takes a single step towards the sofa, one arm outstretched, the barrel within millimetres of Richard's forehead. There's an ominous click as the safety is released. Tom leaps towards them, dropping the heavy bag with a thump, shouting "No!" Michelle, terrified, lurches sideways, grabbing Toby. They fall to the floor in a heap and scramble behind the sofa towards the front door, escape the only thing on Michelle's mind.

But there's a strange zinging noise in her ear, a sudden *thwack* — and right next to them the centre panel of the front door opens up, cracks spreading around a circle of darkness. They freeze, their hands on each other's arms.

"Come out. Slowly."

Michelle puts her hands up slowly, indicating to Toby to do the same. He's behind her as she gets to her feet, taking care not to make any sudden movement.

"Sit down. You too." The gunman, still standing, indicates to Tom. He obeys and sinks to the floor, legs crossed, to one side of the sofa. Richard stays put and Michelle and Toby slide back into their positions, their eyes fixed on the threatening lump of metal aimed at them.

"So, you say you've sent the story. Where and when?"

Richard sighs, studies the fingernails on his free hand.

"I'm warning you. That bullet went into the door. The next one won't." To Michelle's horror, the gun swings from Richard to Toby. "No, no, no . . ." she says, almost rising from her seat — but Richard's hand squeezes hers, holding her down. The entire sofa seems to be shaking and she realizes it's her body causing it.

"I will do it, you know."

She hears his voice as if from a distance, every word slicing into her consciousness. She believes him.

"Now, where and when?"

"It really doesn't matter. What matters is the story's out in the stratosphere, and every second you sit here threatening us, it's growing, reaching further and further around the globe."

"Check it out," the gunman says to Tom, who reaches to his back pocket for his phone. He taps and scrolls for an instant, then gets up slowly, his eyes fixed on the screen. Silently, he hands the device to the gunman, who glances at it, the gun unwavering in his other hand.

The shaking hasn't stopped. If anything, it's worse, because a horrible realization has wormed itself into Michelle's mind. If the story's out, they're dispensable, all three of them. Why would Kimia let them live? The PAN12 sample, still safe in the vault of a high-security bank, doesn't matter anymore. The story will take on a life of its own. The launch will be halted, the authorities will move in. The job is done.

243

But the hitman has failed. He'll kill them out of fury, or to tie up loose ends, or because they've seen his face. Or just because they're there.

It doesn't matter why, he's going to kill them anyway.

She watches in horror as the barrel of the gun angles towards her.

* * *

There are moments in Michelle's life she remembers not for their drama but for their filmic quality. Her memory holds them not in snapshots but in short video clips where the details never change, nor the colours, sounds and smells. She can close her eyes and sense how it was, whenever she wants. The feel of her mother's hand in hers on the way to school, the joy of drawing aside a curtain to reveal the world transformed by snow, Toby running across the garden as a small boy, his fat little legs pumping. She can conjure up precisely what she was doing when someone significant died — drying the dishes, walking to the shops, sitting with friends in the local café. Each of those simple, everyday acts changed for ever after that moment.

Likewise this instant, this fraction of a second in which she thinks she's going to die. The living room and all its contents acquire a Hollywood sheen. The light around her dazzles, colours sharpen, shadows shift and fade. Every ornament, every piece of furniture, is outlined in sharp relief. Every movement slows down. As the gunman takes aim, Richard shouts — more like a scream, she doesn't recognize any words — and hurls his body across hers, while Tom lunges at the man in a rugby tackle, yelling "No!" Toby flings sofa cushions into the fray like in a children's pillow fight.

She's transfixed by the killer's face. She wonders, bizarrely, how he keeps his skin so fresh. But as the scene plays out frame by frame before her, his gaze lifts beyond the sofa, as if he's looking far into the distance. An expression of utter surprise widens his eyes. The blood drains from his face — she can almost see it flowing away through the vein standing out on the side of his neck. He moves forward, side-stepping Tom, ignoring Richard and Michelle, batting aside the cushions launched by Toby. If he was focused before, now he's laser-like.

Richard's the first to make a move.

"GO!" he yells, but something's happened to Michelle's hearing. She knows what he's saying but there's a strange ringing in her ears. A single red rose blooms on the smooth forehead of the assassin. The gun in his hand jerks once, then takes off, flying through the air in a graceful arc to land somewhere behind him. She recoils as a fountain of warm, dark liquid sprinkles across her face, her clothes, the cushions beside her. His body, until now wired, taut as a spring, relaxes all at once. It's like watching a puppet as his controller lets go. His knees hit the floor with a soft thump, his shoulder follows. At last he lies on his side before them, lips working, the look of surprise fading with the life in his eyes. Black fluid seeps around his head.

For a moment she's transfixed with horror. She closes her eyes, waiting for the sense of relief to flood through her: *It's over.* But there's another sound from behind, another scrambling sound, a *whump* like the first one and a grunt of air being forced from someone's lungs. Toby's beside her, frozen with horror, gazing at the dying man on the floor. Richard flings himself to one side, her eyes follow him unbidden.

Just beyond are Tom's legs. They're on the floor, and they're twitching.

CHAPTER FIFTY-EIGHT

A surge of adrenalin sharpens my senses as a car draws up opposite. I peer down and watch as two male figures exit the vehicle. One looks tentative, furtive, looking both ways as he emerges. The other — tall, dark, neat, powerful — strides purposefully towards the back of the building, looking neither left nor right. He's the Other One.

The first figure hurries after him.

I slip my gun into the waistband of my trousers and follow. So my enemy has recruited the traitor. Not bad, something I probably would have done myself, given the simple opportunity he was presented with. I have to give him that.

But I won't give him the chance to do my job. Once I've got them all in a room together, that will be that. I'll be in and out of there, job done, send me the money. After that, I'm off, on my way to paradise. I almost catch myself whistling as I climb the stairs silently, click the safety off and slip to one side of the closed door.

I listen intently, my ear to the doorjamb. A male voice, then a different one, then a female murmur — and then a yell, a scream, someone shouts "No!"

I turn the handle and the door swings open. It almost catches on the back of a large sofa. Facing me, his features turning white with fury, is the Other One. The gun in his hand swivels from an unseen target on the front of the sofa towards me. At the same time a figure dives at me from one side. Instinctively, I squeeze the trigger, noting with satisfaction the perfect hole in the forehead of the hitman before I turn to the other, letting off a second shot.

But something strange happens.

I miss my target — my shot connects with a shoulder when it should have created another perfect circle. I'm losing my grip . . . or is it my sight? My legs give way, I'm falling, falling. Like a single frame of a film, paradise is laid out in front of me. I reach for it but it's fading fast, the divine colours dripping from it, the outlines blurring. My hand closes on nothing but darkness.

CHAPTER FIFTY-NINE

Michelle

"Richard!"

"Stay down!" He turns, grabs the gun and launches himself round the corner of the sofa.

"What's happened?" She pulls Toby's head into her shoulder in an attempt to keep his eyes off the carnage that lies within inches of their feet. "Are we safe?"

There's a long pause, a drumming in her ears now. It's her heart, about to burst.

"I think so." Richard unfurls his body behind them. "But Tom's been hit."

"What?" She leaps to her feet to see Tom prostrate on the floor, blood seeping from one shoulder, his eyes closed, Richard bending over him.

But what really grabs her attention is the other body, lying half in, half out of the front door. A man's body, head to one side, eyes open but empty. Grey hair, cut close to his head, swarthy skin. She blinks once, twice, before she notices the spreading pool of dark liquid around him, the dark stain on his shirt, the gun lying by the wall. Confused, she lifts her eyes to Richard's.

"Who . . . who's that?" Her brain seems to have lost the ability to make connections.

"I have no idea," Richard says. "But he's definitely dead."

"There was another one?"

"Could've been. Could be police or Europol — who knows? He was alone. There don't seem to be any more around. Not right now, anyway."

She stares in disbelief, first at Richard, then at the lifeless body. How could that be? Were there two lots following them, two assassins out to get them? Or did the gunman in the flat just kill someone who was meant to rescue them? It's too much to untangle right now.

The sound of retching brings her to her senses. "Toby?"

He stands, wiping his mouth on his sleeve, his face ashen. His eyes alight on the second body. "Shit, who's that? Mum, what the hell just happened?"

"We appear to have two gunmen in the house," Richard says drily. "Both eliminated, each by the other. And one traitor, injured." Then, seeing Michelle's face, "Oh, he's not too bad. He'll survive, if we let him."

She flinches.

"Sorry, Michelle. Bad joke. Toby, can you get some towels and sheets for Tom, please, and maybe a blanket, while I do something about our killers?"

"What are you going to do with them?" She does her best to keep her eyes averted, but they keep straying back to the blood spatter on the sofa, the walls, the floor. All over Toby, all down her jumper, probably on their faces and in their hair too. If she thinks about it too much, she'll start retching.

"I'm calling the police — and an ambulance. Try not to disturb anything. Don't clear up." Richard disappears into the corridor, his footsteps fading. It takes her a moment to realize their phones in the blood-spattered bag at Tom's feet are evidence. Richard will have to find a neighbour or borrow one from a passer-by. Hopefully there are no more gunmen around the corner. Two, surely, is enough for one day.

Toby reappears, his arms full of towels and sheets. She's relieved to have something practical to do, to keep her mind off the gruesome scene around them. She wants to keep her son occupied too. "Toby, make some tea — with sugar."

Kneeling beside Tom, she places a cushion under his head, turning it so the bloodstains spattered across one side face the floor. He groans slightly. The entry point of the bullet is at the top of his shoulder. She hopes it's gone right through, has missed all his vital organs. He betrayed them, but she doesn't want him to die — he doesn't deserve that. She covers him with a blanket and staunches the blood with a towel, holding it as firmly as she dares on the wound. His pulse feels strong, though his eyes are still closed. Perhaps the shock has rendered him unconscious, or maybe he hit his head when he fell. She daren't move him to look. Somewhere deep in her memory is a rule: you're not supposed to move a person with a head injury.

Toby returns with mugs of tea, some water for Tom. She puts the water to one side. "Better not," she says. "In case they have to operate." Toby's eyes flit towards the other bodies. "Here, Toby, don't look at them. Sit on this side."

His eyes are still wide, a grey pallor to the skin on his face as he squats beside her. He's in shock, as is she. She draws him close, places a blanket around his shoulders.

"It's okay, Toby. We're okay. It'll all be over soon."

Tom's eyelids flicker, then open a crack. "I'm . . . sorry," he croaks.

"You'll be all right, Tom. The ambulance is coming."

His body tenses, as if he's trying to raise his head.

"Keep still, you're losing blood," she says, putting a restraining hand on his arm.

His body relaxes. "Are they—?"

"Dead, yes."

He closes his eyes. "I'm sorry, I . . ." His voice fades away as he loses consciousness again.

She sits huddled on the floor with her son, numb with shock.

CHAPTER SIXTY

Michelle

The hours pass in a blur of sirens, paramedics and questions. In a bedroom, dazzled by the flashlights of the investigators, Michelle answers questions in a trance. There seem to be hundreds of people coming and going, some in white outfits like snow rangers, some in green scrubs, the policemen at the door in uniform. The people who question her, thankfully, are gentle. They give them crime scene suits and take away their bloodstained clothes in plastic evidence bags.

Only the thought of being free, getting cleaned up and sleeping in a safe place keep her going. She answers the questions automatically, skimming over the details of the drug and how she came by it. Once or twice she almost falls from her chair, asleep. She's too tired to think, to wonder how much to tell them, or how little. Toby sits next to her and she stays with him as he's questioned, even though the police don't like it.

She has no idea how much time passes before she hears Richard's voice, remonstrating with the police. "Let the boy and his mother go. Look, they've had enough, you can see from their faces. We're not going anywhere, we can do the rest of this tomorrow, surely?"

Within an hour she and Toby arrive at a nearby hotel, still clad in white suits, their feet in blue plastic shoe covers. Luckily it's very late and there's barely anyone around to stare. They're accompanied by a uniformed police officer, who helps them check in and stays with them until they're safely inside adjacent rooms. He gives Michelle a number to call the next day, and at last they're able to rest.

It's only once Michelle has showered and climbed into bed that she remembers. In all the trauma of the last few hours, she hasn't even checked the news.

* * *

She wakes to a soft knock at the door. It's light outside, and it feels like late morning. Throwing a hotel robe around her, she peers through the peephole on the door. Toby, also in a towelling robe, stands outside.

She folds him in a silent hug for a few moments before he untangles himself.

"Did you sleep?" Michelle takes a quick glance down the corridor as she ushers her son into the room. Nothing to worry about there. Nonetheless, she secures the door from the inside.

"I didn't think I would, after . . . you know, but I was out like a light. It's a quarter past eleven, Mum." The skin on his face is pale and drawn, anxiety written around his eyes. Michelle feels a jolt of concern for her son. It'll take a while to recover from the events of yesterday.

"Have you seen the news yet?"

"Not yet, but I'm starving. Are we allowed to order some food?"

"Of course. First things first. Let's put in an order right away."

Toby turns the TV on while Michelle orders coffee, juice, a full English breakfast for Toby and a continental for herself.

She has no idea who's paying for this, but if it's her, then it's worth it, after all they've been through.

As she finishes, the name "Kimia" rings in her ears. A newsreader with a serious expression sits in front of a photo of the Reykjavik headquarters where she worked until recently, though it seems like years since she was last in that building. The words "evidence" and "life-threatening" stand out in what he's saying, along with "investigation" and "arrest". But without the start of the news piece, she can't tell if it's what she and Richard have been hoping for.

"Try the news channel," she says.

"Has a little-known Icelandic firm found the secret to eternal life?" a newsreader quotes from his autocue.

Rumours have circulated for some time in pharmaceutical media around a secretive Icelandic biotech company, Kimia. It's understood that billions of dollars have been invested in a new wonder drug that's believed not only to arrest ageing, but to reverse it.

The drug, known as PAN12, was scheduled to be launched in just ten days' time to huge fanfare, but in the last few hours evidence has emerged that the formula is fatally flawed, leading to serious illness and even, potentially, death. This raises the question: was Kimia planning to go ahead with the launch, hiding the evidence? Our correspondent, Jan Muller, is in Iceland with this report.

Dressed in a long coat and warm scarf, a presenter stands in the science park in Reykjavik, the Kimia building clearly visible behind him. Michelle feels a chill creep up her spine at the sight of it.

It appears that a scientist working for Kimia, the biotechnology firm which operates from the building behind me here in Reykjavik, became concerned about the results of long-term clinical trials of a new top-secret drug known as PAN12.

253

Rumours have been circulating about PAN12 for some time, with pundits calling it a "super-wonder drug" with remarkable rejuvenating properties, speculating that it could not only transform lives, but the entire world order.

PAN12 was scheduled for public launch in only a few days' time, but the as-yet-unnamed whistle-blower handed the story to an investigative journalist, who has in his possession crucial — and damning — evidence that shows the drug causes serious harm in a substantial proportion of people. The story hit the news media late last night, and speculation has been growing exponentially since then.

So far, we've been unable to interview either the journalist or the scientist. Nor have we been able to gain access to any of Kimia's senior executives — communications with the company seem to have been shut down — and we have not been allowed anywhere near the building. You can probably see behind me that barriers have been placed around the perimeter and there's a strong security presence, allowing nobody without clearance within a hundred metres of the property.

Investigations continue into the potential implications of this drug, but now that the authorities are involved, including the Icelandic Medicines Agency as well as other, global, regulatory bodies, it seems unlikely that the drug will be approved for release any time soon. It looks like there's a lot more to this story than we've seen so far, with far-reaching repercussions for Kimia, its owners and its directors.

"Thank God," Michelle says. She drops her head into her hands, overwhelmed with emotion.

"Mum, why are you crying? It's good news, isn't it?"

Through tears, she says, "It's great news. I'm just so relieved. It sounds like Richard's story will put an end to PAN12. Kimia's directors will be liable for . . . I don't know what, actually — fraud or something. Anyway, I imagine the regulators won't be happy at all. There'll be a serious investigation, and that could mean the end of Kimia. I hope it does."

Toby tucks into breakfast with enthusiasm. "That's great, Mum! You did it — you were a vital part of the story, and without you, it wouldn't have happened."

"I can't take much credit, honestly. Without Richard I'd have been hopeless."

"Where's Richard now?"

The last time she saw Richard was in the flat. She shakes her head before her mind conjures up a picture of that terrible scene. "I don't know. I hope he wasn't up all night."

"What do we do now, Mum? We don't even have any clothes."

"You're right — we can't go out in those boiler suits. Wait, the police gave me a number to call."

"Please don't tell me we need to go back for more questioning."

"I'll resist. Though we might have to, eventually. For now, we need help with the practical stuff. And we need to find Richard."

CHAPTER SIXTY-ONE

Michelle

As it turns out, they don't need to look far to find Richard. There's a soft knocking at the door. Toby's head rises, a hint of fear in his eyes.

"It's okay, Toby." Michelle takes a quick look through the peephole. "It's Richard." Her fingers fumble at the lock.

They gaze at each other for a fraction of a second. Then, without a word, he takes her hand, pulls her into the corridor and folds her in his arms. In that moment, she's in the safest place in the world. Her breathing slows, her heartbeat settles.

It's over in a flash. But before he lets her go, he drops the softest kiss into her hair. When their eyes meet, there's warmth and understanding in their look and her heart leaps.

Back in the room, Toby jumps from his seat, returning Richard's hug with enthusiasm.

"Good to see you, Richard."

"Likewise. Good to see you both."

He turns and gives her a reassuring smile. She smiles back, wondering if Toby can sense the change in them.

"Coffee?" she says.

He nods, and she's grateful for the distraction. It takes a few moments for her breathing to settle.

He looks thin and tired. There's a faint smell of soap around him, his hair wet from a recent shower. He wears a version of the same tracksuit supplied a few minutes ago to Michelle and Toby. Each of these is slightly oversized for the wearer, and in a different colour, but they're basically the same — and on their feet are identical-looking hotel slippers in various sizes. They stare at each other for a second, then snort with laughter. It's a moment of pure release.

"Now we really are a team," Richard says drily. "We have a uniform." From a bag he produces two familiar-looking mobile phones.

"Back to burners, then?" Toby says, a note of disappointment in his voice.

"Only for the moment. We need to be sure we're safe before we go home. I thought we might as well get back in communication first."

"Who are we going to communicate with?" Michelle can barely get her head around what's happened, let alone plan a return to normal life.

Richard smiles. "Good point. You've seen the story?"

They nod in unison.

"Were you up all night working on it?" Michelle says.

"Pretty much." He shrugs. "I got a couple of hours' sleep this morning. Time enough for that after the furore has died down."

"Has it done the trick?"

"We won't know for a while. But I'm ninety-nine per cent sure they can't release PAN12 any time soon. It'll probably never see the light of day. There'll be a massive investigation by the regulators, the authorities and the police, and that will take months, probably years. The preparation of all the documentation, the securing of Kimia's files — it will be a huge challenge. They'll need the courts behind them. Kimia's directors won't give up their secrets easily."

257

"All I can say is, Richard, you were brilliant. Back at the flat—" she hesitates, takes a breath — "I thought you were bluffing when you said it was too late. You were so calm, even with a gun pointing at your head. But you had actually sent the story, hadn't you?"

He nods. "I sent it a few minutes before they arrived. I had the sense that we were on borrowed time and it needed to go."

"Even though you didn't have the evidence you needed?"

He nods. "We had just about enough, with your Icelandic lady. I — we — were lucky, though. It was very close; it could all have ended quite differently."

There's a silence as Michelle and Toby contemplate what that might mean.

"There's so much I don't understand," Michelle says at last. "It all happened so quickly."

"Try me," Richard says.

"What's happened to Lars? Is he safe?"

He says nothing. A cloud passes across his eyes.

"Dead?" she whispers.

"I'm sorry, Michelle. I didn't want to tell you straight away."

So the man who started all this wasn't able to see it through. Though she barely knew him, she feels as if she's lost a friend, and the tears prick at her eyelids.

She swallows a lump in her throat. "How?"

"Professional killing. They found him in his apartment in Stockholm. He was shot in the neck. He would have known very little about it. It's sad. Another day or two and he'd have made it."

Poor Lars. He was brave enough to do the right thing, and look where it got him. A lonely death in a rented apartment. Hunted down and eliminated. It's tragic that only a short time later his courage would have been celebrated. He'd have seen his findings proved correct, and he'd have known how important his actions were. Sadness is followed by guilt, then anger, in Michelle's heart.

"What a tragic end for him. We must make sure his name is known, Richard. He helped save thousands, maybe millions of lives."

Richard nods. "Don't worry, I'm on it. We haven't released his name yet — they're still looking for relatives to inform, though it doesn't seem he had much in the way of family. I'll make sure he gets the recognition he deserves."

"Are you getting loads of money for the story?" Toby blurts out.

"Toby!"

Toby's eyes widen. "It's a valid question, Mum."

"It is a valid question," Richard says. "The answer is yes, Toby. The media are pretty generous when it comes to this kind of scoop; it'll sell papers in massive quantities, send visitors to their websites, go viral on the socials. I'll be okay, and so will Tom and his family. Oh, and you and your mum too, as part of the team—"

Michelle opens her mouth to remonstrate.

"No, I won't hear any objections. Listen, your lives have been turned upside down through no fault of your own. You've lost your job, Michelle, and your home, albeit a temporary one. You'll have to defer your studies, Toby, to give you time to recover from the trauma. When the dust has settled, you'll see it makes sense to include you in whatever financial benefits come from this story. You'll need it. And luckily, there'll be plenty."

Toby grins. "Fantastic! Thanks, Richard."

She's pleased for Toby, but the news about Lars is too upsetting to be glad for herself. Right now, there's something else she needs to know. She dreads the answer, but she must ask.

"What's happened to Helga — do we know that yet?"

Richard shrugs. "Nothing as yet." Seeing Michelle's look of concern, he carries on: "I suspect she's safe. Kimia's not interested in her anymore, they've got other things to think about. You can stop worrying about her."

Michelle breathes again. Helga's escaped and she's safe. "What about us? Are we sure there are no more killers tracking us, waiting for us around the corner?"

Toby looks up, startled at the question, fear in his eyes again. Michelle's almost sorry she asked. But none of them can assume they're safe yet.

Richard nods. "I don't know the answer to that yet. The police are following up the connections between Kimia and the guys who followed us. They'll come down hard on whoever hired them. It's pretty clear they were both professionals working for Kimia — though it's baffling that they killed each other. That may have been an error of communication, or it may have been spur of the moment. Who knows? There's a lot to untangle."

"There certainly seems to be." Michelle's head hurts with all the unanswered questions. Or perhaps it's the shock, or the lack of sleep. She reaches for the coffee jug again, and though it's gone cold, pours herself a cup of dark syrupy liquid and sips it, lost in thought. Richard, his eyes on her, picks up the phone and orders more.

"So when can we go home?" Toby asks.

"When the police say we can. A few more days, I suspect — and there will be more questions at some point. Don't panic, Toby, it won't be today."

"You mean we have to stay here, in this hotel?"

"We have to wait for the all-clear."

Toby's face falls. "That sounds boring."

"More to the point, are we safe here?" Michelle says. She's happy to wait, as long as she doesn't have to worry about gunmen arriving at her door.

"As long as we stay put. There's a security guard on the stairs and the lift to this floor is disabled. The other rooms up here are unoccupied. There's a police watch downstairs. Hopefully it'll only be a couple of days. The staff have been briefed to bring us whatever we need, so if you want a games console, Toby, I'm sure that can be arranged." Toby's face brightens. "Cool! Can we order whatever we want?"

"Within reason." Richard smiles. "Probably not a Ferrari at this stage. And Toby — be careful who you're connecting with. Only people you know, for the moment. And I know I don't need to say it, but don't mention what's happened or where you are. Not to anyone."

A day or two of enforced rest sounds pretty good to Michelle. It's about all she can face at the moment.

* * *

Tom looks away when he sees Richard and Michelle approaching his bed. Michelle hangs back, letting Richard take the single chair.

"It's okay, Tom, we're not here to judge you."

Tom's right shoulder is heavily bandaged, his arm held across his chest by a sling. He looks thin and hollow-eyed, his skin grey against the white of the sheets.

"I'm sorry, Richard," he whispers, his eyes filling.

Richard sighs, shakes his head. "It's okay. I'm not blaming you. I'm here to apologize, Tom. I'm sorry — I was wrong to treat you as I did. I had you down as a private person, not wanting to share your personal life at work. It was a misjudgement on my part and I feel terrible about it. I should be apologizing to you."

"Thank you." A single tear makes its way down Tom's cheek.

"I had no idea about your mum and your aunt, or what you were going through. It was unforgivable of me. But I've made sure they're looked after now, while you're in hospital, and for as long as you need."

More tears flow now. Tom wipes them away with his good hand. "That's . . . that's very generous of you, considering what I did."

"Don't even think about it," Richard replies. Tom's eyes stray to Michelle, standing behind Richard.

"Are you all okay? Toby?"

261

"We're fine, Tom." Michelle feels no animosity towards Tom, only sympathy now. His life was hard, he made a choice. It was a bad one, but everyone makes bad choices sometimes. "Toby's good. He's going back to university — it'll help him to be back to normal." She doesn't mention the therapy for post-traumatic stress disorder that her son will need to combat his panic attacks.

"If it makes any difference, I didn't know he was out to kill you — I thought we were just going to grab the evidence. I wasn't thinking straight. I'm such an idiot . . ." His voice fades; he turns his head away.

"Don't upset yourself. Michelle and I both know you tried to stop him. When you realized what he was about to do, you tried to protect us. We'll give evidence to that effect in court, if needs be."

At the mention of court, Tom grimaces. "That would be . . . thank you so much, both of you. I thought you'd never forgive me."

"There's nothing to forgive, Tom. You were under severe stress; you needed the money for your mum. It was a massive temptation. I don't blame you in the least. Listen, the guy would have found us anyway, eventually. No need to beat yourself up."

As they leave the ward, Michelle notices for the first time the man sitting in the corridor outside. He nods at them as they leave.

"Is that a police guard?" she whispers to Richard.

"Looks like it," Richard says. "Tom's in for a rough ride, I'm afraid, when he's recovered."

CHAPTER SIXTY-TWO

Michelle

The last time Michelle was on a plane she was on her way to Iceland. The thought strikes her just before they land, and her heart lurches with the memory. It seems like decades ago. She'd been so full of anticipation then, so ready for an adventure. Now all that seems naive, frivolous, after all that's happened.

Richard, sitting next to her, senses her concern. Placing a warm hand on her arm, he says, "Okay? Fear of flying?"

She shakes her head. "Not at all. It's not that. I was just remembering the last time I flew. It was to Reykjavik."

"Okay, that would make you a little nervous. But nothing's going to happen to us in Sweden, I promise. Anyway, this time you're with me."

She smiles across at him. "I can't tell you how much that helps. But I suppose . . ."

"What do you suppose?"

"I suppose I can't avoid it, especially right now. We're going to Lars's funeral. It will all come back. I'll just have to handle it."

It's been a few weeks since Lars's untimely death. The funeral was delayed because of the police investigation, which seemed to go on and on. In the meantime, it became clear that Lars had no family at all, no friends in Sweden or Iceland to take on the organization of a service. So Richard and Michelle stepped in and handled the arrangements.

By now, Lars Andersson's name is well known. True to his promise, Richard ensured the scientist's name was released to the media as the man who blew the whistle on the biggest pharmaceutical scandal the world has ever known. He crafted an obituary that was used across the globe, acknowledging the man who risked, and lost, his life to save many others, and Lars's name was mentioned in every news story and feature that followed the initial scoop.

Michelle and Richard are flying to Stockholm to attend the funeral. They've kept the date of the actual service secret, to give Lars a peaceful farewell. After it's done, Richard will meet the media to tell the scientist's story once again. Lars Andersson has become a Swedish hero, his name mentioned at the highest level of government. A memorial service is planned at a future date, a sculpture commissioned in his honour. His story has captured the imaginations of the Swedish people.

"You've done him proud, Richard." Michelle watches from the window as their plane coasts over the lights of Stockholm. "He seemed a modest person, self-effacing even. It's so sad there's no family or friends. I suppose that might be why he was so committed to his work. But he deserves this, he really does. It would have been terrible for him to be buried without any acknowledgement."

Richard looks pensive. "Thank goodness for people with a conscience," he says. "People like him restore my faith in humanity."

Michelle gives him a sideways look. "Are you sure?"

"Well, to some extent," he says.

Knowing what she does about Richard's work, she's surprised he has any faith in anyone.

* * *

At a tiny, traditional church on the outskirts of Stockholm, they bring flowers to lay on the casket. There are no crowds of friends here to say goodbye, no weeping relatives. A small woman with white hair, a thick coat wrapped around her thin frame, snow boots on her feet, slides into a pew at the back of the church. Otherwise it's just Richard and Michelle, the priest and a helper. There was no public announcement, no information put out in the media. Voyeurs, journalists and photographers were not invited.

The simple service, conducted in Swedish, is incomprehensible to the two mourners sitting in the front row but it sounds all the more poignant for its mystery. The songs, delivered as a duet by the priest and his helper, are beautiful and sad. It's all over in less than twenty minutes. As they leave, Michelle and Richard place their bouquets on the polished wood and say their goodbyes. The elderly woman at the back shuffles forward and starts to tidy the few hymnbooks and service cards laid out at the front of the church.

From the graveyard where Lars will be buried, they can see the ocean water that surrounds the city, sparkling in the winter sunlight. Soon it will be dark, the days shortening for the winter months, though Lars will know nothing of it.

They decide to stroll around the churchyard, paying their last respects to the scientist they knew for such a short time, but whose actions had such a profound impact on them. The priest strides out to see them, thanking them in his perfect English for attending. They fend off questions, gently, about their relationship with Lars.

As they talk, Michelle notices a figure in the background, watching them. She's not sure if they're a woman or a man

265

— they're tall and slender, in dark clothing, a hat pulled low on their forehead, a blonde lock escaping at the collar. Under Michelle's gaze, the figure turns and strides away. Something in the person's gait strikes a sudden chord in her mind.

She pulls gently at Richard's sleeve and he pats her hand. "Well, thank you again," Richard says to the priest. "We must go now."

"Of course." The priest nods and smiles as they walk away.

"What's going on?" Richard says.

But the figure has gone. Michelle turns and looks around, but there's nobody there. "I thought I saw . . . someone."

"Who? Someone you know?"

"Well, no, I'm not sure — I only caught a glimpse. It's probably nothing."

He takes her hand. "You're still tired, and you've been through a terrible trauma. Come on, let's get out of the cold. There's nothing more to do here."

She could easily have imagined it. It wouldn't be the first time her imagination has played tricks on her in recent weeks, though usually it involves the dark figure of a man watching or following her. Since the shooting, she has found it hard to rid herself of the images — the blood, the yelling, the deafening gunshots, the bodies on the floor, her total inability to defend her son. Her deep sense of guilt for getting him tangled up in a lethal situation.

The images revisit her with exhausting regularity. Every night and often during the day too, triggered by loud noises, colours, voices. Toby is the same. They've both been diagnosed with post-traumatic stress disorder. They're seeing specialist therapists and they talk to each other often about the process. Whether it's working or not, only time will tell.

In the meantime, she can't trust what she's seeing. So maybe it was her mind playing tricks on her again.

266

CHAPTER SIXTY-THREE

Michelle

Despite everything, all the stress, the terrible flight across Europe, the hiding, the fear, the shocking showdown in the flat — something wonderful has happened, and she can hardly believe it's true.

The moment she met Richard she was impressed by his steadfastness, his calm, his intelligence. His support for her and for Toby through all the trauma has been unquestionable, unwavering and wise.

Since Toby went back to university, Richard has become her lover. Not just her lover, her long-term partner. It feels as if they've always been together, and she can't imagine a future without him. He's seen her at her worst — dirty, unkempt and helpless — but he doesn't care. Every day he tells her he loves her, and she believes him.

It's hard to imagine she once cared so much about ageing, about her looks, about the clothes she wore. She knows now that none of it matters. Ironic that an age-defying drug has convinced her that ageing isn't a problem.

As soon as she's able, she gives the tenants in her old London flat notice and sells up. A few weeks on, she's living with Richard in a beautiful apartment in North London. She wants nothing more than a fresh start. It was Richard's suggestion, and she agreed without hesitation.

They talk for hours about how their future might look. Richard is tired of his work, and when the Kimia story is done, he will have had enough of investigative journalism. It's dangerous and exhausting and though he'll miss the thrill of the chase, he won't miss the dark side of what he does: the injustices, the inhumanity, the violence. There's only so much darkness a person can take.

But for now, the story runs on and on, and Richard will see it through. Every day, he receives calls and messages offering him opportunities. A book, a film, a TV series: all are on the cards, and if Richard accepted all the invitations for interview, he would never be home. Luckily, Richard's experience keeps him grounded. He politely refuses the offers he knows will be flaky, agrees to the ones he knows he can trust, and takes it all slowly. But it looks like the Kimia story will keep him employed for at least a couple of years yet. Then he'll be able to step back. They'll live very well on the proceeds.

Michelle stays in the background. They decide to downplay her part in the story, at least for the moment, to give her time to recover. Her days are busy supporting Richard, helping him in practical ways, organizing his diary, fielding calls, discussing the story as it develops.

Every holiday, Toby returns from university and joins the team. He has decided he wants to be an investigative journalist, and though Richard tries to discourage him, he's adamant. He's learning as much as he can in the holidays, and hopes to take a master's in journalism when he's finished his first degree. The thought of Toby putting himself in danger makes Michelle anxious, but when Toby makes his mind up, it's impossible to change it. It's a few years ahead, though, and he'll be older, more experienced in life.

"Let's face it," he says, "there won't be many situations more dangerous than the one I've already been in. I've got the best possible teacher right here in Richard. And I promise I won't do it for ever."

Michelle has reconnected with Gail. Her best friend spent months bemused and worried about her, but is by nature forgiving. When she hears the story — much abridged, leaving out the worst details — she's incredulous. "You wanted an adventure," she says. "But this!" When she hears about Michelle's new relationship, there are tears in her eyes.

Kimia has gone into receivership, or the Icelandic equivalent. The police impounded everything they could find, including the evidence provided by Richard. Within weeks the workforce was out, the building closed. The directors are in custody — at least, most of them. One has disappeared, a woman called Gudrun Jonsdottir. Interpol is on the case.

When Michelle hears the name, she flinches. "Wait," she says, "Helga's last name was Jonsdottir. You don't think—"

Richard does a quick search online. "It's the most common name in Iceland," he says. "Thousands of women have the same last name. So no, I think it's pretty unlikely. Did she have a sister — or a cousin, maybe — in the company?"

She shakes her head. "I don't think so. No, she would have said so, surely. I would have known." Somehow she's never got used to the idea that Helga could betray her, or that she's disappeared so completely. But it's one of the things she must do to move on.

Nonetheless, she can't help feeling deeply uncomfortable at the thought that one of the directors is missing. It's unfinished business.

* * *

In the summer, there's a hearing, the first of many in the Kimia case. Richard and Michelle travel to Iceland to attend. They sit in the public area. It's a small courtroom, and as it turns out, they sit close to the defendants' box.

Kimia's directors are obliged to appear. When they enter the room, there's a soft gasp. Even Michelle, who has prepared herself, is shocked at their appearance.

There are five of them: three men and two women. They keep their heads down, only looking up once they're seated. Christophe Blanchet, the CEO, is white-haired. This is the first time Michelle has ever seen him, but the few reports of him in the media have all remarked on his youthfulness. Now, lines are drawn on his forehead and around his mouth. His eyes sink into their sockets over heavy dark shadows and bags. He stands with a slight stoop, and blue veins are painted on the backs of his hands. Rapid ageing and prison life have done him no favours.

She's shocked to see Ashley, her former boss, in the line-up. Was Ashley a director of Kimia? If so, it wasn't obvious from her title, and she's pretty sure not many people knew it. Perhaps it was a clever move on Kimia's part, to have directors of the company doing the job of senior managers. Maybe that's how they kept their grip on what was going on at other levels of the organization.

But her initial surprise at this revelation is eclipsed by the shock of Ashley's appearance.

The woman she knew has changed beyond recognition. Of course, she's no longer groomed to perfection. Life on remand is not so luxurious. She's without make-up, her hair has lost its shine, her fingernails are no longer painted. Her blonde bob has turned brown, with touches of grown-out blonde at the ends, and it's long enough to be pulled back into a ponytail. She wears a suit, but it's ill-fitting and modest, not the streamlined designer outfits that skimmed her body so beautifully. The worst is her face. It seems to have collapsed in on itself. Her once-immaculate bone structure has disappeared. Lines from nose to mouth, jowls on her jawline, frown lines between her eyes. Michelle would put her age at around sixty. She can't help thinking how brilliant that drug would have been, had it not been fatally flawed. She kills that thought.

This is a preliminary hearing only, and not much happens. She and Richard are attending not only for the sake of the story, but because at some point in the process they'll both be called as witnesses. It's not something Michelle is looking forward to, but she's determined to see it through, for Lars, for Tom, even for Helga. For all the former colleagues who lost their jobs.

Fortunately for Michelle and Richard, plus the other reporters present, the proceedings are conducted in English, but there are so many indictments that Michelle can't keep up. The legal language drones on and her mind begins to drift. Richard makes copious notes. This is fodder for yet another series of news stories in the Kimia saga — not only the appearance of the directors, which will go viral, inevitably, but the scale of the crimes listed against them.

They're asked about the director who died. They all say it was a "heart attack", no evidence of any connection to PAN12.

As for the missing director, Gudrun Jonsdottir, none of them claims any knowledge of her whereabouts.

CHAPTER SIXTY-FOUR

Michelle

"What does it matter? We got what we wanted," Michelle says. "We stopped the release of PAN12, and the directors are going to prison for a very long time." She and Richard have retreated to a café near the courtrooms, overlooking the ocean. The snow-capped mountains beyond drift in and out of restless cloud formations, appearing at random like ghostly giants in the sky.

"Possibly the rest of their lives — rather shorter lives than they were hoping," Richard says drily. "But the missing director is a loose end."

Michelle nods. "That bothers me too. It seems wrong that one of them won't face justice."

"Indeed," Richard says. "It's not just that, though. I'll bet this woman, Jonsdottir, has the formula."

"But won't the police or Interpol have worked that out too?"

"Probably. But if she hides somewhere they can't access — like North Korea or Mongolia — starts up again and develops the drug in secret, we'd know nothing about it until the shit hits the fan."

"Surely somebody would know about it," Michelle says. "Everyone in the world will be on the lookout for it now. It's had global media coverage, thanks to you. Recruitment alone would be almost impossible."

"Not if she waits long enough — and remember, she's already taking the drug."

Of course. Anything's possible if you have unlimited money and the formula for a life-extending drug. Michelle sighs. "If you're right, it sounds like there's not much we could do about it."

Richard sighs. "Not in the short term, anyway. As it stands, there's plenty more potential in the story today, without imagining what's to come. We've got masses of material already."

She gazes out over the ocean, where a single seabird dips and glides. "I'm beginning to wonder if we'll ever be free of it."

"We will be. When we are, we're going to enjoy the proceeds, believe me. Don't worry, we can slow down soon. It's a great position to be in — we can pick and choose what we want to do. There are plenty of other journalists who'll be happy to follow the story to the bitter end."

"I believe you. I just don't want you to burn out when I've only just found you." She takes his hand across the table.

"Not going to happen," he says. "I've got so much more to look forward to now. We'll see Kimia through, and then I'll retreat to a life of luxury with you."

"Huh. Don't believe you."

"Well, okay. But I won't be doing any more investigative stuff. I'm done with that. I'm going to write a novel."

"A novel? What about? What genre?"

He grins. "It's about an elixir, the fountain of youth. It's, uhh . . . fantasy."

* * *

On a small island to the far north of the Finnish archipelago, where flora and fauna thrive, a few hundred people live in harmony with nature. Few foreigners come here, particularly in the harsh, dark winter, and life's rhythms are governed by the weather and the seasons. So there's a spark of interest when outsiders arrive and build their home here — even more so when that home springs up in the remotest part of the island.

The building that rises from the hard rock is like nothing they've ever seen before. It melts into the background: the sky, the earth, the water reflecting off its soaring, mirrored sides. There are no curves at all, only sharp corners on a huge, oblong box, interrupted by two solid metal doors. Next to the house is a huge steel carport, with space enough for a dozen vehicles, built on a concrete platform. The locals are baffled. Why would anyone want to live like this?

On rare occasions, a passing farmer or a curious walker comes across its owners, a young couple. They nod politely and exchange greetings, but say very little about themselves; nobody knows who they are or why they would choose such an isolated spot to make their home. They remain aloof, staying away from the village on the other side of the island. Like their house, they hardly seem to be there.

What is clear is that they have plenty of money. To build a place like that, here, is problematic, but it's completed in record time. Helicopters are spotted delivering materials; boats arrive in the tiny bay nearby; snowmobiles deliver regular supplies. The locals are curious, but as time goes on and the owners are barely seen, their interest wanes, the gossip stops.

The house gazes out over the roiling sea, and on a good day, a huge panorama stretches for miles. The sky is in constant flux: patches of blue turn into tumultuous clouds within seconds. When the wind blows the sea becomes furious, waves loom and grow to mountainous heights, crashing with deafening blows onto the rocky shore.

Inside, in the warmth generated by the power of the sea and the sun, like all the energy in the house, a woman sits at a silver screen, a single notebook open beside it. She's blonde and fresh-faced, her skin crystal-clear. A smile lingers around her mouth, as if she likes what she sees on the screen. She types quickly at the keyboard, then stands, revealing a tall, slender figure. She closes the notebook, revealing the letters *GHJ* embossed in gold on the cover. She takes it with her.

Walking purposefully, she heads for a well-concealed door to one side of the room. It opens to reveal a wide staircase that takes her down two floors to an underground basement. At a solid metal door, she punches a code into a keypad and pauses for a camera to recognize her face. From a peg to one side, she takes a blue lab coat and slides her arms into the sleeves. She doesn't bother to button it.

The room she enters is a laboratory. A man in similar lab clothing turns to greet her. As she nods her reply, a single earring in the shape of a snowflake sparkles in the bright overhead lights.

Long worktops hold a variety of streamlined equipment. Everything is white and spotless. She walks soundlessly to the seated man and stops behind him. He's watching live video, pausing from time to time to type notes into a report. Four mice scuttle around a large glass box to the left of the screen. Another box to the right contains two mice. These are smaller than the others and thin, their fur patchy, pink skin showing through. Instead of running, they hobble, and one has a large growth on the top of its head.

The woman scrutinizes the report on the screen. It's headed: Test #142: PAN21.

THE END

ACKNOWLEDGEMENTS

Massive thanks to the wonderful Emma Grundy Haigh and Laurel Sills for their help and support in editing this book. Many thanks also to Laura Coulman-Rich and the team at Joffe Books for bringing it to fruition.

I'm so grateful to Emma Mader/Henderson for being an early reader and guiding me on the scientific aspects of my story, particularly the laboratory setting. Your advice was invaluable.

Thank you, Judy Jones, for your company on my research trip to Iceland. What a place! Also for being my first reader, along with my sister, Kate Mercer. I'm not sure it was a rewarding job, but I'm so grateful to you both.

A huge thank you to all my writer friends for their support, and to the writing community as a whole. You're one of the kindest groups I know and without you, this job would be truly lonely.

Special thanks to Adrian, for sparking the idea for this book.

And finally heartfelt thanks to my readers, for reading my work. I couldn't do it without you!

THE JOFFE BOOKS STORY

We began in 2014 when Jasper agreed to publish his mum's much-rejected romance novel and it became a bestseller.

Since then we've grown into the largest independent publisher in the UK. We're extremely proud to publish some of the very best writers in the world, including Joy Ellis, Faith Martin, Caro Ramsay, Helen Forrester, Simon Brett and Robert Goddard. Everyone at Joffe Books loves reading and we never forget that it all begins with the magic of an author telling a story.

We are proud to publish talented first-time authors, as well as established writers whose books we love introducing to a new generation of readers.

We won Trade Publisher of the Year at the Independent Publishing Awards in 2023. We have been shortlisted for Independent Publisher of the Year at the British Book Awards for the last four years, and were shortlisted for the Diversity and Inclusivity Award at the 2022 Independent Publishing Awards. In 2023 we were shortlisted for Publisher of the Year at the RNA Industry Awards.

We built this company with your help, and we love to hear from you, so please email us about absolutely anything bookish at feedback@joffebooks.com

If you want to receive free books every Friday and hear about all our new releases, join our mailing list: www.joffebooks.com/contact

And when you tell your friends about us, just remember: it's pronounced Joffe as in coffee or toffee!